Praise for

The Glamorous Life

"Though hip-hop began in the music industry, Nikki Turner found a creative way to bring the rhythm to print—in fictional novels that give readers a close-up look at urban life."

—*Booking Matters*

"Turner creates colorful yet emotionally driven characters that captivate. Despite the deceit, cruelty, hatred, and unspeakable wrongs, humanity maintains its presence in this glamorous life."

—*Upscale*

"A gritty street tale of a young woman who has to decide which is more important—money or love."

—*Seattle Skanner*

"One of the premier queens of urban literature presents her latest steamy page-turner!"

—*Black Expressions*

By Nikki Turner

NOVELS

Heartbreak of a Hustler's Wife
Natural Born Hustler
Relapse
Ghetto Superstar
Black Widow
Death Before Dishonor
(with 50 Cent)
Riding Dirty on I-95
The Glamorous Life
A Project Chick
A Hustler's Wife

EDITOR

Street Chronicles: A Woman's Work
Street Chronicles: Backstage
Street Chronicles: Christmas in the Hood
Street Chronicles: Girls in the Game
Street Chronicles: Tales from a Hood
(contributing author)

CONTRIBUTING AUTHOR

Girls from da Hood
Girls from da Hood 2
The Game: Short Stories about the Life

Riding Dirty on I-95

*A **Nikki Turner***
Original

Riding Dirty on I-95

A   N O V E L

One World  Ballantine Books
New York

A One World Books Trade Paperback Original

Copyright © 2006 by Nikki Turner

Published in the United States by One World Books, an imprint of The Random House Publishing Group, a division of Random House, Inc., New York.

ONE WORLD is a registered trademark and the One World colophon is a trademark of Random House, Inc.

LIBRARY OF CONGRESS CATALOGING-IN-PUBLICATION DATA
Turner, Nikki.
    I-95 : a novel / Nikki Turner.
        p.   cm.
    ISBN 978-0-345-47684-5 (trade pbk.)
    1. Drug couriers—Fiction.   2. Orphans—Fiction.   3. Women
college students—Fiction.   4. Fathers—Death—Fiction.
5. Interstate 95 Region—Fiction.   I. Title: Interstate 95.
II. Title.
PS3620.U7659I14 2006
813'.6—dc22

                                                    2005055475

Printed in the United States of America

www.oneworldbooks.net

9   8   7

Text design by Laurie Jewell

This novel is dedicated to

All the lives and souls lost at the mercy of I-95,
everyone who has ever taken the chance to ride dirty on I-95

&

The men who put immeasurable time, effort, and devotion
into helping me become the lady I am today: Words can never
express the gratitude I feel for the knowledge and principles
you've given to me. Thank you for giving a girl everything she
could ever need to survive in this cold world.

Craig Robinson
You have been riding with me for over half of my life,
you've seen me at my best and loved me at my worst.

My three uncles
Sonny, Farrest, and Andre.
You are all so different,
but you all love me so!

My late grandfather
Milton L. Scott.
Thank you for being the father I never had.

Riding Dirty on I-95

Do the Damn Thing!

You got to know when to hold 'em, know when to fold 'em,
Know when to walk away, know when to run.

—KENNY ROGERS, "THE GAMBLER"

It was the afternoon of my seventh birthday, and I ran around in our backyard, wearing a pretty white dress with my long braids tied with ribbons, while my momma took pictures of me and the other kids. Seemed like the whole neighborhood was there. I had a huge chocolate cake from the best bakery in town, a piñata, a table covered with pizzas, and not one but two clowns who were making crazy-looking things out of balloons. I'd stopped running to get a big cup of lemonade when I heard a tapping on the glass door and turned to see my daddy, crooking his finger at me from inside the house. I glanced around. All the other kids either were watching the clowns or playing tag, and Momma was yelling at my sister Zurri about something, so I slipped away and went to my daddy.

"Come here, sweet stuff," he said to me. "It's yo' birthday, and I want to have a little heart-to-heart with my favorite girl."

He sat down in his big leather recliner and patted his lap.

"I know I'm your favorite, Daddy," I said, climbing into his lap. I put my head on his chest and listened to him as he hummed the gambler's anthem. My daddy had eight kids. If anybody thought I was just another ashy kid from the projects who wasn't going to amount to nothing, at least I knew I was better than seven other mothafuckas. At that moment I felt that if no one else in the world ever made me feel special again, sittin' up on my daddy's knee was enough to last me a lifetime.

Even though he had a boatload of children, three by my momma and the others by four different women. I was next to last and the baby girl, but Daddy always made me feel like I was his only child. No doubt about it, my daddy was a rolling stone, but unlike most men with kids living all over the place from those rolling years, there were no secrets as far as my father was concerned. I knew who my siblings were, and they knew me. We were one big family, playing together, partying together, and celebrating on the holidays together. My siblings were a big part of my life, and most of us were close. Daddy never dealt with the whole "baby momma" drama. He kept all his kids in check like an army colonel kept his soldiers, walking the straight and narrow. Every now and again, one would go sideways, but Daddy would snatch them right back into line.

Momma stuck her head in the door and frowned at me.

"How come you ain't out here at the party?" she asked.

"She'll be out in a minute," Daddy said. Momma knew there was no use arguing, so she just stood by and waited.

Daddy reached down and pulled a small wrapped box from the floor by the chair.

"Happy birthday, Mercy," he said with a big grin as I greedily ripped the wrapping off the box and opened it. Inside was a small red leather wallet. My very own wallet! I loved it.

"Look inside," Daddy said.

I opened it up, and inside I counted seven ten-dollar bills.

"Thank you, Daddy! Thank you!" I screamed. Daddy just laughed. Then he tapped his cheek and motioned with his hand for me to give him a kiss on his jaw, and I happily did. I loved my daddy more than anything else in the world, including my momma, sisters, brothers, even my new Cabbage Patch doll. None had shit on the love I had for my father. My momma knew it, too.

Daddy looked in my eyes and said, "I don't care how big and grown-up you get, don't ever forget the pieces of wisdom I gave you. I want you to know that everything I ever said to you was all from the heart. You can take each and every one of our talks to the bank." I smiled because this was my daddy and he wasn't like some of my other friends' deadbeat fathers. He never lied to me, ever, not about Santa Claus, the Tooth Fairy, or even the Easter Bunny. There was none of that when it came to me. He kept it real to the fullest degree. Always knowing what the truth looked like coming out of my daddy's mouth would eventually enable me to be able to recognize the BS that came out of every other nigga's mouth.

"Mercy, I need you to promise me that you will never forget anything I've told you. And I want you to always remember, don't let nothing stand in your way. Nothing." He looked into my big brown eyes. "You hear me?"

I nodded, "Okay, Daddy, I promise."

My mother looked on with her arms folded as he hugged and kissed me.

"Now, Daddy got to go and deal with what the world has in store for him," he said as he motioned for me to hop down off his lap. I jumped down.

Daddy stood up. He was dressed to the nines in a silk shirt and tailored suit. And he smelled sweet like money. He gave my mother a hug and went out the door. I ran over to the window to watch my gambling father disappear into the mean streets of Richmond, Virginia.

And that was the last time I ever saw him alive.

See, Nathaniel Jiles, my father, was a stone-cold gambler in every aspect of the word. He bet on everything from darts to car races to sports, dice, card games, and horses. He would place a bet on two cockroaches running across the floor. Hell, my daddy even bet people what their next move would be; sometimes he won and sometimes he lost. My mother once told me that when she was pregnant with me he tried to bet her fifty to one that I would be a girl.

Daddy was respected from coast to coast. People trusted him because his word was his bond. If he said it, then it might as well have been written in stone. If he said a rooster could pull a train, best believe niggas lined up around the corner to buy tickets to see that train move. He was a real stand-up guy, but you and I both know that sometimes the thoroughest of the most thorough can be caught slipping. And that's just what happened to Daddy. Just like any other gambler, he was only one shot away from the big one—so he always thought. Ultimately he gambled his own life away. See, when he won he won big, and when he lost he lost big-time.

Even though he was a gambler, family meant everything to my father. My seven sisters and brothers and I were always his priority. He made sure we had the most fashionable clothes, from our leather coats and boomers to every single pair of Air Jordans that ever came out. We always had new toys, the fastest bicycles, and the latest technology. My brothers were the first on our block to get new video games, and I had my own boom box with all my favorite cassettes. But what looked to be his strength turned out to be a fatal weakness.

That day I sat on my daddy's lap—the last day of his life—was May 5, 1985. Yes, I'm a Taurus, and I am indeed a Taurus in every respect. I'm stubborn, and once my mind is made up, then it's set. My daddy was a Taurus, too, and I think that's one of the reasons we got along so well. Tauruses usually connect well with one another. He was mule-stubborn, and when his mind was set to do something, he did it.

I don't know what was the big deal about turning seven. It had some kind of significance for him. The night before my birthday, he took me and seven of my little girlfriends out for a dinner cruise on the *Annabel Lee,* the party boat that cruised the James River. Then they all stayed for a sleepover and the big party the next day. It was the best birthday I had in all my years.

But my birthday caused the ghetto assassination of my father, and I will never forget that day as long as I live.

That night after all the guests were gone and we kids were all in bed, I heard a knock at the door: *Bam, Bam!* The noise startled me. I heard Momma shuffling from her room toward the door. The knocking grew louder and louder, until it was a banging sound. *Boom, Boom!*

For a minute I thought it was the police until I heard a familiar voice calling my mother's name. "Pearl, open up. Hurry up, Pearl!" I heard my uncle Roland scream over the banging. My brother and sister were fast asleep. I was always the last to fall asleep because I tried to wait up for Daddy to come home from the crap house, and this night wasn't any different. I was wide awake. And I was afraid because I knew the commotion somehow concerned my father. My gut told me so.

At first I had thought my uncle Roland was coming to tell my momma he needed some money to bail my daddy out of jail, but then I thought again. I don't know if it was because of how close I was to my father, like the close connection they say some twins have or something, or if it was that Uncle Roland almost never moved fast. He was always so mellow and cool, like a spring breeze. When he beat on the door like that, I knew in my heart something was damn sure wrong. Something was more than wrong. I knew my daddy wasn't coming home.

I got out of my bed and stood at the entrance of my room as my momma took the top lock, dead bolt, bottom locks, and the chain off the front door to let Uncle Roland in. Out of breath and almost hysterical, he delivered the news.

"Nate is dead! He dead, Pearl! He dead!"

Momma started sobbing. "No, nooo! Nooo!" she screamed.

Tears couldn't even come out of my eyes, because in my heart my life was over. I wanted to die, too. My father was the only thing that mattered to me. I listened to my mother and shared with my siblings because *he* told me that's what I was supposed to do. I had manners because *he* told me every lady does. I made good grades because *he* said I should.

My mother looked up and noticed me standing in the doorway. "Mercy, go back to yo' room," she said through sobs, but I couldn't. I couldn't budge. I couldn't move. My feet were in cement blocks. Then my mother came over and put her arms around me, and my uncle embraced us both. After about an hour of crying, my mother had calmed down a little bit. "Go back into your room now, Mercy. Momma will be in there in a little while. I need to talk to Uncle Roland."

I went into my room, but I listened through the cracked-open door as Uncle Roland talked to Momma. Uncle Roland hadn't smoked in years, but I heard a match strike and smelled cigar smoke creeping into my room. He normally walked around with a chewed-up cigar hanging out of his mouth. That same old cigar could last him almost a week. But on this evening, he lit it.

"I told dat Nate don't be fucking with that nigga Cat. I told him," my uncle said.

"What you talking about, Roland?" my mother asked between sniffs.

"I told Nate never to fuck with that nigga from the beginning. I told him to just pay him. He wasn't hearing it, though. He said he had a tip on the Sunday-night game and would have Cat's money by Monday." He took a pull from his cigar and let the ashes fall on the floor. "Instead of him paying Cat, he went and used the money for Mercy's birthday party."

I felt as if I had been stabbed in the heart. I wanted to throw up. I had been the reason for my father's death. It was all my fault.

"I had no idea that he owed Cat," my mother said, putting her hand over her mouth. "I never imagined that Nate would put himself in a position to be in debt to that man. I heard through the grapevine that those dudes are ruthless. Damn, I wish he would have listened to you, Roland."

"I understood where he was coming from, Pearl. But he slept on Cat and them. He was on niggas' tickets from all over the country." Uncle Roland shook his head. "I mean, niggas from here all the way out to California let him owe them tens of thousands of dollars, so what was fifteen hundred for a local nigga?"

"Everybody in the city knew where to find him if they needed to. They didn't have to kill him," Momma added as the reality of it all began to set in. "I mean, Nate had just left here to go and pay his debts and Cat killed him anyway?"

"Cat wants every nigga to be scared of him, but he knew Nate wasn't scared. Nate wasn't scared of no one, 'specially no local thug like Cat," Uncle Roland said.

Momma put her head down and began to weep. I wondered

who this Cat was, and why he had to go and destroy not just my daddy, but me and my whole family.

"Come on, Pearl," Uncle Roland said to her. "You gotta pull it together for yo' kids."

I t rained for two days as Momma and Uncle Roland planned my daddy's funeral. It stopped raining on the day of the funeral, but the air was misty, and a thick fog settled over the hood. Still, the people turned out to pay their respects. The church was laid out with flowers and wreaths everywhere. Each pew was jam-packed with people, some from the hood and others I had never seen before. Later I found out they were Daddy's gambling friends, who came from all over the country to pay their respects. They were all suited and booted. There were so many gators at the funeral it could have been an alligator farm. The women were sharp as cheddar cheese, and my momma was the fiercest of them all. She looked like the black Jackie Onassis, wearing a little black hat with a veil, a tailored black dress, and sling-back pumps.

"Precious Lord, take my hand." The choir singer took a deep breath and looked up to the ceiling.

"Lead me on. Let me stand," the woman in the choir wailed. And the people wept.

After the hymn ended, the preacher got up and began to speak. Momma buried her head in Uncle Roland's chest, her tears wetting his custom-made suit, so she didn't notice a lot of what was going on around us, but I did. Right before the service was about to start, four nicely dressed guys had entered the church. Each wore a dark overcoat. They brought in beautiful flowers and placed them with the other arrangements. Looking over at my mother, my uncle, and all of us kids, they took off their hats to show their respect.

One of them glanced at a big man across the aisle. He was tall with wide shoulders. Suddenly, Mr. Bigs looked over at me. He had greenish-brown eyes, and his face showed no expression at all. I felt a shiver and turned around quickly.

As I was listening to the hymns, I heard someone gasp and turned to see a heavyset woman wearing a plum-colored dress sitting in the pew behind me. She pulled out her cross and said, "Father, no."

I wondered what was wrong. I didn't get it. None of us did. But she knew. She somehow knew all hell was about to break loose. Just then, one of the four men reached up and fixed his necktie. He left his seat, walked over to the casket, and pushed it to the floor. It landed with a bang. A high-pitched scream came from the woman behind me. And more people screamed as the other three guys hopped out of their seats and together all of them picked up the casket and started running out of the Lord's house.

A couple of my daddy's friends tried to stop them, but one of the guys pulled out a gun and gave them a look that said, "You can join him if you want." I guess they didn't want to catch up with my father after all, because they both sat down like trained seals.

Everything happened so quickly. People were in shock, screaming and running for cover as my father's funeral turned into a circus. Someone tried to grab my sisters, brothers, and me to try to protect us and to keep us from witnessing this madness. Momma looked like she was about to pass out, and Uncle Roland held on to her. Ms. Pat, the only person Daddy trusted to run his numbers, grabbed me. But I broke loose and ran outside the church. As I ran, mud splashed all over my new black patent-leather shoes, and the perfectly tied bow on my blue dress came loose, but I didn't care. I just kept running and running. It was almost like I was running in slow motion. I couldn't get to my dad quick enough no matter how fast I ran. Then I heard gunshots. *Boom, boom, boom.* I froze in my tracks, and when I looked up, I couldn't believe my eyes. Two of those men were firing shots into my father's already lifeless body.

I began to run again. I didn't care if I was caught in the crossfire or not. It would have been worth it. I would have been dying for what I believed in, and my dad was the one thing that I believed in more than anything. If I didn't have him, what did I have?

One of the other guys brought over a gasoline can and poured gas all over my father's bullet-ridden body. The fourth guy, a sorry heartless motherfucker, lit a match. My father's body ignited immediately. I screamed, *"No! Nooo!"*

When I saw nobody doing anything, I took matters in my own hands. If nobody had my daddy's back, I did. I ran straight towards my father's body, but somebody grabbed me. To this day I don't remember who it was. I tried to break loose, but I couldn't—the hold was too tight. As I fought, in between the echoes of gunfire and screams, I could hear my mother.

"Mercy! Mercy!" she cried in despair.

I stopped fighting and turned around, because I wanted to make sure my mother was okay. I didn't need something to happen to her, too. My eyes met hers. I could see that she was relieved she had been able to bring me back to my senses. I don't know what I had planned on doing once I reached my father's body, but I just wanted to get to him. When I saw that Mother was safe, I turned back around. The guys with the guns were like ghosts. Just like that, they had vanished into thin air, gone, disappeared. Then

I saw that green-eyed man. He stared straight into my eyes before he turned and walked away.

When I finally saw my father's body, I cried like I had never cried before. My daddy's corpse lay in the middle of the street burning. In a matter of seconds, several of his friends came over with suit jackets and beat the fire out. Better late than never, I guess.

The street rumors all say my daddy went out in a blaze of glory, but I say there wasn't no glory in burning to a crisp in the middle of the street.

Most girls experience their first heartbreak when they are a lot older than I was, but I had my first heartbreak when I was just seven years old, and after that they kept coming nonstop. Life had dealt me a dirty hand, but I lived through it and I hoped that someday my cards would be different.

CHAPTER 1

Everybody's Got a Hustle

"Would you like to say anything else before I make my ruling?" the judge asked.

Mercy looked directly into the judge's eyes as she spoke. "Your Honor, I would just like to say that I have been a model student in spite of my circumstances and it wasn't the state, my social worker, or any of the foster families I was placed with that made that possible. It was me, my determination, and my drive to rise above being molested, beaten, and mistreated while the state turned its back. I persevered and endured until a better day. This day, Your Honor. The day my life would be placed into my own hands without any roadblocks to hinder me. If allowed, I could be a productive member of society." She paused a minute to wipe her eyes. "So, Judge, I am asking you—I am begging you—please grant me independent living." Her voice went soft as she swallowed. Despair was written all over her face as she prayed for her emancipation. "I can only hope that you don't make me go back to the group home. I am asking you to give me what no one has ever given me since I was seven years old—a chance."

At seventeen years old Mercy stood in front of the judge and pleaded her case. Over the past ten years she had been in eleven foster homes and one group home and had never even come close to being adopted. At the last foster home, her foster mother's boyfriend tried to molest her. He crept up on her in the kitchen and tried to stick his hands under her skirt. She grabbed the first thing she could, a steak knife. Lucky for him, the butcher knife wasn't closer. Once she stabbed him, there were no more foster homes for her. She was hauled off to a group home, even sent to a nuthouse for evaluation at one point. Now she wanted her independence.

The judge looked her over. Her smooth walnut skin bore no makeup, and her short, flat pageboy haircut made her look innocent. However, having a file of her entire life in front of him let him know different. Their eyes met, and he quickly redirected his eyes to the stacks of legal documents before him and began to write on the court documents before him.

Look at this redneck motherfucker, Mercy thought. *I know he ain't going to have no mercy on my soul. He probably gets a hard-on every time a black person comes before him with their life in his hands. Hell, he ought to be wearing a white robe instead of that black one, and a white hood over his head at that. That damn gavel ain't nothing but a torch, and that high pedestal he's sitting up on might as well be a horse. Sittin' up there calling himself a judge when he ain't nothing but the grand marshal of the KKK.* Mercy couldn't help but grin a little, but then quickly hid her smirk when the judge looked up at her. He then looked back down at her file and began going over it again.

I don't even know why I'm getting my hopes up about all this. How could this old white man understand my struggle? He can't. But right now I hope he at least tries to. I just need him to cut me loose from this fucked-up life I've been living. Please just let me go. Release me to the wolves in this big bad world. Let me fuck shit up myself instead of appointing other people to do it for me. I guess it ain't no more I can do. I done prayed all I could, so now it's up to him. I hope he's having a good day. I hope he didn't wake up on the wrong side of the bed this morning. I hope his wife sucked his dick good this morning or something. Damn.

"Mercy Jiles," the judge said as he looked up from Mercy's file. He then took his glasses from the tip of his nose and rubbed his eyes. "Ms. Jiles, this has been a very hard decision for me. Your situation is similar to other girls' who come into my courtroom every day."

Ain't this a bitch? Mercy thought. *I got his card. We all look alike, huh? If he's seen one negra girl, he's seen them all. This Ku Klux Klan motherfucker is going to send me back to that fucked-up-ass group home, I just know he is.* Mercy took a deep breath and sighed.

"But, Ms. Jiles, you are different from those 'other girls.' For some reason, I believe that you are destined to be something. I see your determination and your hunger to rise above your circumstances. And that, I admire about you. However, you must understand because I am going to grant you your motion—"

"Thank you! Judge, thank you so much!" Mercy shouted, cutting off the judge. What else did she need to hear? She had heard enough. Mercy had never been so happy in her life.

The judge continued talking, but Mercy couldn't focus on all the stipulations he was running by her. Thankfully, her court representative later reiterated them. She had to get her high school diploma or GED as well as maintain employment. The program would give her a state-issued check on the first of each month and provide her with subsidized living in a small efficiency apartment. Mercy would be responsible for her utility bills and all her other needs, including clothing and food. If Mercy didn't comply, she would be forced to go back to the group home. At that point she could go before the judge and ask for a second chance. If she was denied, she would have to come back to court every year until she turned twenty-one, when the state could no longer keep her at the group home.

Mercy had no intentions of blowing it. She chose to complete high school rather than cram years' worth of learning into just a few months. Some people say that book smarts only get you so far in life. Well, how Mercy saw it, she was pretty much nowhere as it stood, so however far school could get her was farther than she could have gotten herself otherwise.

In the days following Mercy's court hearing, Mercy applied for jobs everywhere, from fast-food joints to drugstores to retail shops. Things looked promising when she got a call back from McDonald's, where she even had to take a written test, which she passed, missing only one question. She kept checking her pager every five minutes that day, making sure she didn't miss any calls. When the manager called her back the next day, she was certain she had the job in the bag.

"This is the manager who interviewed you at McDonald's yesterday," a man said.

Mercy took the phone from her ear, put it down to her side, and said, "Yes!" She then spoke into the phone. "When would you like me to start?"

The manager paused. "I'm sorry, Ms. Jiles. We're not going to be able to hire you. Your school hours conflict with the hours we need you to work. But we are putting you on the list in case a position should arise with hours you can work."

"Well, guess what?" Mercy said.

"Yes, Ms. Jiles?" the manager said pleasantly.

"You're on my list, too," Mercy yelled, slamming the phone down. One minute after the next it seemed as though doors kept getting slammed in her face.

"How the fuck I can't get a job at McDonald's?" Mercy cried. "Damn, is my luck that bad? It's McDonald's for Christ's sakes. What the hell McDonald's doing having second interviews and tests and shit in the first place when all a mothafucka gotta know how to do is say 'Would you like fries with that?' "

Finally, Mercy had gotten out of the group home, and now she worried that she might not be able to uphold her end of the bargain. She was just about ready to say "fuck it" and let the state take care of her for another year, but she had to give job-hunting another shot.

The next day she met with success. She landed a job at the Ambassador Hotel, which was on the other side of town, and known for its drug traffic, but Mercy didn't give a damn. It kept her in the independent-living program plus put a few dollars in her pocket.

A senior in high school, Mercy was finished with her classes by 12:30 in the afternoon, so she went straight from her locker to the bus stop. She took three buses to get from school to work, and her commute was two hours. After transferring twice, Mercy usually arrived at work at her 3:00 p.m. start time on the nose. However, if the bus was running late, she was late. Sometimes she was able to sneak in without being noticed by her boss, Farrah. Other times she wasn't so lucky and she was either written up or her pay was docked, depending on how late she was.

At the hotel, Mercy was the check-in clerk. Farrah was what Mercy referred to as a BBWA (Black Bitch With Authority). She acted like she owned the whole damn company. Mercy had run across plenty like Farrah in her day, and she hated the feeling that developed in her gut every time she came around. Farrah wasn't mean only to Mercy; she was a bitch to all of the employees. Even when she praised an employee, it was in a condescending manner. "Good job, Mercy," Farrah would say, "but good isn't great."

Farrah knew Mercy's situation and how important it was for her to hold a job. She stayed on Mercy's case and seemed to enjoy the power she had over her. So many times Mercy wanted to snap the fuck-off on Farrah, but just as Mercy was about to beat the brakes off her, Farrah would say, "If I were you, I wouldn't do anything simple that could land your ass right back on the doorstep of that group home you came from."

Mercy would faithfully have to remind herself that this bullshit was only temporary. She could handle Ms. Farrah, but what she didn't want to do was find herself back at one of those foster homes where she could barely sleep at night, trying to guard her pussy from the man of the house. And she sure as hell didn't want to go back to the group home, where she had to fight the ugly jealous-hearted bitches while at the same time trying to stay out of the way of the manly dyke broads who had been turned out many years before. Stealing pussy was all they knew. So Mercy immunized herself against Farrah's snide comments.

One day when Mercy rushed into the Ambassador Hotel lobby at 3:15 p.m., she was relieved to see that Farrah was nowhere in sight. Sam, who had worked there for about three years, was the only one at the front desk.

"About time, Miss Thang," Sam said to Mercy, rolling his eyes. Sam was the tip of a lit match, flaming. He stood six feet tall and couldn't have weighed more than a buck twenty-five soaking wet. He had smooth brown skin and eyebrows that were arched to perfection. His hair was processed with black looped curls. Both ears were pierced, but he never wore his earrings on the job. On the weekends, not only could you find him with earrings in both ears, but you could find him hanging out at Club Colors with pumps and a miniskirt, too.

"I'm so sorry, Sam," Mercy said, rushing in, trying to hurry and take her jacket off and get in her position behind the counter. "My English teacher stopped me to discuss a book we are reading in class. I missed the 12:40 bus and had to wait on the 12:55 one."

"Umm-hmm," Sam said, sucking his teeth.

Just as Mercy was removing her jacket, Farrah got off of the lobby elevator.

"Guyd dayum. Here comes this bitch," Mercy said under her breath.

"Mercy, come into my office," Farrah said, not even making eye contact with Mercy. She was wearing her navy blue work uniform, a jacket and skirt. Her curly roller-set neck-length hair bounced with each step she took in her one-inch navy blue pumps. "Sam, I know you were supposed to be off fifteen minutes ago," she said, stressing the words *fifteen minutes,* "but I just need you to stay a couple more minutes, please."

As Farrah whisked past the two of them to make her way to her office, she left behind her scent of Tabu perfume. Mercy didn't mind the scent at the local department store, or the softness of it when her mother used to wear it way back in the day. However, on Farrah it made her want to puke.

"I already know what this is about," Mercy began as she entered Farrah's office.

"And it's a shame that you do," Farrah interrupted. "You know there is nothing I hate more than a tardy employee. I'd almost rather you didn't show up at all than to strut in here late like everything is okay. This isn't your place. You don't own this hotel, nor are you the manager. You're an employee, and you follow the rules, my rules, or else. And poor Sam had already worked a double shift as it was."

"I apologize," Mercy said, putting her head down. "It won't happen again."

"You don't say," Farrah said, giving Mercy a fake smile, then quickly dropping it. Mercy stood there. Farrah looked at her as if she expected her to say something.

"Isn't there something you want to say to me?" Farrah asked. "Do you want to try to convince me not to write you up? Perhaps you would even like to apologize a little more humbly before I complete this slip?"

Mercy rolled her eyes. "Apologize?" she said under her breath. *You better be apologizing to me for making me put up with that*

strong-ass perfume that smells like you bathed in it, Mercy thought.
*You better be apologizing to me. Bitch, step yo' perfume game up in-
stead of getting that shit off the three-dollar table in Rite Aid. That
fragrance was the shit eight or nine years ago, but today that shit is
played out like an eight-track.*

"I know it's highly unlikely, but perhaps now you'll be on
time," Farrah said, handing Mercy a pen.

Mercy took a deep breath and signed the write-up slip. Farrah
held her hand out to take it back, but Mercy slammed it down on
her desk and headed out of the office.

As Mercy stormed out of the office, the first thing she saw was
Sam standing there with his hands on his hips. "What did the
head beyatch have to say?" he said as he began to gather his belongings to leave.

"I got wrote up," Mercy said, pinning on her name tag.

"Child, ain't that your third one already in four months?"

"Unfortunately, yes."

"Oh, Cruella gon' be all over your ass fo' sho' now just waiting
for you to fuck up," Sam said, throwing his shoulder bag over his
right shoulder. "Watch your back, girlfriend."

"Thanks, Sam," Mercy said. "Oh, yeah, and sorry you had to
stay late on my behalf."

Within minutes Chocolate Smooth, a frequent customer, entered the hotel lobby. Chocolate Smooth was the nickname Mercy
had given him. He was only about five feet, seven inches tall, but
he walked like he stood seven feet. When he strolled into the
hotel, he had that authority as if he owned the place. Watching his
smooth stride, Mercy smiled and thought about the cool-ass dude
from *I'm Gonna Git You Sucka,* the one with fish in the heels of his
shoes. Chocolate Smooth wasn't dressed like he was stuck in the
seventies, but that son of a bitch glided through the doors with
the coolness of an igloo.

Chocolate Smooth always pulled up to the hotel in a fly-ass ride. His gear appeared to be right off the rack from either one of two places: the sales floor or the cleaners. His necklace always seemed like it was fresh out of a tub of jewelry cleaner, and his haircut looked like he had just gotten up out of the barber chair. His sideburns were like a neatly manicured lawn. Chocolate Smooth was just that fine, dark-skinned and smooth as a baby's ass.

It never failed, each time he came to the hotel he had a different broad on his arm, sometimes two. He presented an ID that said Ralph Jones, but Mercy knew that his name wasn't no Mr. Jones. She was sure it was an alias and that he was a drug dealer. And if he wasn't a drug dealer, then he had one hell of a perception game.

"How are you today, Mr. Jones?" Mercy asked.

"I'm doing good," Chocolate Smooth replied in his crisp northern accent. "But I'd be better if you'd look out for me on the price of the room, ma."

Caught off guard, Mercy said, "I can't." She then looked over her shoulder for Farrah.

"Why not? You can do what you want to do," he said. The two women he was with nodded their heads to confirm his statement.

"Yeah, but I can't lose my job over no hookup."

"Check it, sweetheart. I'm just trying to put some money in your pocket plus keep a little bit in mine at the same time."

"How is giving you a hookup gon' put money in my pocket?" Mercy said, putting her hands on her hips.

"Look, I know y'all got a vacant room up in this spot. All you gotta do is hook me up with one. Charge me half of what y'all charge for a room and pocket that shit."

"You're kidding me, right?" Mercy said, chuckling.

"Naw. Ain't you got no hustle about you? Hell, everybody's got a hustle."

Mercy thought about everything he'd said, and she bet he could see the wheels turning in her head.

"Look, it ain't like there ain't ten other hotels you can check mafuckas in at. If you get busted, which you won't, and lose your job, hell, shawdy, you can come work for me," he said, and smiled at Mercy.

Mercy laughed.

"I'm serious, fo' real."

"Okay, look, I see you really trying to get a discount, so I'm gonna give you the Triple A discount. That's like ten percent off," Mercy said as she proceeded to check him in, then issued him a key to his room.

After Chocolate Smooth was gone, Mercy sat at the front desk and tried to do homework for her English class, but she found herself daydreaming instead. She imagined herself as rich as Chocolate Smooth—richer, going on trips first class to the Bahamas, riding in the back of a limo, talking on her cell phone giving orders and then giggling all the way to the bank when she hung up. She wondered, what would her life be like if her daddy hadn't got killed? She damn sure wouldn't have been stuck behind the counter of this place. Her father had always believed she'd make something of herself. Maybe she would, but what?

She heard Farrah approach and put away her books before Farrah could start dishing out more duties that were not in her job description.

"I wasn't going to give you a fifteen-minute break, but I feel like being nice today even though you were late. Go take your break before I leave, and you better not come back late."

Mercy decided to walk to the store right up the street to get something to nibble on. As she passed the hotel parking lot, she noticed that one of the girls who had checked into the hotel with

Chocolate Smooth had run out to his gold Lexus to get something. She was one of the baddest broads Mercy had ever seen him with.

Damn, that girl is lucky, Mercy thought. *She's living the life. Look at her. Hair laid down, mink coat, and her shoes are right.* As Mercy continued on her way, she tried to imagine that girl's life, and as usual, her imagination took over and soon she was making up stories in her head about the girl being a high-class whore and Chocolate Smooth getting abducted by some rival dope dealers. By the time she got to the store, she had created an entire movie in her head.

When Mercy returned to the hotel, she noticed Farrah had placed a bus schedule on top of Mercy's *Sister 2 Sister* magazine. "You better learn to read your bus schedule instead of that gossip column of a magazine," Farrah said. "Because at the end of the day, it's going to be the bus schedule that saves your orphan ass, not that gossip column."

Mercy rolled her eyes and replied, "Yeah, whatever, Farrah." She laughed it off just to keep from hog-spitting on Farrah. Mercy looked at the bus schedule to see if she could maneuver around being late again, but according to the way her buses ran, there was no way to have a backup plan. If she missed one bus, she was basically fucked.

"I need a damn car," Mercy said with a sigh. "Yup, that's all there is to it. I need a little hooptie to get me from Point A to Point B. I'm going to try to save my money and get me a little car. But, hell, what money is there to save?"

For the next couple of days, Mercy couldn't stop thinking of ways she could cop a car. She was at the check-in counter at work plotting hard when an old dude she recognized from the hood showed up. He smiled at her as he paid for his room.

"Y'all got room service?" he asked. "I need me some champagne for my lady friend."

"No, we don't, sir," Mercy said. She was sure he didn't remember her. She glanced past him and saw his car out front with a woman sitting in the passenger seat. One glance was all she needed. There was her momma. *Damn,* she thought. *She's still at it. Fuckin' around with any man who can scrape up a couple dollars to stick in her wallet.* Not that her kids had ever seen any of that money. After Mercy's daddy was killed, the good life was over. If it weren't for the neighbors and people like Ms. Pat and Uncle Roland, those kids would have 'bout starved to death. While her mother rocked the latest fashions, she put cheap shoes and Woolworth's clothes on her kids. While she was out eating steaks, her kids were lucky to have some Beefaroni out of the can.

The man snatched the key from her and ran out like he just couldn't wait to get hold of her momma's worn-out pussy. Mercy felt tears welling up in her eyes. She picked up the phone and dialed the one person she knew could comfort her, Ms. Pat.

"Child, how you doin'?" Ms. Pat asked. "Is school going good? You know, your daddy always wanted you to make something of yourself."

Mercy couldn't bring herself to tell Ms. Pat she had seen her mother, so she told her about her car problems instead.

"You know, I got a cousin with an old car he tryin' to sell," Ms. Pat said. "Let me talk to him and see what he want. It's kinda ugly, though. You too cute for such an ugly car."

"Look, transportation is transportation. I'll look cute when I'm getting out of it on time to work," Mercy said with a laugh.

"Okay."

When Mercy hung up the phone, she felt better. There wasn't

nothing she could do about her skanky momma, but at least Ms. Pat was going to help her find a car. But even Ms. Pat's cousin's ugly car wouldn't be free. She'd have to come up with some money—not just for the car but also for the tag and taxes and insurance and all the rest of the bullshit.

As Mercy wondered how she was going to come up with the money, Chocolate Smooth entered the lobby.

"Hey," he said to Mercy. "Let me ask you something."

Oh, God, now what? Mercy thought.

"Look, do y'all rent rooms by the hour?" he inquired.

"Nope, we don't."

"Oh, I was asking because that's how they do up top where I'm from."

"Nope, we don't do that," Mercy said.

"Look, I need you to stop playing and look out for me for real, and I don't mean no Triple A discount. I need you to let me get a room for about two hours. I ain't really trying to pay the whole sixty-nine dollars for only two hours. How 'bout I give you thirty dollars?"

She thought for a minute about the money she needed for her car and hesitantly agreed. "Just two hours, right?"

"Yup, just two hours," Chocolate Smooth assured her.

"Are you going to mess up the room?"

"Naw." He shook his head.

"You gonna make up the bed right afterwards?"

He smiled and replied, "I got you."

"Don't leave no trash, no nothing in that room," Mercy said in an authoritative tone.

"Look, I got you, ma."

Mercy paused. "A'ight. Don't fuck this up, okay?"

"I got you, I'm telling you. Why I wanna fuck up a good thang? Me and you can help each other out." He smiled as Mercy looked over the list of vacant rooms. She handed him the key as he handed her the money.

"Two hours," Mercy reiterated.

Chocolate Smooth winked.

Mercy looked at the thirty dollars in her hand, smiled, and then tucked it into her bra. *Chocolate Smooth was right,* she thought to herself. *Everybody's got a hustle. Why should I be any exception?*

A monster had been unleashed. For that entire week not only did Mercy rent vacant rooms by the hour to Chocolate Smooth and others, but she took an even bigger risk and rented out vacant rooms for the entire night and pocketed the money. She made sure that the rooms were stocked with extra towels and other amenities. Since the hotel didn't have room service, she didn't worry about that. She had her hustle on lock.

On Friday she caught a cab to work so she wouldn't be late. She would have hated to get fired on the day she was going to take ownership of her new wheels. That night she purchased a 1982 yellow Chevy Chevette from Ms. Pat's cousin. She had to pay a crooked used-car salesman a hundred dollars to write her some thirty-day tags. Although the car was ugly as death walking, she drove it and it got her from Point A to Point B without her ever having to worry about being late again.

Mercy had gotten what she wanted, but just like any hustle, once that easy money came along, the shit was addictive. By the end of the following week she had money from the hourly rental of the rooms from Chocolate Smooth, as well as money she had pocketed for vacant rooms she had continued to risk renting out to others.

Now everybody in Richmond knew that if someone wanted to find a place where there were hustlers, the Ambassador was the hotel where they were all staying and dealing. That was the place the dealers made many sales and got plenty of pussy. Mercy was able to establish a relationship with many of the hustlers. For those who did legitimately check in, she'd check them in under an alias and required no ID. They would always slide her something under the table for that. So if the police or a dealer's main squeeze was looking for him, they wouldn't get the information from the front desk. Also, if a hustler only needed the room for a few hours to cook up or bag up, if the price was right, Mercy hooked them up as well.

Over the next few months Mercy's funds began to grow. The day before her eighteenth birthday she was walking out of Rainbow Plus in Cloverleaf Mall looking for a birthday outfit for herself. Browsing through the racks she noticed the security guard staring at her.

"You need something from me? You see something over here you like?" she asked.

"No, not really, just wondering what's in that bag of yours," the short stubby white security guard said, looking at the huge bootleg Coach bucket bag she was carrying on her shoulders.

"What the fuck you mean, motherfucker? You trying to say that I'm carrying this bag to boost some shit?"

"I didn't say it, you did." He smiled like he was about to get a raise for that comment.

"Naw, boy toy, you don't even get an A for effort on that one." Mercy smiled. "You picked the wrong girl out of a lineup." She continued rummaging through the racks.

"Oh, yeah, then if you know what people like me are gonna think, why would you bring that big bag to the mall, then?" he asked.

"Why?" She chuckled and never looked away from the clothes as she searched for a good buy.

He waited for her answer. She moved around the rack, and he impatiently asked her again, "Now, why would you do that?"

When Mercy moved to the next rack over, she looked up at him. "Well, first off, because I can. The last time I checked I can bring a suitcase in this motherfucker if I want to; it's a free country. Next, I ain't commit a crime," she said, pointing at him, "and I wish you would accuse me of committing one so I can sue the fuck out of you, the store, and the company you work for. And lastly, which is truly none of your fucking business"—she went into her bag—"I keeps me a large jar of Vaseline"—she pulled the Vaseline out—"and sneakers in this bag, in case the wrong bey-atch cross my path on the wrong day and she needs to get dealt with. So, basically, buddy, as long as I shop in this store, and especially in this ghetto mall, this here bag"—she pointed to the bag—"will be on my shoulder."

The guard did not utter a word. Mercy had broke him down and not even raised her voice.

"So Mr. Toy Cop, understand: Stealing, that ain't me. Maybe killing, but never stealing, you heard," she said as she strolled out of the store into the mall.

A few minutes later she ran into Amy, who was one of the city's biggest gossips and seemed to know everything about everybody in town.

" 'Scuse me, ain't you Zurri's lil' sister?"

"Yup." Mercy nodded with a smile although she hadn't seen her sister in years. When Zurri turned eighteen, she had promised to fight the system and get custody of Mercy, but she never did. For a while Zurri wrote to Mercy, giving her hope, but it had been several years since her last letter, when she'd told Mercy she was pregnant. Zurri's focus had then turned to survival; she had her own family to worry about with her baby coming.

Mercy missed her sister and wanted any kind of connection or relationship she could get. So hearing Zurri's name was like music to her ears.

"I knew you had to be," Amy continued, "because y'all look just alike."

"Everybody used to always say that when we were little."

"Well, me and her used to hang out, and she always used to tell me about her lil' sister. You still in the system?" Amy asked.

"Nope, not really. I'm about to turn eighteen tomorrow, and then I'll be one hundred percent rid of them sons of bitches. Do you have my sister's number?" Mercy asked, hopeful to connect with her sister again.

"Her phone cut off, but I just heard there was some drama at her place, that she got to fighting and now Social Services over there looking for her daughter to take her away. Only Zurri won't tell them where the baby at."

Hearing the words "Social Services" made every hair on Mercy's body stand up. "For what?" she asked, worried about her big sister and her niece even more. She had never seen the little girl, but if the Social Services people got their hands on her, she could disappear into the system and no telling what kind of terrible things might happen to her.

"You know how they do," Amy said, sucking her teeth.

"Look, I know you don't know me, but please, I need you to help me. Please help me find my niece," Mercy begged. "You know that we grew up in the system, and I can't let my niece grow up in the system, too. Please, I need you to help me." Mercy's eyes began to tear up.

Peeping out the desperation in Mercy's eyes and in the tone of her voice, Amy said, "Don't worry. I'll help you, girl. Yo' sister is my girl, so I'm going to hook you up." Amy put her hand on Mercy's shoulder like they had known each other forever.

They walked to the pay phone and Amy made some calls. "Look, you got some dough?" Amy asked Mercy as she covered the phone.

"How much?" Mercy asked, as if to say if she didn't have it, she'd get it from somewhere.

Amy replied, "Like a dove."

"Yeah, I got it," Mercy answered.

"Well, the girl who got the baby, your sister's neighbor, said she'll watch your niece until we get there, but we gotta take her a bag of weed."

Mercy agreed.

After Amy took Mercy to a weed spot to cop a twenty-dollar bag, they went to Zurri's neighbor's apartment. Mercy walked in the door and saw the cutest little three-year-old girl with her hair plaited in neat rows and sporting a matching denim jacket and jeans. The girl was playing with an old black Barbie doll with the hair all cut off.

Amy whispered the little girl's name to her.

"Hey, Deonie, I'm your Aunt Mercy," Mercy said. Deonie looked up at her shyly.

"I see you got your doll there. Want me to tell you a story about her?"

Deonie didn't say anything, but handed her the doll.

"See, this here Barbie used to be a fashion model, but then she got in with the wrong crowd," Mercy began. Pretty soon Deonie had crawled up into her lap and was listening to Mercy, completely enthralled.

The next day Mercy called in sick to work so she could get her niece situated. She also visited the Jackson Ward projects to see Ms. Pat and get her advice.

Ms. Pat came to the door in her housecoat. She was a frail-looking woman with salt-and-pepper hair and looked like a sweet little old grandma. Mercy's daddy had trusted Ms. Pat completely. Ms. Pat had even tried to get custody of Mercy and the other kids after Uncle Roland went to jail but never could since she was on disability and lived in the projects.

"How do people do it, Ms. Pat?" Mercy asked, settling down in Ms. Pat's living room with Deonie on her lap. "I've got to work, but who's gonna look after Deonie?"

"Don't you worry 'bout it. I'll look after her. But you need to live closer by. I'm gonna see 'bout getting you a place here in the project. There's a lady I know works at the housing authority, and she owes me a favor."

"That might take a while," Mercy said, handing Deonie a package of animal crackers.

"In the meantime, you can stay here with me," Ms. Pat said, and went into the other room to fix up a place for Mercy and Deonie to sleep.

Mercy was grateful to Ms. Pat, who was better to her than her own sorry mother. Uncle Roland had gotten so disgusted with her mother, Pearl, when he found out she was running after any man with a few dollars in his pocket, even some of those who were known to associate with Nate's killer, Cat, that he'd taken his brother's favorite daughter home to live with him. Besides, the others were either too grown and out of control or had already been swept up in the system.

He'd called himself intervening, but he was a big-time drug dealer himself, and between the late nights, traveling, and living the fast life, she hadn't been much better off with him. Uncle Roland had put forth a good effort, but hell, he could barely take care of his own son, Roe, who was Roland's son by a trick. As soon as his child was born, Roland had taken his son and raised him himself. He'd had good intentions, but the only thing he could pass on to his son was the only thing he knew . . . the streets.

Roland's life had none of the structure that a young child needed. On his son's tenth birthday, Roland felt the only thing his son hadn't had and he was old enough for was a blow job. And on his twelfth birthday, he got him a shot of ass.

However, when Mercy came to live with them, it was different. Seeing firsthand the paths that many raunchy, no-good females take, and where they end up, he'd wanted Mercy to beat the odds. With her being the baby girl and her youngest brother already in and out of trouble, her uncle was very overprotective with her. He'd instilled the principles of the street life in her but had tried hard to keep her a lady. She'd only been with him for about a year when Uncle Roland caught a double homicide charge. He'd beat that, but a month later Roe caught a drug case, and both Roland and his son were sentenced to do a bit, leaving their little princess on the streets to fall victim to the system. Social Services sent her to her first foster family. And for the next few years she'd sampled all the shit that the system had to offer.

"Mercy," Ms. Pat said, coming back in and interrupting Mercy's thoughts. "You know what today is?"

"No," Mercy said.

"You're eighteen. You a free woman now. I made you a chocolate birthday cake."

Deonie loved chocolate cake, and she started squealing and clapping. Mercy had completely forgotten it was her birthday. Then again, birthdays weren't something she really liked to remember, considering when a scheming motherfucker called Cat had killed her Daddy. She had heard that Cat was dead. She sincerely hoped so; otherwise she was likely to spend the rest of her life in prison if she ever saw him.

CHAPTER 2

C-Note

C-Note had been driving for sixteen hours straight on high-way I-95 from Miami back to Richmond. He was exhausted. Al-though it was a drive he could have done in fourteen hours flat, eliminating those two extra hours by switching lanes and driving over the legal speed limit wasn't worth the risk of getting "tow-off" on I-95.

C-Note was happy when he saw the sign that read RICHMOND 38 MILES. The sign gave him that extra burst of energy he needed and confirmed that he was home free. See, many had traveled this same route. Some had good runs, while others, well, they weren't as lucky as C-Note had been. The bottom line was that most cats in the street game knew that I-95 could be the missing link to a baller's success. However, it could be his downfall as well. The traps, the police, the crooked cops, and the women could all be considered the perils and pitfalls of a typical run in the game.

The I-95 stretch had made it possible for plenty of money to be made, babies to get fed, bills to get paid, and countless numbers of women and men to live the glamorous life. The route saw to it that fiends got what they longed for to run through their veins and experience that high they felt they needed. Right off the in-

terstate, plenty of robberies were conspired and played out: an un-
determined amount of body bags were needed each year as a re-
sult of countless drug deals gone bad up and down this stretch.
I-95 was, at times, referred to as Cocaine Alley and at other times
as the Gateway to Riches. Hustlers up north traveled from New
York down south to the small cities, counties, and towns where
the drug prices might be double, sometimes triple what they were
up north, and the competition was almost nonexistent. On the
flip side, I-95 had been the ticket for many southern hustlers who
went up to New York or down to Miami to get drugs at dirt-cheap
prices and bring them back home to make tens and hundreds
of thousands, and if they were both lucky and smart, ultimately
millions. And it just so happened that I-95 had made it possible for C-Note to go from a mediocre hustler, going to his
older brother to re-up, to a dude making major moves in the drug
trade. C-Note had been going to Miami for six months now, ever
since he met Hassim, his drug connect, at last year's Source
Awards.

C-Note turned up the volume on his CD player and blazed the
old NWA song "Dopeman" as he focused on the last thirty minutes of his trip back home to Richmond, VA.

Stay focused, C-Note thought as he drove, bobbing his head to
the music. *A nigga really ain't home free until I pull up in my drive-
way and get in the motherfuckin' house. These state troopers don't be
bullshitting. Niggas always talking 'bout "watch out for those Geor-
gia and North Carolina troopers," but shit, Virginia troopers ain't
nothing to fuck wit' either.*

As C-Note drove up I-95, he thought how life could change in
the blink of an eye. He smiled when he thought about how things
could sometimes go sour before shit could get sweet, which was
how the cards were dealt to him. He went from getting robbed to
having one of the sweetest connects in the city. It wasn't too long

ago that C-Note had gotten caught slipping. It was Source Awards weekend 1998 in Miami, Florida. C-Note was outside of a trendy Miami club checking out the scenery, which consisted of tricked-out cars and half-naked, beautiful women on the prowl. Although it was 2:00 a.m. on an October night, the temperature was still a muggy eighty-five degrees. This was nothing in comparison to how hot the women were. Everywhere C-Note looked—to his left, to his right, behind him and in front of him—eye candy surrounded him. If he wasn't used to having some of the baddest bitches that Virginia had birthed flocking to him, then that night he would've been super fucked-up in the game, not to mention rolling back to VA broke as a broke-dick dog, falling victim to having his cash, jewels, and his riches tricked away. He was out by himself because his boys were up in their room tricking and treating themselves. They couldn't resist making some pimps rich: and these chicks didn't look like the ordinary prostitutes. Nope! These weren't the average hookers standing on the corner trying to make a dollar out of fifteen cents. These bitches looked like superstars or models. The fashion of the day was the "come fuck me" lace-up-the-leg sandals. Every top-flight pimp in the country had brought their hoes to Miami for this event to walk the halls of the luxurious hotels, hoping to find a paid baller who liked what he saw and didn't have any problem paying to play. And C-Note's homeboys, especially his right-hand man, Jus, had fallen victim to the game.

However, C-Note was different. He wasn't paying for any pussy. Every now and again he might jerk off a couple of dollars on a broad, but only when *he* felt like it. It was never because some trick-ass broad roped him in and set the price. In the past niggas might have robbed him blind because a killer he wasn't, but nobody's ho was about to jack him for a little bit of his paper for a sexual favor. It just wasn't happening, especially after being raised by a mother who was a first-tier gamestress herself. Observing all the trickery his mother, Lolly, dished out, he became well schooled when it came to female game, and he decided at a very young age that he wasn't going out like a lame. Besides, his older brother had schooled him to the power of his magic stick. Between C-Note taking notes from his mother and brother, he was certain that he was doing a chick a favor by blessing her with some of his *good dick game*. Plus, he felt that he had enough charisma to pull any broad he desired, so paying for pussy was definitely out of the question.

C-Note sat in the cut of Los Bravos Nightclub, observing and playing the background like he always did. Handsome, he was a dark-skinned chocolate specimen. Black as tar with the prettiest white teeth, and boy could he wear a baldhead. He had big round eyes and long eyelashes that gave him sex appeal. He was tall, slinky, and had big feet. Now, any woman from the hood or the suburbs knew what that meant.

C-Note was dressed good enough to taste in his all-white sweat suit, and his spanking new, "straight out of the box to his feet" white-on-white Nikes. The necklace he had borrowed from his brother sealed the deal. The eight carats of flawless diamonds dripping through the "Richtown" pendant were worth more than his 5 series BMW. Although C-Note was exactly what most of the women in the club were looking for, the average chick didn't spot him because he stayed in the shadows, positioning himself where he could conveniently see what he wanted to see. Two foreign beauties caught his eye as they sat in a corner. He tried, but couldn't figure out what their exact nationality was—Dominican, Panamanian, Puerto Rican, or what? But he was certain of one thing: Those two women were bad! He was intrigued with the way they were all over each other.

Damn. Dem bitches is lesbos, he thought, shaking his head. *Seems like that shit is a fad, the in thing.*

C-Note couldn't keep his eyes off of them. Once the girls noticed him looking, they held eye contact with him and put on a show, just for him, that had him so caught up his eyes were glued to their performance. For a minute he thought about breaking his main rule. If a nigga was gon' trick, it was gon' be with some original broads like them. It was like picking out furniture. He didn't want the shit that he could get at any ol' department store that everybody seemed to have in their front room. He wanted that shit that a mothafucka had to get shipped from overseas.

The two exotic women continued to perform for him, kissing and licking each other. One put her finger in the other's mouth, and the one doing the licking stared at him the entire time. The two girls smiled, whispering in each other's ears, then pointed at him between their bewitching laughter. The more docile one whispered something in the aggressive one's ear, who smiled, giving her friend a high five. She then looked over at C-Note and seductively mouthed the words, "Want to join us?"

With a mischievous smile carved on his face, C-Note headed over to the girls' table so they could make the necessary arrangements to take the party elsewhere. He never noticed the two cats watching him the whole time he was distracted with the chicks. Before he knew it, the two guys were up on him.

"Whad' up, VA?" one of the dudes asked.

C-Note didn't even look up, because he was still caught up into the broads. Besides, his name wasn't VA. The other dude said it again, a little louder this time.

"Whad' up, VA?" he said.

C-Note then gave them the universal hood greeting, the "wassup" nod. As he threw his head up to acknowledge the jokers, he noticed the imprint of a pistol through the guy's shirt. C-Note was sure that shit wasn't right, but he didn't let on. He decided to try to play past them.

Damn, how the fuck I let these niggas get up on me? he wondered. *These bitches got me slippin' like a motherfucker fo' real. My momma ain't never lied when she said that pussy is power.*

"You got me at a disadvantage. Do I know you?" C-Note said, locking eyes with the aggressor.

"No, but you can get to know me," the spokesman of the two replied to C-Note's comment. He then pointed to C-Note's necklace. "Slim, that's a nice piece. What you tryin' to get for it?" At that moment, C-Note knew for sure that these were some grimy niggas and they were on a greasy mission.

C-Note arrogantly replied, "Naw, I don't sell jewelry." Just then he felt the cold steel of the pistol press against his side.

"Run the chain, niccka," the spokesman said through gritted teeth.

C-Note's first instinct was to pull his own burner, but then he thought again. *Never do irrational things on fucking impulse. Let me think this shit out.* C-Note's brain was working in overdrive. *I'm on a major strip with a good five hundred people, which translates into five hundred witnesses. Three things can happen: I can give up the chain, be forty thousand late, and have to explain to my brother that his chain is gone. Or I can pull out my burner, lay these motherfuckers out here and now, and take the chance of going to the penitentiary for the rest of my life for a piece of money. Or three, I can get killed in the process.*

C-Note made a decision that night that some might have thought was the soft, sucker route: He gave the chain up, which made him able to live, and fight another day.

"Empty dose pockets, too, niccka," the less vocal one said after

C-Note proceeded to hand over the necklace. C-Note noticed his tattoo, the five percenter symbol on his hand.

The beauties watched the whole episode as it went down. Once the two bandits walked off with C-Note's goods, the more aggressive of the two women strutted over to C-Note.

"Damn, papi, we was trying to get with you," she said, rubbing her hand down the side of C-Note's face. "We couldn't help but notice you, I mean with that eye-catching chain and all. But since that shit is long gone along with your money, you probably ain't in the mood to pay what we cost. So I guess we gon' have to holla back another time, Richtown!" Just then her girlfriend walked up, put her hand around her waist, and the two walked off.

Damn, these motherfucking bitches done got my chain taken and won't even give a nigga no play, he thought. For the first time in his life, he felt like a lame. That couldn't be what Jay-Z meant when he rapped about a chain reaction.

"Bitch, go suck a dick!" C-Note shouted as he made his way into a nearby bar to try to gather his thoughts and convince himself that he wasn't really a sucker after all.

He sat at the bar and ordered a drink with the few hundred dollars he had in the other pocket, which he hadn't turned over to the two stick-up kids.

"Let me get a double shot of Henny," C-Note said to the bartender.

A guy who looked to be in his late thirties came and sat beside C-Note. The guy ordered a drink.

"Rough night, huh?" the man said, noticing the disgusted look on C-Note's face.

C-Note gave a slight chuckle. "Hump!" he grunted. "That's an understatement."

"Well, you can't let shit get you down," the guy said.

"Yeah, funny you should say that. Man, I just got robbed a few minutes ago."

"No shit?" The guy had a Spanish accent, but he spoke good English.

"For real." C-Note nodded.

"Did you make a police report?" the guy asked.

"Fuck the police! I don't call them sons of bitches for shit," C-Note spat.

The guy smiled and said, "I like yo' style."

"However, my momma might be calling them after my brother kills me." C-Note picked up the drink the bartender slid in front of him and took a sip.

"Why yo' brother going to kill you?"

"Because niggas robbed me for his shit. His chain cost a lot of money. I had no business with it."

"Don't worry; it's only material. Plus you can get a hundred more chains, but you can't get yo' life back."

"Now all I got to do is convince my brother of that," C-Note responded.

"Look, I'm Hassim," the guy said, extending his hand.

"C-Note." They shook hands.

"C-Note, huh? Ah . . . ," Hassim said, nodding his head as if something was on his mind.

A guy walked by and acknowledged Hassim. "Peace," the dude said.

Hassim acknowledged him back with a nod, and C-Note laughed.

"Let me in?" Hassim asked, wondering what C-Note found to be so funny.

"Thinking 'bout the greeting 'peace.' That's all. Funny how people quick to say 'peace,' but a nigga can't really have peace.

Every time I try to have peace of mind, a nigga is trying to get a piece of mines."

"It's like that from time to time," Hassim said nonchalantly. "So, what you going to do about them guys that got your chain? You gonna give them beef?"

"Naw, man. My name is C-Note, and I'm about money. I can't get money and fight a war at the same time."

There was a long silence between the two men before Hassim looked into C-Note's eyes and said, "Look, man, I like your style. I saw that bullshit go down, and I liked how you handled yourself. You put your mind before your ego." He nodded, never breaking eye contact. "My friend, you have a good head on your shoulders, and I know I can help you get a thousand more of them chains."

C-Note looked over Hassim's clothes, trying to figure exactly how a man in some dirty white Adidas and a Marlboro T-shirt was going to help him. Then it popped in his mind that a book could never be judged by its cover. He took into consideration Hassim's swagger and the way he talked so authoritatively, and C-Note knew what was up and asked, "What's it going to cost me—I mean your help?"

"Loyalty."

Is this motherfucker bullshitting or what? C-Note thought at the time, but from that day forward, Hassim had been dishing out bricks at rock-bottom prices, and like a gymnast, C-Note was flipping them with ease. So far, so good. Neither one of them never put any bullshit in the game.

"Hey, Don Corleone, you out there? Breaker-breaker, Don Corleone. Come on in," C-note heard as he snapped back to the present. He was swiftly brought back to reality when he heard a trucker over his CB radio. Riding down the highways and byways, C-Note had always thought that he didn't need anybody or anything except for his faithful Ford LTD work vehicle. He quickly learned that the truckers were the true rulers of the highway, and especially of I-95. No four wheels were able to compete with their eighteen wheels. Since they were the governors and the chiefs, it paid to be in their union.

C-note quickly grabbed the mouthpiece to his CB and pushed the button to reply. "Go ahead, Lil' Lost Chicken," he said.

"Keep your eyes open and look over your shoulder, because two full-grown bears are coming up fast through your back door," Lil' Lost Chicken said from an eighteen-wheeler that was riding about three miles behind C-Note.

"I'm on it," C-Note said. Then he heard the trucker make a long whistle before he heard the voice of another trucker come over the radio.

"Shaggy Dog, what bones you got?" C-note asked the animated trucker who was about five miles ahead of him.

"I'm up here. Just blazed exit sixty-nine at the cigar plants, and the Bandit is in the cut," Shaggy Dog replied.

"Is he rolling or taking pictures?" C-Note asked. He realized Shaggy Dog had just passed the Phillip Morris buildings.

"He a sitting bear, taking plenty of snapshots." Shaggy Dog informed him that the trooper was lying in the cut with his radar on.

"A'ight, keep the front door open for me, Shaggy Dog," C-Note said.

"You ain't got nothing to worry about. I'm up here three exits ahead with my eyes wide open. I'll keep the doghouse dry for you." He ended with a long dramatic whistle and then said, "This Shaggy Dog on the run to the end of the stretch," letting his fellow truckers know that he was going to Canada.

C-Note checked his speed and his car's secret compartments

and smiled at the heads-up from his trusty newfound trucker friends. As much as C-Note wished he had someone who could ride along to keep him company or share the driving, there was no one he felt he could trust. There was no way he was going to risk giving his connect up to a soul. Who would blame him, as sweet as his prices were? He was getting keys at thirteen g's a pop when the going rate was anywhere from eighteen to twenty g's. On top of that, Paula—his right-hand, get-money, ride-or-die bitch—had a priceless "whip" game. She cooked coke so good that she could easily take ten keys of this 93-percent raw and turn them into twenty. So not only were his prices low, but his product was the best in town. C-Note's money flowed like the Jordan River. By no means would he jeopardize that bringing along some local clown playing cutthroat with him, or even worse, being able to sing like the damn Pips if Smokey got lucky for the ride.

Damn, I wish my brother was here so we could do this shit together, C-Note thought. His brother, Lynx, had introduced him to the game and was now in prison doing a five-year bit.

C-Note arrived into Richmond at approximately eleven o'clock in the morning on the fifteenth of the April. He knew he couldn't drag his feet on dumping the work, because he planned on taking another trip down to Miami before the first of the month. Dressed in the same matching brown khaki Dickies work uniform with the same wheat-color Timberland boots he wore every single time he made his trip, he stopped first at a mini-mart to get a Red Bull. Just as C-Note got back in his car, his cell phone rang. He looked down at the caller ID and then answered it.

"Yo, I'll be there in thirty minutes," C-Note said into the receiver.

"Cool," Paula cooed. "I'll be waiting."

C-Note hung up the phone and smiled. That's what he liked

about having Paula on his team. There was never any useless small talk. If he said he was on his way, no questions were asked.

Thirty minutes later he was at Paula's, and while she had his coke brewing, he made phone calls to a few worker bees to get the show going. While talking on the phone, he couldn't help but notice how phat Paula still was as she moved about the kitchen in some old green sweatpants. He didn't want her to know he was watching her, because the minute she thought he was admiring her, she would be all over him.

It's too bad that she's a straight ex ol' ho, C-Note thought, shaking his head. *Or else I would have her ass.*

He thought about Paula's travels displayed in pictures on her octagon mirror stand: to heavyweight boxing matches, on cruises and to Cancún.

Paula was a washed-up, watered-down, burnt-out ho from way back in the day, when hustlers were really getting real money. Paula was still beautiful in her own right, but she could never be made into a housewife. Her reputation of chasing if not every baller but damn near every hustler that ever walked the streets in Richmond from 1986 to 1993 was too much to overlook. For a while she was the best gold digger for as long as anybody could remember. Known best for her lockjaw pussy, she was given the name "Sweet Pussy Paula."

Sometimes mistaken for an Indian, Paula had long, black, wavy, thick hair that she wore in a neatly maintained ponytail. As thick as her hair was, it demanded a serious Revlon perm, but she wasn't trading in her naturally wavy hair for bone-straight hair. Besides, her fierce sex game just sealed the deal.

Sweet Pussy Paula had a good run. She ran through ballers' cash and stash like Marion Jones in a two-hundred-meter sprint. Everybody wanted a piece of Sweet Pussy Paula. If a hustler hadn't either sexed or turned down the opportunity to hit Paula, he hadn't arrived in the game yet. But before she knew it, her stock fell extremely low and she found herself being propositioned to do things that were way out of character.

Since she had a reputation, and not for doing good hair, Paula couldn't get a steady clientele in the beauty salon she owned. It wasn't that other chicks thought she was a moral disgrace. No, broads were funny like that. They were lightweight jealous of the rumors of just how good Paula's pussy was, making them second-guess what they were workin' with up under their own thongs. It didn't help her at all that her hair game was only okay, and when it came to doing hair in the VA, okay was just not good enough. The only stylists she had in her shop were either chicks with un-steady clientele or ones who had been kicked out of damn near every shop in Richmond. But together they somehow made it.

Besides stripping, Paula tried it all: nails, massage therapy, and selling drugs. However, when it came to dealing drugs, she could never keep the re-up money straight, spending it as quickly as she made it. While trying to stretch her product out so that she could make as much money as possible off her drugs, she learned that she had a hell of a "whip game," something she acquired from watching some of the best ballers to ever do it cook their own stuff up because they didn't trust anyone to cook their shit, not even a naked bitch in pumps.

At first she became Lynx's best-kept secret, but he passed her on to his lil' brother because her loyalty had never been questioned. Because Lynx or C-Note never sexed Sweet Pussy Paula, somehow she was convinced that they really cared about her.

By the time Paula had finished up her entree, C-Note's phone started blowin' up. The word was out that he was back in town and the shop was wide-open.

After Paula served him all of his coke on a platter, C-Note peeled off several bills from a stack of hundreds like he always did.

"Are you sure?" Paula asked, looking at the money. "I know you just got back in town. I can wait till you dump some of that work. I don't have anything that dire to be paid. My bills are on point from when you came through and gave me that money two weeks ago."

"Naw, I'm good," C-Note said, shaking his head from side to side. He was impressed by Paula's lack of greed. The way she was lookin' out for a brotha's pockets instead of her own was a bonus. But still in his eyes, once a ho always a ho. He replied, "I was going to go and get you something nice, for all the work you be puttin' in for me, but I ain't have the time. So go ahead and hold on to that."

"Thank you!" she said, pocketing the money. "You ain't gotta say it more than once. Is it anything you need me to do? Because you know today is Monday, and I'm off work from now to Wednesday."

"I might need you to come by my house and take my clothes to the cleaners. And see if you can take my watch to the jeweler to get a link taken out for me."

"A'ight, you know I got you." She smiled.

C-Note's phone rang again. He looked down at the caller ID screen to see who was calling him. "Damn, I swear I don't feel like fucking with this larceny-hearted-ass nigga, let me go. I'ma hit you up later," he said to Paula as he gave her a brotherly hug, then grabbed his duffel bag and answered the phone.

"Yo," he said as he walked out the door.

"Nigga, where you at? Why I gotta call you a hundred times to get you to answer?"

"Stop tripping," C-Note said, sucking his teeth.

"Look, man, I need to get some of that. I'm doing bad as a bitch," he heard his brother's right-hand triggerman, Cook'em-up, say.

"You know this ain't even your MO." C-Note knew that Cook'em-up wasn't a hustler. He would rather kill a nigga and take his instead of going out to get his own.

"When the chips is low, a nigga gotta do whatever. So help a nigga out," Cook'em-up reasoned.

C-Note took a deep breath and said, "Look, holla at me on Friday and I'm going to look out for you real decent."

"Friday? What you mean Friday when shit is fresh out the oven today? I need to have shit today!" Cook'em-up said in his attempt to try to strong-arm C-Note.

Damn, I know this nigga ain't going to fuckin' pay me. He never does, C-Note thought. Cook'em-up already owed him five g's from last month and was still asking for more work. Cook'em-up wasn't somebody that C-Note could just give a half ounce to in order to get him out of his face. He knew Cook'em-up would want at least a big eight or better. But it wasn't happening today.

"Look, man," C-Note said with a sigh. "I can only throw an OZ yo' way, straight up."

"An OZ?" Cook'em-up spat. "Man, come on. This me, baby. This is Cook'em-up."

And that's why, C-note said to himself. Finally Cook'em-up saw that he wasn't going to do any better, so he and C-Note hooked up and Cook'em-up copped the ounce of coke. Just as C-Note called it, on Friday Cook'em-up called for more, and just like always, he had no money to pay for what he had gotten before. C-Note talked a little junk to Cook'em-up but always looked out, because he knew that if push ever came to shove, it would be Cook'em-up who would gladly, at the drop of a dime, be the muscle behind his organization. Cook'em-up had been working with the family a long time, even before C-Note's father was killed, so C-Note had to do right by him even if it was a losing proposition.

CHAPTER 3

Kiss My Grits

"Late again? Your ass is about to be hauled off to the group home," Farrah said, with her voice full of contempt.

"Oh, for real," Mercy challenged, hands on hips.

"Remember a few weeks ago when you signed this last warning?" Farrah said, slapping a copy of the write-up with Mercy's signature on it down on the desk. "Bam!" she said with a Kool-Aid smile. "You're outta here and on the road to the group home, boo." Farrah got in Mercy's face and Mercy could smell the Chinese food she had eaten earlier for lunch on her breath. Mercy almost gagged.

"Get out of my face," Mercy said with no emotion as she sat down in the chair while Farrah roared into laughter.

"Don't you know I *liiivvvve* for this?" Farrah stressed. "I live for these days when I can shut down you little grown-ass girls who think you know everything. You ain't nothing, and you ain't going to be nothing. Now get out of here and carry your ass back to the group home."

"Bitch, kiss my ass," Mercy said with emotion and stood up. She scanned the room for something to throw at Farrah. Then for a split second she wanted to spit on Farrah. However, she knew she had to leave. She walked calmly to the door, then turned and said, "The next girl that comes through here might not be as nice as me, so you better watch who you fuck with. And I mean what I said: Kiss my ass, bitch!" And Mercy pulled down her elastic uniform pants, bent over, and smacked her butt. She quickly pulled her pants back up and said, "I am eighteen years old, and I don't have to deal with your bullshit ever again. So stay the fuck out of my way."

A week later, Mercy still hadn't found work. She looked for jobs in the mornings, and in the afternoons she took Deonie out for her exercise, which was usually a ride on her tricycle. With Deonie being so hyper, activity was a must. In fact, this was the only way to tire her out and get her to take a nap. Deonie loved her bike, and she rode it at top speed without ever slowing down. To keep up with her, Mercy would have to speed-walk beside her. She didn't care, because it helped keep her voluptuous hourglass figure intact since she couldn't afford a gym membership. They usually did three laps around the whole neighborhood.

On this particular day during the first trip around the block, Mercy saw the same old hoodrats whose total ambition was to become hustlers' wives, doing what they do best, hanging on the corner or sitting on the bench at the bus stop, wasting their lives away. These broads were looking for any hustler, didn't matter what kind—part-time, full-time, nickel-and-dime, or big-time drug dealer—to come and move them out of the hood. The leader of the hoodrat coalition was none other than Brianna, who just happened to be Farrah's niece. Brianna had so much potential but wasted it, instead devoting her life to picking on other people and making fun of them instead of looking in the mirror at herself.

When Mercy and Deonie passed the group of girls, they had jokes big-time, and, of course, Brianna was the ringleader. Like good little flunkies, the others followed suit, as they always did.

"I bet her baby have to eat with all that safety equipment on!" Brianna teased, making fun of Deonie's safety helmet, knee, and elbow pads.

"Ha! Ha! Ha! Ha! Ha!" the other girls laughed.

"Now we all know that she rides the short bus." Brianna couldn't stop because she was on a roll. Mercy shot her a mean look.

How could these bitches be so fucking cruel? she wondered. *To make those kinds of jokes, about a child? I swear I wish my niece wasn't with me. I would beat the brakes off of her and anyone in her crew who wants any part of me. I'm not going to stoop to their level, though,* Mercy thought, trying to calm herself down. *But fo' real this shit seems to escalate every time I walk around this motherfuckin' block. It's one thing for these chicks to hate on me, but what the fuck my niece gotta do with this?*

Brianna kept going on with the jokes as if she was purposely trying to push Mercy's buttons, and on Mercy and Deonie's last lap around the block, Mercy gave Brianna a nasty look and Brianna laughed loudly. Mercy kept walking. She knew that she couldn't act a fool while her niece was with her. She knew her temper and that if she responded there would be a fight, and those girls would surely double-bank her.

Later that evening, Mercy was playing catch with Deonie and the two little kids that lived next door when Brianna and her crew came walking by. Brianna had more jokes when she saw Deonie without her safety equipment.

"Oh my God, look at her," Brianna said, pointing to Deonie. "Poor thang. It ain't her fault. She's the one that's backwards," she said, nodding toward Mercy. Brianna continued, "Don't that stupid girl know you suppose to wear safety equipment when you playing ball, not when you ride a bike. But that lil' girl don't have nowhere to get no sense from. I betcha if you put her brain in a bat, the bat would fly backwards."

Brianna's followers roared into laughter as if they were watching the queens of comedy.

Mercy had had enough of Brianna and her crew.

"What? What did you say?" Mercy snapped.

Before Brianna could respond, Ms. Pat called out of her door, "Mercy, come here. I need you for a minute."

Lucky bitch. She has no idea that Ms. Pat just saved her life.

"There's a job opening at the cookie factory," Ms. Pat said as Mercy and Deonie entered her apartment. "Give this man a call. You can probably start right away." Ms. Pat handed Mercy the number, and Mercy sighed with relief and called the man. It wasn't much, working in a cookie factory, but it would pay the bills and she and Deonie could move into their own apartment.

Ms. Pat pulled some strings and was able to get Mercy an apartment across the hall from her. Mercy wanted to move to a better neighborhood, but she felt her job at the cookie factory was unstable. Although it paid fifteen dollars an hour, they laid off on a regular basis. It was an unwritten rule that when work was available, they would call her back, but there was no telling how long it would be before that call came. Sometimes Mercy worked for four months straight; she'd get laid off for two months. But when she did work, she could rack up on the overtime. And she did. Sometimes she brought home over a grand a week. When she worked, she worked like a slave, on any shift they would give her. During her days of being laid off, she was eligible for unemployment checks, but that money wasn't half of what she raked in when she worked. During months when she didn't work a day and her unemployment had been exhausted, she would still somehow be able to scrape together enough to pay the low rent for her apartment in the hood.

When she did work, her rent would increase. She didn't want to report her income, but she had to or Brianna would be sure to tell someone and get her kicked out for sure.

One day when she hadn't been working for a couple of weeks, she went over to visit with Ms. Pat, who asked her to go to the store and pick up some Kool-Aid.

Although she didn't feel like it, she could never say no to Ms. Pat. Mercy left Deonie with Ms. Pat while she went off to the store.

Mercy noticed that dude C-Note that everybody had been talking about as he rode past her in his brand-new GS 400 Lexus. Although she knew of him, they had never been formally introduced. Mercy tried to stay clear of all the neighborhood boys, especially C-Note. She knew that all the girls wanted to ride his dick, including Brianna, and Mercy wasn't trying to be just another statistic.

The word on the street was that C-Note was a good dude, and she never really heard any dirt kicked on his name except that he was soft. He was known to get money, and he would go out of his way to duck the drama and the gunplay. He's what some would call a finesse hustler. She had heard that his older brother, Lynx, a renowned player, introduced him to the game. Lynx wouldn't let him accept anything less than a hundred dollars, so the fiends gave him the name C-note, a name that stuck with him. He was a nice guy, and on the strength of his brother, he could have any woman that he wanted. But he never entertained any from the hood. Not that anybody knew of, anyway. It was to no one's surprise that over a few months C-Note started coming up in a ghetto-fabulous way. He was pushing a new Lexus and slowly beginning to have three sets of projects on lock, which was making his name ring. Not only was he a stand-up dude, he was making major moves right in the footsteps of the brother, who was now in prison.

Mercy had never noticed how sexy he was until she saw him getting out of his car as she walked across the parking lot to the Chinese-owned store.

Damn, that nigga is sho' wearing the fuck out of that wife beater, looking like a chocolate pop, Mercy thought, licking her lips. *I'm always looking for a brother in a suit, but shit, I will take this wife beater any day.*

Brianna was standing on the corner with her hoodrat crew. As soon as Brianna saw C-note pull into the parking lot, she rushed over so she could be heard and seen. Loudly, she screamed out, "Girl, you sooo funny, ahhh haaa-haaa." Then she fell into laughter, trying to get C-note's attention. But he went into the store and never acknowledged her. Mercy laughed to herself and went to the back of the store to get Ms. Pat's Kool-Aid.

Brianna came in right behind her.

"Hey, C-note," Brianna asked in a flirtatious manner. "How you doing?"

Mercy pretended not to be watching, but she saw that he never opened his mouth; he only threw his head up to indicate "What's up."

Brianna bought a cherry blow pop while C-note went over to the grill side of the store and ordered food in a soft voice. "Yeah, let me get a, ummm, cheeseburger sub with no onions and a large fries cooked hard." He leaned up against the counter to wait for his food. As soon as Brianna made eye contact with C-note, she began working the blow pop overtime, licking it as if it was a dick with a cherry on top. For a split second she had C-note's undivided attention. That is until Mercy came up to the counter with her packages of Kool-Aid and three cans of ravioli for Deonie.

Mercy never claimed to be anybody's beauty queen, but many people told her she was pretty. Although she was a bit on the thick side, she carried her weight well. She was one hot dog away from a size sixteen but often squeezed into a fourteen, always telling herself that she was going to lose weight. She had tried every diet known to man at least once. At five feet and eight and a half inches tall, she was voluptuous and curvy. Her white teeth complemented her dark brown skin. Never letting the gap between her two front teeth slow her down, she constantly reminded herself that it was only temporary. Since her job's health insurance plan didn't offer dental, she was saving her extra dividends to get braces. However, her well-maintained spiked short haircut was her trademark, and each piece was always intact.

Mercy's appearance snapped C-note out of the trance Brianna had him in. Brianna had mastered the art of how to get to the center of the blow pop, but now every ounce of C-note's attention was directed to Mercy. He was absolutely mesmerized by her in her pink stretch Twirk jeans and the Twirk baby tee to match. She was wearing her brand-new 5411 white-on-white high-top Reeboks.

Walking past C-Note, Mercy could feel his eyes glued to her body. She didn't make eye contact with him, but she knew he could smell the faint scent of her Victoria's Secret Rapture.

As Mercy stood in line with her items, a man in front of her called out numbers to the clerk, a tiny little Chinese lady, to punch into the lotto machine's computer. C-Note finally caught her eye, looked her up and down, and then locked eyes with her.

"Whad'up?" C-Note said to Mercy.

Mercy saw Brianna gritting on her, so she worked the moment like it was a cow, milking it for all it was worth. She looked him up and down and in a very seductive voice replied, "Hey, boo, how you doing?"

"Not as good as I could be, and you?"

With a little sexy laugh, Mercy said, "Not as good as I should be."

"I can't tell. But later with all that. What's yo' name, boo?" he asked. Brianna's mouth dropped, shocked that he was even entertaining Mercy.

"Mercy," she said in a sure but confident way to give him a smile.

"Let me guess, that's short for Mercedes or something, huh?"

"Nope. It's just Mercy."

C-Note mumbled under his breath only loud enough for Brianna to hear him. "Damn, but I sure hope she rides like a Mercedes."

The smile that Mercy dropped on him had C-Note feeling like an M&M, only he was melting in the palm of her hands, not in her mouth. There was no way C-Note could hide or handle it. He might as well have written all over his face that he wanted to be Mercy's candy man.

"I don't know what you smiling up in his face fo'?" Brianna got up in Mercy's ear and said. "He don't fuck wit' no Reebok broads."

"There's an exception to every rule," C-Note said with a slight cockiness. "Besides, I make the rules around here."

Mercy laughed like it was something funny, but she did not want to get in a verbal war with Brianna right then.

"Bitch, I don't see nothing funny," Brianna spat. "You got a nerve to be laughing. Get yo' teeth fixed before you start laughing and smiling up in somebody's face!"

"I'm not even going to stoop down to your level," Mercy responded, and laughed again in Brianna's face.

"It'll be too hard for you to, you too-tall, linebacker-looking-ass bitch. Bitch, you can't get on my level."

"Whatever, but I know I ain't about to be too many more bitches. And when you wanna address me as a bitch, make sure you address me as a real bitch, you hear me?"

"A real bitch with a retarded baby?" Brianna laughed.

"Ho-ho-ho, wait a minute. Yo, enough is enough. Fo' real," C-Note said, getting in between the girls. He could see that the argument was about to escalate to something physical.

"Look, ladies, chill," he told both of them. He then pointed to Brianna. "You can't talk about nobody's baby being retarded. Yo, that shit ain't cool." He then looked at Mercy. "And you got too much going on for yo'self to be out here fighting."

"I'm cool, trust me," Mercy said. "You want a piece?" She offered him a piece of gum.

"You know I do," he said, taking the gum.

Mercy paid the clerk for her items. "Can you triple-bag my stuff, please?" Mercy asked the clerk. "I'm walking, and I don't want them busting through the bags." She then gestured toward Brianna. "I would've offered that thing a piece of gum, but this kind of gum ain't for no gorillas."

"That was a good one, shawdy," C-Note said laughing with her.

"Laugh now, cry later, beyatch!" Brianna said under her breath. Brianna was madder than ever, but she wasn't going to try anything with C-Note, the king of the projects, right there. Mercy walked out of the store, and C-Note followed behind her.

"You gon' be a'ight, shawdy? I can take you home," he offered, wanting to showcase his new whip.

"I'm okay, trust me," Mercy said. "She's the least of my worries. Her bark is worse than her bite."

"What make you say that?"

"Because that's all she does, don't you know? Her and her girls always be joking on my baby niece."

"Oh, that bitch is foul."

"I usually don't say nothing because my lil' niece be with me, but not today."

At that moment, the store clerk came to the door and called C-Note to inform him that his food was ready.

"Hold up," C-Note said to Mercy. "I'll be right back. Don't go nowhere, now."

"I won't," Mercy responded with a smile, but just as soon as C-Note entered the store, Mercy started walking home.

Before Mercy knew it, out of nowhere, Brianna was in her face. "Oh, bitch, you want to play with me?"

Mercy knew what time it was, and she didn't give Brianna a chance to say or do anything before she hit her with a quick left hook and a hard straight right using the cans inside of the bag as her weapon, gripping it tight. Brianna neither saw nor expected it. The hook caught Brianna on the jaw while the straight right hit her on the chin, knocking Brianna straight to the ground. Mercy grabbed her by the braids and dragged her for a split second, then kicked her in the face four times before Brianna's friends jumped in to help her.

One of the girls hit Mercy from the blind side, and Mercy hit the ground hard. They tried to advance on her. She was too quick for them, though. Since she was mentally prepared for the fight, she would not let them take her. In a blink, Mercy reached for the bag with her ravioli cans, gripped it tight in her hand, and came up swinging. Mercy hit one chick on her hip, and she fell like a bad hairdo. The other girl was still throwing a bunch of quick baby punches at Mercy, looking like she was in fast-forward mode her licks were coming so quick. It's too bad she had no idea that she was about to get the hell beat out of her, courtesy of Mr. Franco-American Raviolis. Mercy swung the cans in a wide upward loop, coming down across the girl's head, sending her into la-la land. She continued to beat the heifer until she realized the girl was out cold. She threw her cans in the big Dumpster and was about to throw in the towel until she saw Brianna scrambling, trying to get up off the ground. She could not resist. Mercy knew what she had to do. Brianna threw her hands up in defense; all the fight had been taken out of her. Mercy didn't give a damn that she had just knocked Brianna out one time; she had to give her a bonus round. She reached out and grabbed Brianna's braids and yelled, "This is for my niece, bitch!"

Brianna tried her hardest to fight Mercy off, but there was no hope, especially when Mercy head butted her. Not once, but four times. Mercy had fought with so much emotion that she had not realized that her shirt had come off. She had blanked out and was living out her dream of being the heavyweight champion of the hood. She had no idea just how much damage she had done to her foes or herself. Mercy too was bleeding and in need of a few stitches.

It's funny how in the hood everyone can be in the house, but let a fight break out and people come out like the roaches do when the lights are turned off. But when the police come, they scram like roaches when the lights are cut on. Luckily, somebody had told Ms. Pat about the fight. Equipped with her butcher knife, she showed up in just the nick of time. It was only by the grace of God that she was able to get down to the corner and pull Mercy off Brianna, leaving the police clueless as to who was the gangsta-ass chick who had punished the neighborhood troublemaking bitches.

Ms. Pat drove Mercy to the hospital to get stitches and a wrist brace. When Mercy woke up the next morning, she had a headache that would not quit, every bone in her body was hurting, and her right eye was swollen shut. She got up and walked into the kitchen, where her friend, Chrissie, who had been with her in the group home, and Deonie were having cereal.

"Hi, Auntie," Deonie said. She then looked up at Mercy and scrunched up her face. "I don't like that makeup on your face."

Mercy snickered. "I don't either, baby," she said, smiling at her niece.

"Girl, you look like shit," Chrissie said.

"I feel like it, too," Mercy replied.

Just then there was a knock at the door.

"Damn, I hope that ain't none of these nosy hoes coming to borrow shit or being fucking nosy," Mercy said, groggy.

"Who is it?" Chrissie screamed.

"Damn." Mercy held her head to try to ease the pain that ran through it at the loudness of Chrissie's voice.

The visitor at the door screamed back, "Where Laila Ali at?"

CHAPTER 4

In da Joint

"What in the hell you want, man?" Chrissie asked, protective of her girl as she swung open the front door.

"Damn, shorty, chill. I'm looking for Laila Ali. I want to see if the champ is a'ight." Chocolate Smooth spoke through the screen as he used his tongue to play around with the toothpick in his mouth.

Mercy came into the living room with her pajama short set on. After her brawl with Brianna, she felt like her head was about to implode. The slightest whisper was amplified by a thousand. Surprised, but not wanting to let on, she said, "What the hell you want? And why you showing up at my shit unannounced? I haven't seen you since my days at the hotel."

"I just happened to be around here taking care of something and saw you from a distance. You went into the ring before I got a chance to say hi or get your number. And I came over to check up on you," he said.

"I'm living. And?" Mercy said, folding her arms.

"Look, ma, don't give me a hard time. I had to bribe some little kid to show me where you live."

Chrissie had her arms folded, looking Chocolate Smooth up and down. He did the same to her.

"Damn, y'all sure are some hateful-ass women in this house. I ain't come here for no fight, because I know it ain't no win. Y'all some ruff necks in disguise for real!" Chocolate joked.

"Let him in, Chrissie," Mercy said, walking over to the green, faux-leather sectional sofa that she had gotten from a secondhand furniture store. Chrissie unlocked the screen door so he could come in. "But don't get too comfortable," Mercy added.

To Mercy's surprise, when Chocolate Smooth walked in, he held a giant basket of fruit and a gift box in his hand. "For you, champ," he said, winking and handing them to Mercy.

Looking at the fruit basket, Mercy showed the beginning of a smile, "Oohhh, this is cute. What's in here?" she asked before slightly shaking the wrapped box.

"Open it and see," he said proudly, as if he knew he had picked out something she would like. Then he walked over to the couch and sat down next to Mercy.

She eagerly tore through the mystery box as Chrissie stood by the sofa, just as eager to see what was in it. Mercy pulled out a pair of boxing gloves with a card inside that read: "Let's go a few rounds." Mercy laughed out loud.

"Ma, for real, I want some boxing lessons. You fight like Muhammad Ali. No bullshit. I'm from the rough, and I ain't never seen a girl fight like that."

"Looks to me like Mercy did more than a lil' fighting. Look at her eye," Chrissie interrupted.

"She do look like Popeye, don't she?" Chocolate Smooth chuckled.

"I was basically fighting for the respect of my niece," Mercy said in a serious tone. "Even if I would have gotten my ass kicked,

I still wouldn't have lost because I was fighting for her. I love her that much. Shoot, she's all I have."

"I respect you for that," he said. "I really do."

A pair of eyes peeped around the corner from the kitchen.

"Hey, cutie pie," he said. Deonie ran and hid. A couple of seconds later she peeped around the corner again, smiling at Chocolate. He started playing peekaboo with her. That went on until they all heard someone blowing his European-sounding car horn like crazy. Chocolate ran to the window and looked out and saw the Richmond Police Department racing up to the door. Before he could prepare himself, the police were banging at the door.

Mercy told Chrissie to take Deonie to the back and then glared at Chocolate, certain that they were there for him.

"I ain't gonna hide in here or none of that, because I know your niece is in here. Just open it."

Mercy opened the door and stood there with the nastiest disposition, but it was one that the Richmond Police got on a regular basis when they went to someone's house to start some drama.

"Yes?" Mercy said, with a confused look on her face.

Chocolate could tell that the po-po was about to trip on Mercy, and to avoid a scene he stood up and basically surrendered. "Yo, yo. Let's just take this outside," he said, raising his hands in surrender. "Let's just take this outside."

"Who are you?" one of the officers asked Chocolate.

Chocolate walked towards the door as Chrissie walked into the front room.

"Hold it right there," another officer said, drawing his gun. "We're looking for a Ms. Mercy Jiles."

The room fell silent as both Chocolate and Chrissie turned their attention to Mercy.

"I'm Mercy Jiles." Mercy hesitated. Before she knew what hit her, the police were slamming her against the wall and handcuffing her.

"Hey, hey," Chocolate said, and started to go towards Mercy.

"Hold it right there, mothafucka," an officer said, "unless you trying to take a ride with her."

"I'm cool," Mercy yelled over her shoulder, catching a glimpse of Deonie walking down the hall. "Chrissie, get Deonie. Keep her out of here."

The police began reading Mercy her rights as they led her to the squad car. "You are under arrest for aggravated assault . . . ," they informed her.

"What?" She scrunched up her face. "What the fuck?" Mercy yelled as she started jerking away from the cops.

"You wanna add resisting arrest?" one of the officers snapped.

The police proceeded to try to take Mercy out of the house in her pajamas. But with all of the confusion and commotion going on, Ms. Pat came running right over and talked to one of the officers, and they let a female officer go with Mercy to her room so she could slip into something else. Once Mercy was dressed in jeans and a sweatshirt, they led her straight out of the house to the police car.

"Don't worry about it, ma," Chocolate yelled out the door to Mercy. "I got you. Don't worry, you'll be okay. Just don't say shit, because they'll use it against you. They some real pigs, too. They eat they own shit. Just look at them with these smiles on their faces. So keep your mouth shut, and I'll be right down there to get you. Believe that."

A couple of the officers shot Chocolate dirty looks. Mercy just nodded to let him know that she heard what he was saying, but he hadn't said anything she didn't already know. After all, she had been raised by the thoroughest of the thoroughbreds. Her father was a stand-up type of dude straight out the gate, and it didn't stop there; the genes had been passed on to his daughter.

Mercy couldn't believe this was all happening as the police car pulled off. Not once had it crossed her mind that Brianna and her low-life friends would go and file charges against her. After all, it was a mutual battle, and Brianna had asked for it. When Mercy got down to the Ninth Street Station to be booked, she was charged with three counts of aggravated assault, malicious wounding, assault with a deadly weapon, and two attempted murder charges. Bail was set at fifty thousand. She needed five thousand ninety-five dollars to get out with a bondsman.

Now where the fuck am I going to get that money from? Mercy wondered. *I know Chocolate ain't gon' come up off all that for my black ass, and I ain't got shit. I can't believe these cave-rat bitches. They been fucking with me and my niece for months now, and when I beat them down, it's a damn problem. What kind of shit is that?*

The bullpen was cold and smelled like piss, shit, vomit, and menstruation mixed together. She couldn't figure out if it was the stench seeping through the cracks of the concrete or the woman that was balled up in a knot over in the corner shaking. It could have been the old lady wearing the twisted wig who kept running to the toilet to hurl. Mercy could tell she was a dope fiend and prostitute. As she observed all of the women around her, tears started spilling out of Mercy's eyes.

"Don't cry," a girl said to her, placing her hand on Mercy's shoulder. "It's not that bad." The girl paused, waiting to see if she was going to get a response from Mercy. Mercy wiped her tears, but said nothing. "What you in here for?"

Mercy looked up at the girl, and easy on the eyes she was not. Her hair was a mess. She had been forced by the prison guards to remove the tracks of weave from her hair. It was evident that they'd been painfully ripped out. There were traces of brown hair glue clinging to her hair and scalp. Her skin was a little rough, but it wasn't nothin' that a little makeup couldn't cover up. Mercy looked at the girl's hand that was resting on her shoulder and noticed that two of the five nails on her hand were on point, like the Koreans had just finished airbrushing them. The other three were chipped up or broken down to the skin. And those nails were acrylics, so Mercy knew that shit had to hurt. She frowned when she thought of the broken nails and the pain they inflicted. For some reason, even though they were both in the same predicament, locked up, Mercy pitied her.

"Assault," Mercy answered, making a long story short.

"I don't know why they got you in here. From looking at your face, it looks like the other person should be in here. Did yo' nigga beat you up or something?" she asked, observing Mercy's eye.

"No," she said with a whimper. Her head was still pounding.

"Girl, don't worry. You'll be okay."

"Shit, I don't know where these motherfuckers at?" another girl interrupted. When Mercy first saw this girl, she could have sworn she was on the wrong side. She could have easily been placed on the men's side of the lockup. The girl had on some brand-new Timbs, and a sweat suit sagging off her butt. She was a little chunky and even walked around the holding tank with a slight pimp, cupping her private area like she had a nut sack. Her hair was braided in zigzags like Allen Iverson. It didn't take a rocket scientist to figure it out: She was as gay as a bird.

The gay girl continued, "These mafuckers better bring they ass. Ain't nobody trying to sit down in this motherfucka all day and then have to be moved to the jail. This is some bullshit."

"What you in for?" the girl who had been talking to Mercy asked the gay broad.

"Petty larceny," she replied.

"How much yo' bail?" the girl asked.

"Five hundred."

"Damn, all you need is fifty dollars, and you can't get out? Shit, I wish my bail was only five hundred. I keeps that type of change in my pocket."

"Oh, my peoples is coming. You better believe that. You can lay flat and bet that my peoples will be here." She looked the nice girl over, not believing the girl was getting slick out the mouth with her.

"What you in for, Big Money Grip?" the gay chick asked the nice girl.

"Murder, and I ain't got no bond," she snapped.

"Damn," Mercy said, looking up at the girl. At that moment she didn't feel so bad after all. Mercy knew enough about the law to know that half of the stuff they were charging her with would eventually be dropped. But even then, the little crappy charges that would still be hanging over her head weren't for murder, that was for sure. She knew that she had a bond, and even if nobody came and got her she was going home one day, but ol' girl was a completely different story. She had a murder rap. She was going to be sitting for a minute, if not for the rest of her life, if found guilty. And in Mercy's eyes that was far worse than her own predicament.

Mercy could feel a little tension between the two chicks. She also heard the guard approaching the cell, jingling keys getting closer and closer.

"Alice Smith," the guard called. "ATW."

The gay girl jumped up, and at that moment she looked at the other chick. "All The Way means I'm all the way out of this bitch." She grabbed her sweat-suit jacket and said, "I told you my peoples was coming."

"How about ATW don't always mean you going home," the girl said, pissing on the gay chick's parade. "Shit, don't let them fool you. You could be going to the next jurisdiction to get another stack of warrants." Nonetheless, the guard escorted the gay girl out of the holding cell with her blowing a kiss to the other chick on her way out.

"By the way, my name is Yorkey," the nice girl said to Mercy.

"Mercy," Mercy responded.

"Want a piece?" Yorkey asked Mercy as she pulled out a Snickers bar.

"Thanks," Mercy said. The two of them were soon talking as if they'd known each other forever. Yorkey explained that her murder rap was really self-defense. Her ex-boyfriend had gone crazy when he saw her with another man, and he had attacked her in her own house. She had to kill him or he was damn sure going to kill her.

"What about you?" Yorkey asked. "Who did you assault?"

"Oh, nobody important. Just this jealous-hearted bitch who wouldn't shut her mouth, so I shut it for her. I tried to knock her teeth out."

"Well, she'll probably drop the charges, soon as word gets out on the street about it," Yorkey assured her.

They talked for a few hours, and Mercy told Yorkey all about living in the foster homes and how she just wanted to take care of her little niece. Yorkey listened to everything. Then she said, "When you get out of here, and I know you will, you need to try to do something with your life. I can tell you ain't the kind of person to just lay around and let people walk all over you. Your daddy was right. You better than that."

"I hope you get out, too, Yorkey. You don't need to be spending your life in one of these shit holes."

After a while they ran out of things to talk about. They watched as the deputies brought the male inmates in from court, and Mercy sat on the bench wondering what she could do to get out. As her thoughts continued, she heard a familiar voice call out her name.

"Mercy? Is that Mercy in that cell?" the voice asked.

Mercy ran to the bars. "Who is that?" she asked.

"Who you think? It's Shawn, yo' brother," Nayshawn said. "And what the fuck you doing in here?"

"Long story," Mercy sighed.

"I'm listening," he shouted back. Although Nayshawn was the younger brother, he seemed like the older brother. The system had turned him into a man before his time.

"I got da fighting. Some broads jumped me. They all took warrants out on me and shit."

"You just like Daddy was, strong as shit. You know Daddy would beat a motherfucker down."

"I know."

They both were quiet for a minute thinking about their father until Nayshawn broke the silence. "Damn, that's fucked up about dem bitches."

"Ain't it?"

"Yup. I wish I was out there. I would beat them bitches just on GP," Nayshawn said, letting his sister know that he had her back no matter what.

Nayshawn was really her half brother. Same father, different mothers. He was two years younger than she was, but he'd been sentenced to juvenile life only three years ago for an armed robbery after he ran away from a foster home. His mother had turned into a straight junkie after their father got killed. It had been a few years since the last time they had seen each other—when they were placed in the same foster home after being separated for four years.

Mercy thought back. It was the middle of the night, and as Mercy lay in bed she could feel a presence standing over her. When she opened her eyes, it was Nayshawn.

"Let's play," Mercy remembered him saying.

The next thing Mercy knew, Nayshawn had climbed into bed with her and tried to touch Mercy in places that he shouldn't.

"I'm tellin'," Mercy threatened, although she would never have snitched on her brother. If she had learned nothing at all from her short stay with her uncle Roland, she'd learned that snitching was never an option. Her uncle had murdered two brothers who were the triplets to the dude who had snitched on his brother. He believed that when a man told, the only proper thing to do was go to his mother's house and hurt somebody to make a snitch feel the heat. So Mercy had only used the threat against her brother to scare him off. After that night it didn't go farther than that, but Nayshawn was embarrassed every time he looked at his sister. He'd started acting out until he was sent away. She never blamed her brother for what he did that night and loved him dearly. She blamed the system. It was the system's fault, for separating siblings. Brothers and sisters should always know each other. Never should they be apart.

"So, how you doing?" Mercy said, bringing herself back to the present.

"I'm maintaining. Just trying to knock these last years out."

"You know I got Zurri's baby staying with me while she doing her time."

"I know. That's good lookin' out."

"How you know?" Mercy asked curiously.

"Because you my sister and I keeps up with you."

"A'ight now. Y'all know males and females not supposed to be talking," a female deputy said. Of course Mercy and Nayshawn ignored her.

"I know when and if I get up out of here, I'm going to keep up with you, too. Fo' real. I'ma write you and hold you down. I promise," Mercy said.

"Write me for real," Nayshawn said in a sincere tone.

"So, what you doing down here now?"

"I got a street charge. A nigga tried me, so I had to handle my business."

"So, you running up yo' time, huh?"

"Naw, just handling my business. You know you got to in here."

"Well, know I'm here for you if you ever need me," Mercy said.

At that moment, the deputy called out, "Mercy Jiles, ATW. I'll be there to get you in a minute."

That minute seemed like the longest of her whole entire life. She was smiling, and in spite of the reeking odor in the holding cell, the deputy's words were a breath of fresh air.

Yorkey looked at Mercy and said, "I told you it won't be so bad after all. And if you want to get the charge dismissed, just take out a warrant on those bitches."

"I do want it thrown out of court, but I don't do warrants," Mercy replied. "I'm a real bitch, and real bitches do real things. And taking out warrants is some fake-ass, bitch-type shit."

The cell door popped open, and Mercy gave Yorkey a hug and her phone number so they could keep in touch.

From the other cell, Nayshawn yelled, "Mercy, if I ever need you, I'm going to write you at Ms. Pat's house."

"A'ight, I got you. But I'ma write you as soon as I get home and get situated so you can have my address. Make sure you call me. I love you, bro."

When Mercy got to the last door to finally exit the lockup, the first thing she saw was Chocolate Smooth standing there with Deonie in his arms asleep. A smile immediately crossed her lips. Mr. Bones, the bondsman, was also standing there with his Polaroid camera to take her photo in case she skipped out. He snapped his pic, damn near blinding Mercy, then was on his way.

"Yo, I'm glad to see you," Chocolate said. "Your lil' baby been going off all day. After she heard me tell Ms. Pat that I was going to get you out, she wouldn't let me out of her sight. When I tried to leave, she held on to my leg and wouldn't let go. Ma, that lil' girl is strong as shit."

Mercy quickly pulled Deonie out of Chocolate's arms and took her into hers.

As they started to walk away, Chocolate asked, "So how was your four hours in the Ninth Street Hotel?"

Mercy just shook her head. She didn't even want to think about that place anymore. All she wanted to do was go home and hold Deonie. She hadn't realized how much she missed her in just that little bit of time.

"Look, ma, sorry I took so long, but Mr. Bones was late," Chocolate apologized. He continued apologizing for taking so long and not getting her out any quicker as they rode home.

Mercy stared out the window, suspicious of Chocolate. She didn't know why he went out of his way to bail her out. She didn't mean shit to him. As far as he was concerned, she was just some clerk at a local hotel who used to let him get rooms by the hour. But, hell, it wasn't like she had given him the rooms for free. He paid for them, so they were even. It was a business transaction; nobody owed the other squat. So why was he doing something for nothing now? Nobody had ever looked out for Mercy. So why now? she thought. What did this dude want?

As Chocolate continued driving, Mercy looked over at him and said, "Thank you." Mercy paused because she didn't know what to call Chocolate. She had always referred to him by the nickname she had given him. Then there was the fake name he used to check into the hotel under.

"I don't know what I would have done without you," she continued. Then she shook off that emotional shit and changed the subject. "I couldn't believe them bitches couldn't wear them ass-whippings like women."

"Don't worry, ma, I got this one. No one wants to be labeled a snitch, not in the damn hood anyway."

"Shit, or anywhere else for that matter," Mercy added.

"When they get tired of people calling them five-oh, they'll come clean. Plus I'm going to holla at them myself."

Mercy looked over at Chocolate again, surprised that he had her back like that. "Thanks," she said.

"I told you, don't worry, I got you," he reiterated. "I'ma hold you down." He glanced over at her.

"Why?" Mercy couldn't help but ask.

"Because. I can tell you's a real down-ass chick. I know you'd look out for me if I needed you to. I look out for people who look out for me."

"But I really ain't did shit," Mercy said.

Chocolate, just like the nickname Mercy had given him, smoothed right on over Mercy's comment. "I like you and your style," he said, concentrating on the road as he busted a right. "You gon' let me take you out tomorrow, right?"

Mercy stared at him and thought for a moment. Every fiber of Mercy's mind told her to decline, but her body did all the talking. "How about next week, when my face heal up?" she suggested.

"That's cool." He smiled as he pulled up in front of Mercy's building.

Mercy went to get Deonie from the backseat of the car where she still lay asleep.

"I'll get her," Chocolate said as he proceeded to scoop Deonie up.

He carried Deonie up the stairs and laid her on her bed. He then walked back down to the living room. "I gotta go try to make this bail money back," Chocolate said. "I'll be by tomorrow to bring you some stuff to help nurse your face back so you can hurry up and get better and we can go out." Chocolate smiled and winked.

"Look, what's your real name?" Mercy asked.

He looked down, then chuckled. "Raheem," he said. He then walked over to Mercy and kissed her on the cheek. "I thought you'd never ask."

That was usually Raheem's test to distinguish bitches from real bitches. Most hoes could not have cared less about his real name. The only name they ever gave a fuck about was Benjamin. At that moment, he knew Mercy was something special.

As Mercy watched Raheem glide away with his smooth stride, she was glad that she had let her body do the talking.

Just like he promised, Raheem came by to check on her the next day. He arrived with a Happy Meal for Deonie and soup for Mercy. They watched some movies that he had rented until the wee hours of the morning. The next morning he went to handle his business, but came back before dark with food and movies again. It didn't take long for this to become a routine.

Finally, one night Raheem and Mercy didn't bother with the movies. After they put Deonie to bed, Mercy took a nice long bubble bath. Raheem waited for her in her bed. When she came out, wearing nothing but a towel, Raheem's eyes told her he appreciated every inch of her. It was time, she knew, for her to let him get as close to her as he wanted to. And when she crawled into bed with him and felt his hard dick rub against her, she knew she wanted it, too.

Before long, Raheem wasn't living in any hotels anymore. Mercy was his girl, and they shared the same address.

CHAPTER 5

The Getting Gets Good

Right off the bat, Raheem, AKA Chocolate Smooth, rolled out the red carpet for Mercy, introducing her to things she never imagined would be in her reach so soon. He banned her from the Rainbow clothing store and got her VIP at Nicole Miller. He stepped her up from the Ten Dollars Store to Bebe and from Hills department store to Macy's, but most important he updated her imitation Coach bucket bag to a Gucci tote bag.

Like Cinderella's fairy godmother had done, Raheem took his magic wand and turned Mercy's Chevette into a Nissan 240. He turned her secondhand furniture into a brand-new rich mahogany leather living room set that filled the entire apartment with the scent of leather. Her status changed from hoodrat to hoodstar all in a matter of three short months. And Brianna dropped the charges against her faster than a dealer drops a bag of dope when the po-po come around. In fact, Brianna was hardly anywhere to be seen lately. If Mercy came walking down the street, Brianna suddenly remembered she had somewhere to go and she was gone. Her little followers didn't have much to say now.

The getting was good, and soon Raheem became the first man, outside of her father and uncle, to ever show her any kind of love.

Although Mercy was much younger than the women he had kicked it with in the past, Raheem spoiled her all the same with sneakers, jewelry, hairdos, and all kinds of gifts whenever he made a trip to New York. Whatever Mercy needed or wanted for her and Deonie, he provided. Not only did he provide her with the material things she desired, he gave her his love.

"You're a very special lady," he said on Valentine's Day as he gave her a diamond tennis bracelet. It was the nicest gift he had ever given her, and she was awed by it.

"What makes you think I'm so special?" she asked, clasping the bracelet around her wrist.

"You got heart and you got brains. And I can tell you're loyal. You got it all, boo."

Not one nigga could fuck with the way Mercy felt for Raheem, and he knew it. Mercy still had big dreams. She wanted to do something great with her life, something that would have made her daddy proud. Maybe with Raheem her luck had finally changed.

CHAPTER 6

Fuck Nigga$, Get Money

Mercy was in the kitchen, washing up the morning dishes while Deonie sat in the living room watching cartoons on TV, when she heard the doorbell rang. It was probably Ms. Pat coming over to take Deonie to her house for a while so Mercy could go shopping. Before she could get out of the kitchen, she heard the front door open.

"Hey, baby girl, it's me!" she heard someone yelling in the other room. "It's your mommy."

Mercy's heart fell to her feet. She ran into the living room to see Zurri with a big smile on her face, holding a lollipop out to Deonie. Poor Deonie stared at Zurri as if she didn't know what to do.

"You don't know your own mommy?" Zurri asked. Deonie hesitantly reached out for the lollipop. "That's my baby."

Zurri swept Deonie up in her arms while Mercy stood there in shock. She had always known this day would come, but in the nine months she had been raising Deonie she had fallen in love with her as if she were her own child, and now she didn't know if she could face it. Zurri turned to her with a huge grin and gave her a hug with her other arm. "Hey, Sissster," Zurri whined.

A dry "hey" is what Mercy gave Zurri.

"You are just the best sister ever, Mercy. Thank you so much for making sure they didn't take my baby away."

"When did they let you out?"

"Ummm, I've been home for about a month now."

"Oh, for real. Well, why you didn't come by here sooner?"

"I had to get my shit together and make sho' I'm a'ight first. Plus I knew you had it under control," Zurri casually said, then looked into Deonie's eyes. "Auntie Mercy was treating you good?"

Deonie smiled and nodded. "My auntie Mercy is the best."

Mercy so badly wanted to be excited to see her sister, but she wasn't. She wanted them to bond, to catch up on lost time, but things were not going how she had always imagined they would. The connection that the two sisters should have had just wasn't there.

"You gon' let me take her stuff or what, because I got a ride waiting for us." Just then a horn blew.

Mercy nodded and said, "I'll get her stuff for you."

She quickly gathered up Deonie's things, thinking she might break down any minute but not wanting to cry in front of her niece. Deonie gave her a sticky kiss on the cheek, and just like that she was gone.

As Mercy stood in the doorway and watched, Deonie waving from the car seat in the back as the car drove off, tears ran down Mercy's face. *Damn, I'm gonna miss the hell out of that little girl,* Mercy thought. *Who am I going to have now?* Mercy hoped that Raheem would pull up in his car. Mercy needed him at that moment. She didn't want to go back in the apartment alone. She'd never been there alone. That had been her and Deonie's place. She'd probably still be living back at the rooming house if it weren't for Deonie. She had only moved into the apartment for

Deonie's sake. She didn't know what it was going to be like living there now. Mercy heard the phone ring. She quickly ran inside and grabbed the phone before it went to voice mail.

Out of breath, looking down at the caller ID, she saw Raheem's cell phone number. "Hey, baby," Mercy said with a sigh of relief.

"What's the deal?" Raheem asked in his regular confident tone.

"Nothing," Mercy lied, not knowing her man would hear the real truth in her voice.

"Where cutie pie at? What she doing?"

"Her momma just showed up out of the blue with a lollipop and took her."

"Damn, baby."

"But normally I think I would have been okay with it, but she was just so casual about the whole situation. She said she had been out for a month, and you know she didn't even come by and see Deonie until now."

"Well, kids know who really love them and who bullshitting them."

"I know, but I am going to worry about my niece. Her mother takes the whole being a mother thing too lightly," Mercy said sadly.

"Well, she knows you are there for her, right?"

"Yup, she knows I love her. I used to tell her every day."

"Damn, baby, the house is going to be so quiet with her gone." Raheem sighed.

"I know." Mercy wiped away a tear that had formed in her eye. "I miss you. When are you coming home?" she said, clearing her throat.

"Well . . ."

"Well, what, baby?" Mercy asked curiously.

"Shit is crazy as a motherfucker."

"What happened?"

"Niggas tripping. My little man was supposed to be coming up, but he hasn't even left yet. Now he holdin' me up."

Mercy knew better than to ask any incriminating questions, especially over the horn. That was the main rule in the hustler's wife handbook.

"Damn, baby. I just really need to see you," Mercy said. "With Deonie being gone and all . . ." She paused. "I just miss you, is all."

"I miss you, too," Raheem said. His other line beeped. "Hold on a second, babe." He clicked over to answer the call, then clicked back to Mercy. "Look, boo. Let me call Amtrak and see what time the train leave to get up here."

"Okay, boo," Mercy said, relieved her man was taking care of her.

Arrangements were set, and Mercy would soon be on her way to see her man. There was just one thing Raheem needed her to do first. He wanted her to stop by a house that he hustled out of to pick up his bags and bring them when she came up. Mercy packed her own bag and then did as she was told. It wasn't until she was on the train and she decided to look inside the heavy bags before she put them in the overhead compartment that she realized they contained guns. Although she felt like her freedom had been jeopardized without her consent, she brushed it off. She didn't want Raheem to know that she had gone in his bags; he trusted her, and she didn't want to ruin that. But she didn't want to piss off the one person, other than Ms. Pat, who had her back. Now it was her chance to have his.

Once Mercy stepped off the train and planted her feet on New York soil, Raheem upped his game to a whole 'notha level. If Mercy thought she had been treated well before, she hadn't seen nothing yet.

Over the next couple of days, Mercy's life consisted of shopping at Neiman Marcus, Macy's, Saks, and other fine stores; eating at the fanciest restaurants; and staying in a deluxe suite at the Waldorf Hotel.

On their final day in the Big Apple, Raheem took Mercy up to Spanish Harlem for lunch. In the middle of their meal, Raheem excused himself from the table and went to the back, past the kitchen area, to cop his work.

When they got in the car to head back to Richmond, Raheem took a paper bag from inside his jacket and pulled out a Baggie full of white powder.

"What you got there?" Mercy asked, looking at the Baggie. She knew it was drugs but didn't know what kind. She didn't really care but thought maybe she ought to know something about his work.

"Rent, food, clothes, nice cars. Everything we need to live the good life," he said. He had copped a clean spoon from the restaurant and scooped some of the powder into a smaller bag. He slipped the smaller bag into his pocket and placed the larger Baggie back in the paper bag. "We got to stop off in B-more and deliver this little package. I want you to keep the rest of this in your pocketbook in case we get pulled over and they start fucking with me," Raheem said, like he was handing her a brown-bag lunch.

What could this hurt? Mercy felt it was the least she could do for her man after the way he'd treated her while they were in New York. And in a way it made her feel closer to him that he trusted her to take care of things. Her daddy's motto had always been to take care of those who take care of you, so she was determined to be the same way.

As soon as they hit the Maryland House, they stopped for a minute. Raheem would rather piss in a Coke bottle than pull over at the Maryland House rest stop, but he wanted to catch a power nap. Besides, there was something about those plush hotels that made Mercy step up her sex game. She had really put something tough on him this weekend. Mercy was worn out, too—not from the sex but from all the nonstop shopping, eating and sight-seeing. They both dozed off. An hour hadn't gone by when Mercy was awakened by a Maryland state trooper knocking on the passenger window. Mercy's heart began racing while Raheem went into action.

Raheem quickly swallowed the heroin that he had separated from the main package. The trooper noticed his movements and drew his gun. He then ordered Mercy to open up the door, but she froze.

"Fuck the police," Raheem responded.

At that point, the only commands Mercy obeyed were those of her man. As the trooper reached for the door, Mercy fumbled around for the automatic lock but was too slow. The trooper took one of his hands off of his gun and swung open the door. He then quickly replaced it on the gun.

"Get out!" the trooper yelled at Mercy. He yanked her out of the car as she gripped her purse in her hand. "Get down on the ground!" Mercy dropped on her stomach. "Driver, hands on the steering wheel." Not even giving Raheem time to do it, he screamed it again: "Hands on the steering wheel!"

As Raheem attempted to put his hands on the wheel, the trooper reached over and tried to open up Raheem's mouth as he was swallowing the last bit of the drugs. The jaw used the strongest muscle in the human body, and Raheem's mouth was glued shut.

"Open your mouth, you fuckin' cocksucker! Open up, I said!"

"Ouch!" the trooper screamed when Raheem tried to bite his finger off. When the trooper looked at his finger, Raheem took a huge gulp and began choking until he swallowed again, clearing his throat passage.

"Get the fuck out of the car," the trooper said, cocking his gun.

During the showdown between the trooper and Raheem, Mercy managed to slip the drugs out of her pocketbook and throw them off into the grass without the trooper seeing her. But once the trooper got the situation under control, Mercy was sure that Raheem was going to jail.

Mercy lay on the ground and watched as the trooper leaned Raheem over the trunk of the car and patted him down.

"What you got here, son?" the trooper said as he grabbed at the wad of cash in Raheem's front pants pocket. "Traveling with cash, huh?" The officer pulled the money out of Raheem's pocket. "And a large amount of cash, too. Didn't your mother ever tell you never to travel with large amounts of cash? You could lose it all, or better yet," the trooper said as he slipped the money into his front shirt pocket, "someone could steal it from you." He then laughed. "Now where are the drugs?"

"I ain't got no drugs," Raheem said.

The trooper slammed Raheem down on the trunk of the car and handcuffed him. "Get down on the ground," he said as he pulled Raheem up off of the car and made him lie on the ground. He proceeded to search the car and didn't find anything but a small bag of weed under the seat. "Since you like to eat stuff, eat this," the trooper said, holding up the bag of marijuana.

Raheem turned his head in defiance. The trooper got down in Raheem's face and shouted, "Eat it, cocksucker, or go to jail."

Raheem had several warrants out on him, so his decision wasn't hard at all. He ate the weed.

The trooper walked back over to the car and pulled out a small blue cooler that was full of water from melted ice. The cooler had been there for over a week, and the water was starting to reek. "Here, drink the water out of here so that shit don't get stuck in your throat," the trooper said, setting the cooler down and helping Raheem up into a sitting position. "It wouldn't look good if you died out here."

Raheem gagged as he drank the water. The trooper laughed. He then uncuffed Raheem and left him and Mercy sitting there on the side of the road as he drove off with his unexpected bonus. Two months and four trips later, each time carrying more and more drugs, Mercy seemed to have found her niche in life: hustling.

Mercy sat in the prison visiting room, waiting to see her brother Nayshawn. She was supposed to have been there two weeks ago. But she was here now. This visit would change the game for her forever.

"Damn, your name been cleared my visiting list forever. Why it took you so long to get here?"

"Been traveling."

"Where?"

"To New York with my man," she said, stressing New York like it was on another planet or something.

Nayshawn grew upset and asked, "Do dat nigga got you running up and down the road with shit in your pussy or toting his shit?" He wasn't new to this thing; he saw dudes from all over come through the system discussing their ride-or-die chicks.

Mercy was almost embarrassed to say yes, the way her brother was deep in her ass. "It ain't like that."

"That's what yo' mouth say. Well, do dat nigga be paying you?"

"Yeah, he pays all the bills, and takes care of me and I ain't never broke."

" 'Fuck dat. You can do that shit yo'self." Nayshawn threw his hand up. "Baby girl, that nigga ain't doing nothing but using you."

"It ain't like that."

"Listen to me." Nayshawn grabbed Mercy's hand. "Listen, Sis, you know I ain't going to let no nigga play you out pocket, right?"

Mercy didn't respond, but she listened.

"Look, that nigga ain't doing shit you can't do for yourself. You can't give up the goods for free and mule the pack. That nigga is getting over like a fat rat."

Nayshawn broke the game down to her even though Mercy didn't want to believe him, but she started to think about the way Raheem played his game, the way he sweetened her up at first and then slowly tricked her into helping him out. It was true—he was getting paid, and she wasn't even on the payroll. The truth hurt like a motherfucker.

"And, Mercy, if you gets busted, you'll wind up in the penitentiary and he'll have some other girl quicker than a New York minute doing your old job. Boo, I'm sure you're not the first. You're just the lastest."

On the long ride back from the prison, Mercy thought about everything Nayshawn had said to her. She replayed bits and pieces of his conversation over in her head, and she reflected back on the hotel scene when she had first met Raheem—the girl that was with him. She digested the whole situation and saw how easily their relationship had turned eighty percent business and twenty percent anything else.

Once she got back home, she watched as Raheem sat at their kitchen table bagging up his dope. She began cooking dinner. Once the food was almost finished, Raheem came up behind her and put his arms around her.

"Tonight I should be done with this and we should be ready to hit the highway tomorrow," he whispered in her ear.

For a minute she was going to agree just like she had in the past, but something flashed through her mind: *You gotta know when to hold 'em, know when to fold 'em, know when to walk away, know when to run.*

That gave her the strength.

"Stop, Raheem," Mercy said, squirming away from him before heading to the cupboard to get some plates. Raheem stood there shocked. Mercy had never rejected him.

"What you mean 'stop'?" he snapped.

Mercy sighed, set the plates on the counter, and turned to face him. "Look, I know what's up. I ain't green for real."

"What?" Raheem said with a puzzled look on his face. "I'm over here in the right field, how you just gon' throw some shit out in left?"

"You heard me," Mercy said, as if she had just visited the Wiz and was given some courage. "See, you think I'm stupid, right? Oh, is it because I'm from down South, huh? Poor little country Mercy, huh?" She looked into his eyes as she stepped in closer to him. "I know how you New Yorkers do. Yeah, I been schooled, motherfucker. Y'all come down here tryin' to find y'allself one of them country girls to buy a few presents for, then you throw a little dick at 'em and get her sprung. Why? Just so she can do what you need her to do."

"Man, stop it. You know better," Raheem said, gritting his teeth. "Man, who been in yo' ear?"

"You are right, I do know better," Mercy agreed. "So you need to make a decision."

"What kind of decision? What are you talking about?"

"Look, I ain't going to be running up and down the highway for you, carrying yo' shit." She emphasized yo', pointing at him. "I ain't going to be laying up, letting you fuck me, doing your dirty work while I settle for a Chanel bag with matching shoes.

Fuck that," Mercy spat, now more bold than she had ever been in her life.

Raheem chuckled while shaking his head. He couldn't believe Mercy had finally caught on. "So?" he said, throwing his hands up in defeat.

"So, you need to take your pick: Either we can get money together or we can lay up together. Take yo' pick, New York."

Raheem looked Mercy up and down, admiring her curvaceous body and her beautiful face. He knew by her body language that she meant every word she was spittin'. He smiled and licked his lips.

He had come into Mercy's life and accepted her with a black eye while she rolled in a Chevette. Raheem had helped build her up, and although he didn't own her coochie, he owned something that was valued much higher than a piece of ass—her undying devotion.

"All right," he said in a sincere tone. He pulled Mercy toward him and moved her chin closer to kiss her passionately on the lips.

Mercy melted as she aggressively began to kiss him back. She couldn't believe it. For once in her life someone had made her feel like there was nothing in the world more important than her, not even money, and a hustler's money at that. That said a lot.

Raheem pulled away from Mercy and wiped his mouth. Her eyes were lit up as she waited for him to speak.

"All right, Mercy, you win. Let's make this money." Raheem then turned away to finish his business.

Mercy stood there feeling stupid. How could she think for one minute that a nigga would have chosen a bitch over money? So just like any dude on the come-up, Raheem had picked the money over Mercy. Mercy was hurt. There was a part of her that wished he would have chosen her, but it was cool. She was used to not being chosen. All those years in foster care, no family ever chose to keep her either. But hopefully, like Yorkey, that girl in jail, had told her, things wouldn't be so bad after all.

But from here on out, I'm not thinking with my emotions, because every time I do, they get crushed, she thought. Lil' Kim couldn't have said it better than when she put it on wax: "Fuck niggas, get money!"

CHAPTER 7

Rules to Surviving the Game!

The whole block seemed to be on vibrate from the bass in C-Note's truck when he pulled in front of his mother's house. His mother, Lolly, wearing a baby blue housecoat with matching slippers and her fake Louis Vuitton scarf on her head greeted him at the front door.

"Is you motherfucking crazy?" she yelled. "Have you lost your damn mind? Coming round here with that loud-ass music. I don't know who's fucking worse, you or your guyd damn brother."

C-Note brushed her off as his cell phone began to ring. He walked right past his mother, down the hall, into the den and answered his phone.

"Yo," he spoke into the receiver.

"What's the deal, man?" Jus, his right-hand man, said from the other end of the phone.

"Ain't shit going on at this end. At my mom's house, chillin'. What's good?"

Lolly entered the den, still fussin'. "I know one thing, you know how these folks is on this block. You know they'll call the police in a New York minute and you still blasting that loud music." She pretended like she had come into the den to straighten up, fluffing toss pillows that didn't need fluffing. But really she just wanted to pop trash.

"Ma, I'm on the phone," C-Note said with an annoyed look on his face.

"You think I give a shit about you on a motherfucking phone? You shoulda been thinking about keeping the peace when you rolled up with all that loud-ass music in front of my fucking house."

He ignored his mother and walked out of the den and into the kitchen. "Man, what's the deal?" C-Note continued his phone conversation with Jus as he opened up the refrigerator.

"Man, I got this bitch coming over and she bringing a friend. You trying to fuck or what?" his childhood friend asked.

Jus and C-Note had raised so much hell together. They swindled together, got money together, spent it together, and without a doubt tag-teamed broads together. So without even needing the details on the chicks, he responded, "No doubt."

"They want us to take them out and then afterwards, you know what's up."

"A'ight."

"So, I'ma hit you up in 'bout an hour after I see what the bitch friend look like."

"Don't have me coming to see no Skeletor bitch." They both laughed and began cracking jokes like they always did.

"I'm at my momma spot now, so hit me up when shawdy get there." C-Note hung up the phone.

Lolly walked into the kitchen and put a stack of mail in front of her son. "Hump," she huffed. "And your brother wrote you, too. You need to be going to see him."

"Ma, he know what's up. He da one that said it best: 'Visitors make prisoners.' " He then tore the envelope open to read his brother's letter. His brother, Lynx, had been locked up for a good year and had never written him before, so C-Note knew that this letter was probably going to be an earful.

"Well, at least write him back," Lolly said, placing a pen and paper in front of him. "Ain't no need to get up from that table until after you write your brother back."

"I hear you, Ma," C-Note said before adding, "Damn," under his breath so that she couldn't hear him cursing her. He then started to read the letter.

What's up, my lil nigga?

That's right, I said it. You gonna always be my lil' nigga no matter how much bigger than me you get. Well, let me jump straight to the point. Your name has been ringing bells around here on the yard. Word is that you doing major things. I had been meaning to write you for about two weeks now, but I been caught up doing shit up in here. When Ma came to see me this weekend, she told me how you was living. Ma ain't stupid, you know. She confirmed what I already knew. She demanded that I write you and give you a pull up. Before I get into that, I want to tell you thanks for the money slips. Good looking out. The pink slips been looking healthy, and you know a nigga likes that shit.

When Ma first asked me to write you and give the law to you about the streets, my initial thoughts were that gangstas don't write about the streets, the streets write about us. But after some persistent solicitation (by Ma) and further deliberation (by me), I decided to do it. I know I may sound like I'm preaching to you, but peace, my little nigga. Just be patient. I promise to keep it short, and to the point.

You probably asking yourself, "Who the fuck this nigga think he is, locked the fuck up trying to tell me how to do mines? What makes him so bona fide?" Peace that, soldier, I feel you! And I'm not claiming to be a guru of the streets. I don't profess to be a master of the game, nor do I hold any "hustla of the year" awards. And as you know, I'm not, or wasn't even, the best hustla in our family. You know that title is held by our father; may he thug in peace. But I am yo' big brother, the one who taught you everything you know and would die for you. I'm also one of the few soldiers that has paid his dues and made his bones in order to obtain what most every street soldier covets. The most elusive street dream. The reason why we lay those bricks and blaze those burners, the holy trinity to the streets: Money, Power, and Respect!

I'm not going to glamorize, trivialize, condone, nor condemn the type of life that the men in our family have lived. It started out with Grandpa and moonshine. Then our Pops with heroin and PCP. This legacy was then passed to me. And now to you. This is truly not what I wanted for you. I wouldn't wish this type of life on my worst enemy. The chances of survival are slim. The chances of maintaining your freedom are almost nonexistent. Some may ask, why do we do it then? In the beginning it is to eat, but then to be totally honest with you, most of us love this shit. . . . It's a "G" thang.

As for us, we were born with a disease. We contracted it from our mother at birth. Actually it's more of an addiction than a disease. The worst vice any man born with nothing can have: Good Taste! But I'm not mad at her. The game was good to me. You know it. I was driving some of the best automobiles, wearing some of the tightest gear, and fucking some of the finest bitches on the planet. But like they say, excessive amounts of anything is not good for you. The street maxim "Ball till you fall" couldn't have been more true. I literally balled until I fell.

Remember when you told me that you wanted to be a gangsta and move more weight, and I told you it gets greater later? Well, I can see that later is finally here for you now. So, I can only pass on what was given to me by Pops long ago.

*THESE ARE THE TEN MOST CRUCIAL RULES FOR
PROSPERITY AND SURVIVAL IN THE GAME:*

10. *Death B4 Dishonor*
9. *Kill or be killed*
8. *Never trust a shadow after dark*
7. *Never talk B-I over the phone*
6. *Trust no one! Even down to never letting anyone ride in
   your backseat! No one can be trusted! No one!*
5. *The only way three people can keep a secret is if two of
   them are dead!*
4. *Beware of the cross: crisscross, holy cross, and the double-
   cross*
3. *Protect what's yours by all means necessary*
2. *Never use your own product!*

*But the last and most crucial rule is the most invaluable of
them all. If you can only remember one rule, this is it:*

1. *THERE ARE NO RULES!!!!*

Always remember that I am here when you need me.

Love, Lynx

PS: Play at your own risk.

A smile came across C-Note's face as he folded up the letter and
placed it back in the envelope. He sat at the table and digested
everything that his brother had just spoon-fed him in the letter.
C-Note's meditation was interrupted by his greedy, money-hungry
momma. Just that quick she had gone from housecoat to a tight-
fitting jogging suit.

"C, I need some money to go to Bingo," she said, lighting up a
cigarette.

"Ma, come on, I just gave you money."

"Well, you only gave me three hundred dollars, and that's gone.

I had to buy some groceries and pay the man to come and do the yard since you too busy to do it. And I told you that I want to get a new kitchen set."

"So why you asking for money to gamble it away at Bingo, then?"

"Because I was trying to make it easy on you. That's why I was going to go to Bingo to win the money for my kitchen set and make it easy on your pockets," Lolly said. "If I was asking you for the money to buy the kitchen set, it would be for a hell of a lot more than some three hundred dollars."

C-Note shook his head as he went in his pocket and pulled out his bankroll. "Ma, you don't make no sense," he said, and gave her a hundred-dollar bill.

Lolly, with one hand on her hip, extended her other hand out for more money. "You know it takes money to make money," she said.

"Damn, I got niggas in the street trying to get me for what's mines, and now my own momma, too. Now, ain't that some shit." He handed her another Franklin. "I hope this'll do you. And I hope you ain't going out here with that tight-ass shit on either."

She tucked the two hundred dollars in her bosom, and as she walked away, she yelled over her shoulder, "And watch your mothafuckin' mouth. I don't know where you get that talk from."

C-Note shook his head as he smiled, thinking about his crazy momma as she switched down the hall. He wouldn't trade her for the world.

CHAPTER 8

Work on Greyhound

"Hello, you have a collect call from—" said the automatic recording.

"Raheem," Mercy heard Raheem's voice jump in. She pressed five to accept the call.

"What's the deal, baby?" Raheem said.

"Nothing much, same old same," Mercy replied. She was stretched out on her big king-sized bed. She'd been sleeping alone for the last three months, ever since Raheem had chosen money over her. A week later he had gotten busted on I-95; she was grateful that she wasn't with him. She had gotten a stomach virus the day he was leaving. He needed some work and couldn't wait for the virus to pass.

"You heard from dude?" Raheem asked.

"Yup, I just sent you some money that he gave me for you. Did you get it yet?"

"Naw, it ain't come yet, but I'll probably get it today."

"Yeah, you should've got it yesterday, but since you didn't, you'll probably get it today."

"So Hyena and them been holding you down, huh?" Raheem asked.

"They good people," she commented.

Hyena was the New York connect that Raheem had been dealing with before he was hauled off to a federal prison. Mercy felt Hyena's name should have been Buck-Eye because of the black patch he sported over his right eye, but the name seemed to fit him. Built like a bowling ball, Hyena was a short, stocky guy who stood at five feet, five inches tall and weighed in at 230 pounds. He wore his long, coal-black hair in a ponytail.

Once Raheem was behind bars, he hooked up Mercy with Hyena, and from that moment Mercy's chips started rolling in like never before. Hyena arranged for Mercy to transport drugs throughout the East Coast corridor. She handled herself so well that he kept giving her more and more assignments. Hyena loaded Mercy with so much work that she had to recruit Chrissie and a few other good chicks to help her get the packs from Point A to Point B. Hyena only dealt with Mercy directly, though, and Mercy moved the most work because if she couldn't trust anyone else, she knew she could trust herself. She kept her cookie packer job, but trafficking was what really paid the bills. And using plain old common sense with a combination of street savvy and trial and error, she mastered the job.

"Oh, yeah, I just took seventy-five hundred to the attorney. Hyena gave me five of that, and I put the other twenty-five hundred to it. I'm going to do some lil' odds and ends work so I can give the attorney five more," she told Raheem.

"Damn, baby. You looking out for the old boy, huh? You be holding me down."

"I ain't got no choice. You know real bitches do real things."

"When I met you at the Ambassador, I never knew that you would turn into a real soldier for me. You could have run out on me just like everyone else did when the damn *America's Most*

Wanted show splattered my pictures all over the country," Raheem said. "You know I 'preciate you."

Mercy had seen those pictures on the TV as well as the pictures of two men he was supposed to have murdered back in New York. Whether Raheem did the murders or not, Mercy didn't know, but now he was sitting in a federal jail trying to rumble with the government to give him liberty.

"You know I got your back," she said.

"All right, ma. Well you know I'ma get at you again real soon."

"Stay up, baby," Mercy said as they ended the call.

Mercy had basically been footing Raheem's whole attorney bill, holding him down better than any of his so-called loyal niggas ever could or would. She prayed that somehow the attorney would find a loophole in Raheem's cases and that Raheem would be released. And once he was, he would appreciate her for what she was and would make her wifey. Somehow she managed to make it all work: visits, letters, cards, calls, keeping the commissary stacked, and knocking the lawyer's bill down, all in between her drug runs. Mercy laid in the bed for an hour thinking about Raheem. Before she knew it, it was time for her to go and punch the clock on I-95. She took a shower, grabbed a few things, put them in her Fendi bucket pocketbook and was out the door.

I swear to God, I don't want to catch no stinking-ass Greyhound with all this work on me, Mercy thought as she headed for the bus station. *Last time that shit had me good and miserable the way it hit every single bump in the dag'on road.*

She was catching the express bus to Richmond. She had one more run after this one, and she was hoping to get back in time to go to a big party on Friday night. She continued her thoughts as she approached the Greyhound bus at the Port Authority in New York. She knew she had to play it safe. She couldn't drive with all the shit on her, and Hyena said that the car with the stash box was in the shop. She didn't have time to sit around New York and wait, so she decided to go ahead and leave the driving to Greyhound.

This was the third time that Mercy had ridden like this with the work taped down to her body under her clothes with a body girdle on top. Something had to give. When she'd been dealing with Raheem, the heroin was just taped and wrapped up like a dick, which she stuck up in her canal. But back then it had only been a hundred or two hundred grams. Dealing with Hyena, the game had been stepped up to a whole new level. More money brought more work. Work that couldn't be shoved up in her pussy.

Mercy was anxious to get her job done so she could get herself together to go to the party that everybody in town was going to. Since she traveled everywhere picking up money and delivering drugs, she was able to shop at any of those destinations. And she did, big-time. So her outfit was never the problem. The finishing touches—hair, nails, pedicures, and accessories—were the problem. She had to be home in plenty of time for all that.

As the bus rolled down the highway, Mercy drifted off to sleep as she thought about how much fun she would have at the party and what she had to do when she reached home and was done working. She had managed to get into a comfortable deep sleep when she was awakened by flashing blue lights as the bus started slowing down. Mercy didn't know what the hell was going on, but she immediately reached in her Prada tote bag and put her Air Max on. Once her sneakers were tied tight, she got up out of her seat.

"Excuse me, excuse me," she said politely to the people whose elbows or shoulders hung off a little into the aisle as she headed to the rear of the bus. She went into the bathroom and locked the door behind her. Someone must've gave her up. She had to think quickly. She took the drugs off of her body full tilt and looked for a place to hide the packs, but couldn't find anywhere in the compact bathroom. When she felt the bus pull off the road and come to a complete stop, she had no choice but to flush the drugs down the toilet.

She threw some water on her face and was back in her seat before the police got on the bus. As the police officer slowly made his way down the aisle, checking IDs of the passengers on the bus, Mercy's heart began to beat faster and faster. Trying not to look worried, she buried her head in her book, *Whoreson,* just to keep from falling apart. She was sure that her name was the one that the police were looking for.

Damn, what ID should I show him? The real one or my fake one? Mercy thought. *If he's looking for me, what name would he be looking for? I know this motherfucker is coming to get me. Somebody had to drop a dime on me. Shit, I knew I shouldn't have taken Greyhound. This shit is too risky.*

"May I see your ID, ma'am?" the officer asked Mercy.

"Yes, sir," Mercy answered, handing over her ID, wondering if she should play it cool.

The police barely glanced at her ID before handing it back to her. Mercy exhaled once he was two seats behind her. But he still had to check the restroom, and she'd been the last one to come out.

She prayed that the dope hadn't floated back to the top. Then all of a sudden another thought came across Mercy's mind. What was she going to tell Hyena? What if he didn't believe her? Was he going to kill her, or what? She definitely wasn't going to get paid. Her mind raced every which way.

The police finally exited the bus and she knew she was okay. It was a close call, but at least she had her freedom. Once she reached Richmond, her brain began to operate more clearly. She had to get the dope out of the toilet to make sure that it got where it was supposed to be. She would do everything in her power to keep Hyena from knowing she had lost control of the situation. So she waited until the night crew came on and watched as an old man got on to clean the bus. Mercy followed behind him.

"Hey, how you doing?" Mercy asked.

"Fine," the older black man said. He looked like he should have been retired and not cleaning anybody's buses.

Mercy didn't want to scare the man, because he was her only chance at getting the drugs. So she decided to turn on her sweet and innocent girlish charm.

"Sir, I really need your help," she said, looking helpless. "I was taking my little niece to the bathroom, and she dropped some very important stuff in the toilet by mistake. Is it anyway possible you can get it out for me?"

"Stuff?" he questioned, with a peculiar look on his face.

"Yeah, uh, some important papers," Mercy lied in the most convincing tone she could muster.

He looked her in the eyes as she continued to pour her heart out. "I'll pay you. I just really need your help."

"Pay me?" he asked.

"Yeah, I'll pay you," Mercy repeated.

"Just for getting some paper out the toilet for you?"

"Well, it's more like some packages," Mercy said, batting her eyes. "The packages are important, but I'll pay you a hundred dollars."

Upon hearing the dollar amount, the man agreed with no more questions asked. "Consider it done. You don't have to worry your pretty little self anymore. I'll take care of it. You just go on out there and wait."

"It's five packages altogether," Mercy informed him as she exited the bus.

In a matter of twenty minutes, the man came off the bus with five packages in a bucket covered with feces and piss. He then handed the bucket to Mercy. It was absolutely disgusting, but mixed in the feces and piss was something Mercy needed. She set the bucket down and then reached in her purse. She peeled off two hundred-dollar bills and handed them to him. His face lit up.

"Thank you so much. Thank you, ma'am," he said as he pocketed the money. "If your niece ever drops anything else down the toilet, my name is Ben, and I'll get it out for you." He winked as he walked away, a happy old man.

Mercy hurried and took the bucket into the bathroom of the bus station. She dumped the contents of the pail into the toilet and got out her five packages. After rinsing off the goods in the bathroom sink, Mercy was on her way. Mercy made Ben one of her workers and put him on her payroll.

CHAPTER 9

Black Beauty

"What you got planned for tonight and tomorrow?" Hyena asked Mercy as they sat in a restaurant in the heart of downtown Richmond and ate lunch. Hyena had never been to Richmond, but since he was driving down south, he'd decided to stop in Richmond to check Mercy out.

"Well, I just plan to relax and then get myself ready for this party that I am going to the day after tomorrow," Mercy answered.

"Is this the same party you been talking about for a month now?" he asked. She nodded. "Well, I need you to come through for me again. You should be back tomorrow morning if you can jump into character right away."

She would never say no to Hyena. She knew he depended on her, and she wanted to come through for him. She loved being a part of a team, and a team player she was.

"You promise I'm going to be back by noon? Because my hair appointment is at two," Mercy said, patting her hair.

He put up his finger and said, "Hold on." He picked his cell phone up and made a call. Before she knew it, he was speaking in a language she could not understand. As he talked she gazed into his one eye.

What is under that patch? she wondered. *Is it a wandering eyeball, or is this nigga just trying to look like Slick Rick or something?* Mercy's imagination took over, and she began concocting all kinds of different scenarios to explain what had happened to his eye. *Maybe he had been tortured, maybe stabbed in a fight.*

Hyena's conversation only lasted a good two minutes before it was over. After he hung up the phone, Mercy had looked him over completely. *How could a nigga with so much money not have an eye?* she asked herself. *I wonder why he ain't ever get a new eye? Damn, I want to know the answer. When Raheem calls I'ma ask him about that patch.*

He put the glass up to his mouth. "You got my word. Everything is worked out. I just need you to make this happen. The work is easy," Hyena said convincingly.

"You know I got you," Mercy assured him. "Now, what do you need me to do?"

He leaned in closer and spoke in a soft tone. "I need you to catch the Greyhound and get off at the Baltimore Travel Plaza. Go across the street to the truck stop and look for a truck called Blue Thunder. Hop in the rig and keep the driver company until he gets to Columbia."

"Keep him company?" she interrupted.

He chuckled, covering up his laughter. "Your mind is always in the gutter. Don't nobody want your little tight pussy," he said jokingly, but she could tell by the way he looked at her that if it had been another time and place and under different circumstances, he would pursue her.

"As I said, keep him company on his ride down to Columbia, SC, where he's going to change rigs," Hyena continued. "Once he changes rigs consider your job done. I'll have a car to pick you up, pay you, and drop you at the airport to catch your flight home. There's a flight that leaves out at 9 a.m., so as long as everything goes as planned, you'll be able to get your hair done."

"Shoot, sounds easy enough," Mercy said, taking a sip of her water with lemon.

"You'll have to check in every hour on the hour to let us know everything is copacetic. No need to worry—someone will be following you anyway—but it's still important that you check in."

After Mercy was given all the particulars by Hyena, she sprung into character and went to take care of business. Just like clockwork, everything went as planned when she arrived at the truck stop. As she waited for her ride to show up, she got firsthand knowledge that the whole truck stop had a world within itself. She silently watched the obvious drug dealing, using, and prostitution going on. After sitting there twenty minutes, she saw the rig and hopped up in Blue Thunder. She was surprised to find her driver was a fat, sloppy, dirty-looking white guy wearing dingy farmer johns and looking like Uncle Jesse from the *Dukes of Hazzard*. When Mercy jumped in the truck, he simply tilted his dirty baseball cap at her and pulled off.

There wasn't much for Mercy to do on the ride to keep dingy Farmer John company. He seemed to have plenty of friends on his CB radio. So Mercy just pulled out her book and read it. However, she couldn't seem to focus because of the ruckus going on over the CB radio. She couldn't ask Farmer John to cut it off because it was his truck. When she was little and rode with her father, he would always say, "Passengers have no say-so on the entertainment. The driver is the DJ."

So for a minute she just sat there and listened. Farmer John kept trying to encourage her to get on the CB and play around with a few fellas out truckin', but she didn't. She was more interested in being a spectator.

"Yeah, I got a black beauty with me that I picked up on the side of the road. She was hitching down to Miami," Mr. Farmer John said, winking at Mercy for her to play along, "and oooweee, what a sight she is."

"I'll take her off your hands," some guy sounding exactly like Wolfman Jack responded.

"No, I can't do that. I promised her I'd get her there safe and sound."

"Let the black beauty know if she needs a ride back from Miami, holla at Don Corleone," Mercy heard a sexy voice jump in over the CB. There was something about his voice that made her want to get on the CB and take Don up on his offer, but she didn't.

"Y'all see that. You put a beaver at stake and Don Corleone wakes up. We thought you was napping off in the truck stop, partner," Farmer John said.

"Lil' Lost Chicken, I'm always moving, baby. I had to stop and get me some petrol, but I'm on the road again. I just couldn't wait to get on the road again." Don Corleone started singing the lyrics to the country song.

Mercy smiled as she heard Lil' Lost Chicken say, "Stick to hip-hop, Don. Leave the country alone."

"Lil' Lost Chicken, what's the deal with the black beauty? Is she my type?" Don continued.

"I don't know, but she's the original black beauty," he answered, looking Mercy over and winking at her. "A real thoroughbred."

"Black Beauty, come in? Bat those eyes one time for me, Black Beauty," Don Corleone requested.

Mercy ignored him, but once she realized that they were in a traffic jam and there was an accident up ahead on I-95, she finally got on the CB, realizing that the trip was going to be longer than she had anticipated. "Where you at, Don Corleone?" Mercy said. "You in the middle of handling some Mafioso business?"

Don laughed as he and Mercy talked down the highway all the way until she got to her destination.

"Was it a match made on I-95?" the trucker asked Mercy as she climbed out of the truck.

"You never know." Mercy winked. "You never know."

Once she hopped out of the rig, Don Corleone was erased out of her mind. Her only focus was the exchange she was being paid to make.

CHAPTER 10

Get Ur Freak On

The party was sold out like a Michael Jackson concert. With so many people there, the old Thalheimer's building was packed like a sardine can.

"Glad we were able to get in VIP," Mercy said. "Otherwise my ass would be headed back to the south of the James on my way home."

"Or worse, still standing in line," Chrissie said as they both giggled, giving each other a high five.

"Girl, I know. I am so glad that we ain't have to pay the money to get in here," Mercy said, happy that she didn't have to dish out three hundred dollars to pay both her and Chrissie's way into the club.

"Girl, I say we toast to those Gucci pants," she said, looking Mercy up and down, "because those were the hook for the night." Chrissie put up her glass.

"I say we toast to real chicks who know real niggas who don't mind spending."

They toasted as they swept the room with their eyes, searching out their sponsor for the night.

Although Mercy would have coughed up the money to get in

VIP, she was grateful she didn't have to. Thanks to Herb, a guy whose attention Mercy seemed to have captured, Mercy had three hundred dollars in her pocket to spare. Herb had been staring a hole in her from the other side of the room all night long. He must have been under the impression that just because he threw out a few yards Mercy was going to be up under him the entire night. He would be sadly mistaken.

Herb and his boy had pulled up into the club's parking lot at the same time as Mercy and Chrissie. Herb parked his midnight-blue 600 Benz right beside Mercy's brand-new 320 Benz. When he stepped out of his ride at the same time she did, she was impressed as she took in his whole package. He was wearing his hair in neat zigzagged Allen Iverson braids. He had on gators, Cartier frames, and jewels; and his swagger was on point. Tall, slim, with a creamy caramel complexion, straight dappa don she could not deny. His boy was okay, but Herb was exactly what the doctor had ordered.

"Hey, love," Herb said as he looked Mercy up and down.

"Hello to you too, boo," she replied as she looked him over again.

"I see you in those jeans. I see ya, baby," he said in a slick tone, sliding his glasses down to the tip of his nose.

"That's why I put them on, so you could see me." She was confident, and her walk confirmed it as she stepped with one foot in front of the other like she was auditioning for a position on the runway during Fashion Week.

"You looking real good. Baby, Gucci can stop making them shits now," Herb said. He had no idea that one of the finest girdles ever manufactured was holding her in place, creating a mirage. Lord only knew that if she ate one chicken wing or even farted, these pants would've popped like a bottle of Cristal.

"Thank you, darlin'. You ain't looking bad yo' self," Mercy said.

" 'Y'all got VIP?" Herb asked.

"Ummm, Chrissie, did you ever get the VIP situation straight?" Mercy asked, trying to play it off.

Before Chrissie could even respond, Herb said, "Don't worry 'bout it. I got y'all," he said and waved his hand, signaling them to come on.

As soon as they arrived in VIP, Herb started popping bottles like firecrackers on the Fourth of July. He attracted so much attention that Mercy slipped away, letting him have the spotlight to himself. Well, not exactly just slipped away. The cutthroat hoochies were trying their damnedest to get Herb's attention. If she didn't get out of the way, the sac chasers would have trampled all over her. Had it been any other day of the week, month, or year, she would have dealt with them. Plain and simply, she would have opened up her Gucci bag, nicely put on her Gucci sneakers, politely placed her Gucci boots in the bag, Vaselined her face up, and inflicted serious pain on the guttersnipes. However, this night was different—her pants were too tight, for one, and plus she was glad that the skeezers were able to assist in putting distance between her and Herb. Shit, who takes sand to the beach anyway?

"Damn, that nigga act like he ain't used to shit," Mercy said as she watched Herb act like a nigga with new money.

"Naw, them bitches see the dollar signs and they come around like flies on shit," Chrissie said, laughing.

"Let's fall back." Mercy motioned for Chrissie to follow her as they slid off.

Mercy and Chrissie found themselves at a table over in the cut. When the waitress came over to take their order Mercy asked to borrow her tablet and pen for a second. Mercy proceeded to write a note. She then folded it up and handed it to the waitress. She ordered a bottle of champagne for her and Chrissie and asked the waitress to give the note to Herb.

The note read: *"I ain't the ride a nigga's dick type of bitch on the first night. Go ahead and get your freak on. I'll call you tomorrow."*

After a few minutes the waitress returned, with a smile and the bottle of bubbly they had ordered.

"How much I owe?" Mercy asked, opening up her Gucci purse to pay the waitress.

"Nothing," the waitress replied. "The guy over there in the burgundy suit with the plaid vest on took care of it."

"Burgundy suit?" Mercy asked, squinting up her face.

The waitress came in a little closer to Mercy and said, "And, girl, it's a Zanetti suit at that."

Mercy and Chrissie scanned the club like a couple of surveillance cameras. Finally, Mercy locked eyes with the man responsible for quenching their thirst. He smiled, nodded his head, and sipped his drink, never letting his eyes leave hers. Mesmerized by his eye contact, like a zombie, Mercy was on her way over to say thank you to C-Note when Herb approached her and grabbed her hand.

"Why you send me that letter?"

"No harm or disrespect intended. Just keeping it real. No hard feelings, baby," Mercy said, still trying to keep her eyes on C-Note.

"Don't be like that," Herb said, almost in a whine.

"I'm not. As a matter of fact, give me your number so I can call you tomorrow."

"Come on, baby. You know you ain't going to call me tomorrow. Why you trying to play me?"

"Yes, I will. But I can't if I don't have yo' number."

Herb paused and looked Mercy up and down, trying to determine if she was on the real or not. "Yeah, you right. You got a pen in your purse?"

"No, I sure don't," Mercy lied.

"I do," Chrissie said, digging down in her purse. She retrieved a pen and handed it to Herb. Mercy shot her a sharp look.

"Good lookin' out," Herb said as he grabbed a napkin, wrote down his number, and handed it to Mercy. "Don't take it unless you gonna use it."

"Look, you ain't gotta be pressed about a phone call the way bitches is all up in your face," Mercy said, snapping her neck. "Boo, that shit don't intimidate me at all. You need to understand that no hoochie can run me away. I'm just going to let you breathe tonight because I ain't fucking tonight. So, I ain't the best thing for you to gamble on for the after party."

Just then Missy's song "Get Ur Freak On" came on. "I couldn't have said it better than Missy," Mercy said to Herb. "I'll holla at you." Mercy walked away, leaving Herb looking dumbfounded.

She managed to make her way over to C-Note with Chrissie right beside her.

"You got 'em chasing you down, huh?" C-Note said to Mercy, referring to Herb. Then he added, "I better keep my security close." C-Note had the prettiest smile Mercy had ever seen.

Feeling the effect of the champagne, Mercy got a little bolder. She embraced C-Note with a hug, throwing her leg up like she had recently seen someone do on television when she was greeting someone. "Thanks for the champagne, darling."

"It ain't nothing," C-Note said, bobbin' his head, running his tongue across his top row of teeth as he checked out Mercy from head to toe. "How's your lil' niece doing?"

"She's good," Mercy answered. "She went back to live with her mother. She calls me every single day, though."

"So who living with you now? Dat New York nigga?"

Mercy pulled her head back because she was caught off guard. She had no idea that C-Note knew her business like that, or would even bother to concern himself with it. "Nobody. My girl Chrissie be hanging out sometimes, but that's it.

"So who living with you?" Mercy shot back. She looked him in his eyes, then took a sip of her drink.

"You could be."

"Naw, I don't shack up with no niggas unless I got a ring. That ain't my thing. Been there, done that!"

"I feel you." He smiled. "But we can work towards that," he said, popping trash.

"You know how many times I done heard niggas try to kick that same game?"

"As good as you look," C-Note said, looking her over, "I can imagine. But look, baby, I can't rap with you like I want to in this here club."

"Is that right?"

"You know I done wanted to holla at you for like a year now. The last time I saw you I told you to wait for me and the next thing I know you sending blows to the head like Zab Judah." Both Mercy and Chrissie laughed as C-Note continued. "Then I was sure I was going to run into you again, and here we are. I never thought it would take this long, though."

Mercy could only blush as her pussy began to throb and fire-crackers seemed to ignite over the club's ceiling.

Damn. This nigga is kicking game to me. I swear I ain't had no good dick since Raheem, and I might just fuck this nigga here tonight. I done seen head-sprung in the back of the club before, but never thought I'd be one of them hoes. But a bitch is horny as hell.

"So, look, the bottom line is I've seen all I need to see tonight," C-Note said as he rubbed his fingers across her face.

"Is that right?" Mercy said, putting her head down, all of a sudden turning shy. For reasons she didn't quite understand he made her feel like no other. The way he looked at her, like she was so beautiful. She wanted to feel safe with him; she felt like he would protect her from the world.

"Yeah, so look, let's go and get breakfast," C-Note said, telling more than asking.

Just then some girl interrupted their conversation. " 'Scuse me, C-Note," she said. "Jus is drunk as shit. He over there wildin' out."

"Thank you, baby," C-Note responded to the girl, and then turned back to Mercy. "As I was saying, let's go get something to eat. But I got to go take my nigga, Jus, home, because he been drinking and that nigga can't hold liquor. You know I can't leave him out here to fall victim."

"I feel you," Mercy said, understanding.

"You can follow me to drop that nigga off, and then I'll keep my other nigga with me to keep yo' girl company while we kick it."

"A'ight," Mercy said with a smile.

"So, I'm going to get him and then I'll meet you outside up there at the corner in fifteen minutes."

"Which corner?"

"Seventh and Broad. Look, lock my number in your phone in case for some reason we lose each other," C-Note insisted.

Mercy read off his phone number before she locked it in and then gave him a hug.

"Fifteen minutes," he whispered in her ear as he embraced her.

Mercy smiled as she sashayed away. Her heart was beating fast because she knew in her heart that she had just met her knight in shining armor. C-Note was a take-control type of man who had the game all figured out, according to his street credibility—someone who wouldn't expect her to carry his pack or jeopardize her freedom, because he was a stand-up type of guy, the type of guy she just had to have. And if a street guy was what she had to have, her daddy would have approved of him.

CHAPTER 11

It's about to Go Down

After C-Note snatched Jus's drunk butt up, they headed towards the exit. C-Note stopped and waited at the bottom of the steps of the club when he realized that Jus wasn't right behind him.

Where the fuck is that nigga? C-Note thought as he looked around. He must have stopped off somewhere or got mixed up in the crowd. C-Note stepped outside of the door of the club to wait for his partner.

"Move along!" the four-hundred-pound, seven-foot bouncer shouted. "Move along."

C-Note thought the bouncer was talking to someone else until the big guy tapped him on the shoulder. "My man, you need to move the fuck along. I need to keep this area free."

"I'm just waiting on my man," C-Note advised him. "He should be coming any second. He was right behind me when I was walking down the steps. He's drunk and ain't in no kind of condition to be left and shit. You know how it is."

"My man," the bouncer said, filling his chest up with air, "move the fuck along. I don't give a fuck about yo' nigga being drunk. I want this area clear."

"Peace, G," C-Note said in a calm tone as he walked over to the bouncer. "I'm not trying to start anything or be rude, because I know you got a job to do, but my man is pissy drunk. He was right behind me and should be coming out any minute now. So I'm going to wait here by the door for the next minute or so."

C-Note turned to walk away. Catching a glimpse of Mercy, he put his finger up to tell her to wait a minute. He then motioned with his lips, "I'm coming."

The next thing he saw, or didn't see, was the lights go out. The bouncer hit him with a fist the size of a sledgehammer. The punch was so hard it sent him straight to the concrete and stretched him out cold. The crowd was silent for a few seconds, and a group of people surrounded C-Note.

"Damn! That's fucked up," one of the clubgoers said.

The bouncer was standing off by the door, still popping junk. "I bet when I tell a motherfucker to move along next time, motherfuckers will move."

"That's fucked up," another clubgoer said.

"Naw, man, I'm just doing my job," the bouncer insisted.

When people saw that it was C-Note stretched out on the ground, somebody walked past the bouncer and said, "Nigga, you done fucked up. I hope your family got some insurance on you."

"Look at that lame. The bitch-ass nigga is stretched out. Look like he da one that needs some insurance." The bouncer laughed. "A nigga like him ain't got none. It's cool, though, because the students at MCV will see him."

Seconds later, Jus came out of the club along with Cook'em-up and a few other homies.

"What da hell happened out here?" Jus said. They were shocked when they saw their boy out on the cold concrete.

"What the fuck?" one of the homies said with an incredulous look on his face.

By that time, Mercy was kneeling down by his side trying to get him up off of the pavement. C-Note came around and looked up at her, half embarrassed and half groggy. He jerked his arm away from her and said, "I got it. I don't need no help."

Someone pulled Cook'em-up aside and told him what happened, while his other homeboys hurried up and got C-Note off of the pavement, pushing Mercy aside. As they walked down the street to get into the car, a police cruiser slowed down and stopped two bystanders and asked them what was going on. Neither of them said anything. However, as folks saw Cook'em-up and the rest of his team, they all started clearing out. They knew what time it was. It was time to get the hell out of Dodge. If Cook'em-up had any reputation at all, it was that of a stone-cold murderer. He didn't take any shit and usually left no witnesses. The bouncer had violated, and you could smell the murder in the air.

Cook'em-up and C-Note stood at the back of the truck. "Go 'head and get ghost. I'll take care of this clown as soon as shit calm down," Cook'em-up said.

"Nope, not this time," C-Note said in a quiet voice.

Cook'em-up couldn't believe what he had just heard. He knew C-Note didn't like to get his hands dirty when it came to the rah-rah shit; that's why he offered to take care of the BI himself. He knew if they let this "Suge" Knight–wannabe clown get away with this stunt they would be the laughingstock of the entire city. By morning every little joker in the game with a pair of nuts would be trying to carry his man's little brother for weak.

"Not this time?" Cook'em-up repeated what he had just heard. "I got the utmost respect for you, Note." Cook'em-up didn't want to offend his man's manhood. "No doubt, yo' hustle game is on another level, but ain't no room in this car for no Martin Luther King, Jr. tonight." Before C-Note could respond, Cook'em-up continued. "Just go ahead and roll out, and I'll meet up with you later with the details. Trust me."

C-Note pulled back the cover where the spare tire was supposed to be.

"You got me twisted, Cook," C-Note said, finally getting a word in edgewise. "I appreciate the offer, trust that, but I gotta bake this cake myself."

Cook'em-up knew C-Note couldn't give the bouncer a pass. He watched as C-Note went under his spare tire and pulled out an M-16, identical to the one Al Pacino had in *Scarface*. Before he knew it, C-Note had changed his clothes. He put on a pair of jeans and a black Champion hooded sweatshirt. He always kept a few spare pieces of gear in the truck. C-Note then walked off, heading around the corner to the club. Cook'em-up saw murder in his eyes. It was like C-Note had transformed from a gentleman to a gangsta in a matter of seconds.

The homies were all in awe, trying to talk sense into C-Note. They knew he wasn't a killer, and they didn't want him to hesitate in the heat of the moment and get himself killed. So they began to chase behind him and try to take control of the situation themselves.

"Let him handle his business," Cook'em-up called out to the fellas. "He feels he needs to handle this one himself."

It was indeed time for C-Note to let the world know how he would hold his own. Although Cook'em-up had warned the homies, they all continued to trail closely on C-Note's heels. But Cook'em-up didn't budge. He was certain that C-Note had the situation under control and didn't need any assistance from anybody. Cook'em-up got in C-Note's car, turned on the ignition, and let the engine run so it could be good and ready to peel when

C-Note returned. Cook'em-up lit a cigarette, shook his head, and smiled.

C-Note never stopped walking as he used one hand to pull the head of the hoodie over his head. His face was now partially covered. He turned the corner and had the bouncer in his sight. It enraged C-Note to see that the big guy was still throwing his weight and position around, talking to people with no form of respect at all. As C-Note got closer, the bouncer knew something was wrong by the facial expressions of a whole new crowd of partygoers who had no idea what had gone on fifteen minutes before. As he turned to look around, in a split second the smile plastered on his face turned into despair. C-Note had locked eyes with him, and the expression on his face made C-Note fully aware that the big bad guy wished he was someplace else. Anywhere but here. He was so scared of what the big gun had in store for him that he shit his drawers. The bouncer fixed his lips to start pleading for his life, but whatever he was fixing to say never left his throat.

"Chop! Chop! Cha! Cha! Chop! Chop! Cha! Cha!" Sounds of gunshots roared, echoing through the sky as C-Note dumped the whole clip into the bouncer, never letting his eyes leave his target. He saw the life leaving the bouncer's eyes as the big man lay on the ground.

With a wicked smile he said, "Game over, Biggums." Then he quickly walked away from the scene, strutting right past his homeboys as if they weren't even there. He strolled like he had made a major accomplishment, and he was wearing a badge of honor on his chest that he wanted displayed to the world.

Once C-Note bent the corner he saw that Cook'em-up had turned the car in the opposite direction. C-Note hopped in the backseat and lay back to let all the chaos in his mind settle. Jus hopped in the front seat, while the other homeboys got into Cook'em-up's car and fled the scene.

"Nigga, is you fuckin' crazy?" Jus said from the front seat, looking back at C-Note. "You could've waited to do that shit. Man, you know how hot you 'bout to make us? Nigga, it was a million mafuckers out there, and somebody gon' tell."

Cook'em-up was quiet.

C-Note smacked his lips and replied, "Ain't nobody gonna tell because them so-called witnesses was too busy running for they fucking lives." Jus turned around and looked from the front seat as C-Note continued in an ice-cold voice. "Praying that I didn't give them none." Then a low chuckle escaped his lips.

Everybody in the car was silent. There was no radio playing, no conversation going on at all for the next few blocks. They were digesting C-Note's unexpected reaction. Then Jus finally said, with his whole high now blown, all of a sudden sober as a preacher man, "Man, you crazy as shit, C-Note."

C-Note looked up at Jus. "Man, don't call me C-Note no more. That nigga died with Biggums back there at the club. C-Note was that nigga that was all about getting money. He wasn't no soldier. He didn't want war. He toted guns but wouldn't kill for his army. That dude wouldn't protect what was his. He was a good nigga, but he just wasn't built like that." Nobody responded. The fellas just listened. "As a matter of fact, pull this motherfuckin' car over."

Cook'em-up did what he was told. C-Note grabbed one of the Heinekens out of the floor in the back of the car and hopped out. The homies didn't know what was up, but they followed suit. He popped the Heineken and the others homies did, too. He poured some out onto the ground.

"Like I said," C-Note continued, "that nigga died and a good nigga he was, but for every nigga that did it in this game, when he dies or goes to jail, it's a better nigga that takes his place. And Cleezy took that nigga C-Note's place."

He talked in the third person like he, in fact, wasn't C-Note. Jus didn't say a word. He was dumbfounded. But Cook'em-up loved every word that C-Note was kicking. So he poured some beer out and said, "May that nigga C-Note rest in peace."

"My niggas, shit is about to change. I ain't taking no shorts, halves, or parts," Cleezy said. "None whatsoever. No mo' sucka shit. This here is an organization. If and when the Feds come, we going down for organized crime, CCE, and all that bullshit. So we gon' run this shit like a fucking organized drug ring, straight gangsta style all the way. If in doubt, take the motherfucka out. This nigga right here, Cleezy, done hit this town and shit is 'bout to change. Y'all niggas got me or what?"

"No doubt, my nigga," they said, giving pounds, knowing that Cleezy meant every word he said. This night had been a life-altering night. And they all knew it. C-Note was dead. Cleezy had been born. Cook'em-up and Jus were certain that the boy they had all grown up with and protected for many years had been killed, and there was no doubt with Cleezy walking the streets, the city limits would never be the same.

They all piled back in the car.

"Man, you going home?" Cook'em-up asked Cleezy.

"Naw, man. Just keep the car and drop me off at Paula's. I gotta go get some shit together over there," Cleezy said. C-Note's plans with Mercy had been forgotten. Cleezy had other things on his mind.

"You handling yo' business, huh?" Jus said as Cook'em-up pulled the car in front of Paula's house.

Cleezy hopped out of the car and took in a breath of fresh air. He had just found a power that he had no idea existed within him. He had the power to take life and to be able to breathe life into himself. As he walked up to Paula's house, he was glowing, and his boys in the car saw him in a new light.

CHAPTER 12

The Mouth or the Box

It was almost four o'clock in the morning when Paula's phone woke her up out of a deep sleep.

"Hellloo," a sleepy Paula said after fumbling to get the receiver to her ear.

"You sleep?" Cleezy asked her.

She yawned and looked at the clock.

"No, I'm up," she lied.

"Stop lying."

Paula paused. She could hear something different in C-Note's voice. "You okay?"

"Yeah, I'm good. You got company?" he asked.

"Naw, not in here. Don't no niggas be laying up in here."

"That's what yo' mouth say."

"Why, what's up? You need to come through?"

"Yeah. I'm at the door now. Come open it," he demanded.

Still half asleep, Paula walked to the door with her Hampton University T-shirt and a pair of white panties on. The T-shirt was so short that her butt cheeks were hanging out. She opened the door and headed back to her bedroom and hopped back into the bed. Cleezy walked right behind her. She figured he was just going to do what he had to do and she was going to go back to bed. But Cleezy turned on her bedroom light and startled her.

She squinted her eyes, then focused in on the knot on his head.

"Oh, my goodness," she said, jumping out of the bed and walking over to touch his head gently. "What happened?"

"Nothing. I got into a little altercation, that's all," he said nonchalantly.

Paula raced to the kitchen to get some ice and returned to place it on his head. "Here, let me put this on it."

He pulled away, and then he remembered that gangstas need love too, so he let her be his nurse. As she held the ice on his head, Cleezy looked in the mirror at her. He noticed her ass cheeks hanging out from under her T-shirt. He was seeing Paula in a different light. He was seeing her through the eyes of a different nigga, a nigga that was high off of adrenaline, the rush that he had got from murdering someone. A dude who had just been transformed to a real gangsta, a man who had been resurrected. He couldn't help himself as he reached out and palmed her ass.

Paula was shocked but didn't mind at all, especially when she felt his manhood rise against her. Her eyes grew wide because she was finally going to get the big black dick that the women been talking about. She had always wanted a piece of him but hadn't wanted to be the aggressor. She didn't have to now, not this night anyway. She just let herself go with the flow as she allowed Cleezy to take control of the situation.

Cleezy pushed Paula down on her bed. She lay there panting, waiting for his next move. He watched her, waiting for a sign that it was cool for him to do what his body was telling him to do. The look in Paula's eyes told him everything he needed to know. Cleezy stood at the edge of the bed. Paula sat up and began undoing his pants for him. He just stood there as if it was her job and he didn't want to intrude by helping her. Every now and then

Paula looked up to make sure that she was following the boss's unspoken orders. Cleezy stepped out of his pants, then quickly turned Paula over onto her stomach.

"Oh, God," she said, caught off guard as Cleezy snatched her panties off and entered her fully from behind. She closed her eyes as Cleezy lay there inside of her as hard as a rock, not moving a muscle. There was absolutely no movement at all. He just stayed there breathing heavily in her ear.

Slowly he pulled out, leaving nothing but the tip inside of her. Afraid he was going to take that from her, Paula flexed her pussy muscles tightly around his dick, trying to activate her lockjaw pussy while holding on for dear life. Suddenly, he rammed himself back inside her; again he teased her by pulling out and leaving only the tip inside of her.

Paula began pushing her ass up against Cleezy, allowing his pubic hairs to brush up against her and tickle her ass. "Ummm," she moaned.

"That's right, do that shit," he whispered in her ear.

Trying to push up against the weight of Cleezy with her ass, Paula pushed Cleezy into her. The feeling of Paula's warmth wrapped around his dick like a blanket started feeling so damn good that he found himself in sync with her, stroking her softly. In and out, the strokes became faster and more passionate until Cleezy found himself hammering away at Paula's pussy like a jackrabbit on steroids.

With fists gripping the sheets, Paula began to moan, cocking her ass up, taking in all that Cleezy had to offer. In the heat of the moment she called out in between moans, "C-Note, oooh baby."

He gripped her tightly around her waist and whispered in her ear, "C-Note is dead. It's Cleezy that you wit'." The long intense strokes of pipe that he laid up in her began to get more aggressive. "What's my name?" he asked, pumping her hard as if he was stabbing her with his dick, waiting for a response in between thrusts.

"Cleezy," she barely got the words out as the pains of passion ran through every bone in her body and he dog-dicked her from the back.

"Whose pussy is this?" he asked her surprisingly.

"It's . . . aump, aump," she moaned. "It's . . . it's yours, baby?"

"Whose?" he asked as he punished her forcefully. In all of her days of ho' hopping, she had never had it laid down to her like Cleezy was giving it to her.

"It's . . . it's Cle . . . Cleezy's," she said. "It's yours, baby. It's that nigga Cleezy's," she said as he lightened up on her a little to the point where she could throw it back to him.

"For how long?" he asked, enjoying every minute of Paula's sweet pussy.

"Huh?" she asked, caught up in the sexscapade.

"I said, for how long?" He began hitting a spot that she never knew existed. "How long is this my pussy?"

"Forever and ever, until death do us part."

"Don't say that unless it's official."

"Cleezy, it is, and that's on everything I love. Cleezy, this is yo' pussy," she said as she stepped up her game, poppin' that pussy like she was a Luke dancer.

"Oooohhh, you better mean it," he said, thrusting in and out of her. Hearing the name Cleezy only made his dick harder. He was high off of who he was, that nigga, that shoot-'em-up bang-bang nigga who had the world at his feet. Hundreds of thousands stashed, keys of coke waiting to be moved, a hell of a team who would die for him, and he owned the hottest, wettest, juiciest pussy in town. Damn, life was good. Just the thought of every-thing had Cleezy's nut boiling inside of him like a volcano about to erupt.

"That's right. This is Cleezy's pussy. This is my pussy. Oh shit," he moaned as he felt his cream running through his veins. He pulled out and let it shoot all over Paula's ass like it was a tsunami.

As the white thick cum oozed out of his big black stallion, Paula quickly fell to her knees, taking the sexual session to the highest level, completely throwing Cleezy off balance when she licked every ounce of the cum she could manage to lick off of his dick and swallowed like it was Kool-Aid.

Damn, damn, damn. That nigga C-Note ain't never got this kind of treatment from no broad, Cleezy thought. *Now that shit I just had was some real gangsta loving. Here it is that nigga thought he had experienced some of the best sex any nigga could get. I can't figure out if it was her box or mouth that was the best. Now, that shit right there is deep.*

When it was all said and done, Cleezy knew why Paula had acquired her nickname, Sweet Pussy Paula.

Paula had no idea who this man was: C-Note, Cleezy, whoever. But whoever she had just been with, whoever the outlaw was, had made her feel like she had never felt in her entire life. He was what she wanted, and she would sacrifice and do whatever she had to do to keep him in her stable. Being an old-school ho, she knew the power of the pussy. Paula was familiar with the fact that when a man gets a good piece of pussy he will say anything in the heat of the moment, but she hoped like hell and prayed like never before that everything he said in her bed was gospel.

Cleezy and Paula screwed until the sun came up. Then Paula got out of bed, showered, and went into the kitchen to prepare breakfast. Cleezy kicked back, looking like a king in her king-sized Victorian-style bed. As he flipped through the channels, he came across a news report showing the yellow tape outside of the club and the bouncer being taken away by the coroner. Hearing the reporter say, "The authorities have no leads on any suspects, nor have any witnesses come forward yet" was music to his ears.

He had indeed gotten away with murder, which made his dick hard all over again. It led him into the kitchen to put Paula on the dining room table to get the lovemaking started all over again.

CHAPTER 13

A Dream Come True

"No, it's no problem," Mercy said into the phone. "I understand. Okay, I'll be ready day after tomorrow." She hung up the phone and thought, *Damn. Now what?* She needed to get some work done on her car and wanted to replace her broken DVD player for her TV set, but she didn't have any money, and Hyena had just postponed her next run.

Maybe she could hang out with Chrissie for a couple of days, but she doubted it. Although Chrissie had a room at Mercy's apartment, Deonie's old room, she spent most of her time laid up in some paid man's house. Chrissie raked in the men from here to Anaheim. She had no dreams, aspirations, or goals. She had no oomph about herself or nothing, but the men seemed to love her anyway. Some days she would be sitting on a few grand and other days she would be as broke as an old floor-model television.

Mercy strode into Chrissie's room at the end of the hall and found her standing in front of her closet with an open suitcase on the bed.

"Where are you going?" Mercy asked.

"Girl, that fool I met last week wants to take me to Vegas to do some gambling, and I got about ten minutes to pack."

Mercy sat down on the edge of the bed, disappointed.

Mercy never understood how Chrissie came across those men. She was like a magnet for men with money, men you would presume wouldn't be seen with a broad less than a Halle Berry look-alike. Chrissie was easy on the eyes, but she was no dime piece. She had an okay face, a creamy peanut butter complexion with a minor case of acne that her liquid foundation pretty much covered up, and a firm petite frame. She didn't even have an apple-bottom ass or big titties to fill in what she lacked in looks. The rich men Mercy had always seen on television, from rap stars with a fine-ass video ho on-screen and a model wife off-screen to Donald Trump with his exotic-looking wives, always had a trophy on their arm. Chrissie was no trophy—a plaque maybe, made out of nice cherrywood, at best. But a trophy, no way. Yet she still managed to snag NBA and NFL players, major big-time drug dealers, CEOs, young entrepreneurs with new money, and dirty old rich men with money two times as old as they were. Chrissie attracted all kinds of men with paper.

"Mercy, which one of these bags should I take? The Fendi or the Gucci. Never mind. I'll take both of them. Now, tell me, which one of these dresses I oughta take? I just got this one. Do you think it looks good on me?"

Chrissie held a slinky little slut-red dress up to her chin and glanced in the full-length mirror. Bitch had bags and clothes by Prada, Gucci, Fendi, Dior, and Chanel, just to name a few, all piled up in her closet. And it wasn't even her apartment. It was Mercy's.

"You know it looks good. Thank God you ain't never had to work for your clothes, girl. You wouldn't work in a pie shop if you was starving to death," Mercy joked.

"Why work when I got a perfectly reliable, clean pussy, which makes certain I get all the desires of my heart?" Chrissie said.

Chrissie threw the dress into the suitcase and closed it shut. She then laced her feet with the best footwear that money could buy.

"Bye, girlfriend," Chrissie said, and kissed her on the cheek. Then she tottered out of the room on her stiletto heels, dragging her rolling suitcase behind her. Mercy followed her to the front steps and watched as Chrissie got into her mint-green Thunderbird convertible with customized plates that read HATE ME. Some NBA star she spent a week with in Maui paid for that.

Almost every female clique has someone like Chrissie. She's the one who's not the cutest in the bunch, but from the moment she steps into the club, every male in there tries to get at her. She just has this certain confidence that seems to consume any room she steps into. She walks up on the scene, acting as if she's looking like a million bucks. Her long straight hair, which she purchased from the Korean hair supply store, is never out of place. It's always sewn in, never glued in, and paid for by the flavor of the month. Her makeup is always applied to perfection, and she's usually sportin' the latest diamond earrings, two-carat total weight minimum, that damn near blind the men in the club. Dudes figure, if her swagger is that tough, then she must be a bad-ass bitch. And when guys step to her, she looks them up and down as if deciding whether or not they are good enough to even be saying "hi" to her.

Chrissie's parents had abandoned her, so she'd been placed in a foster home when she was nine. A few years later, Mercy met her in Chrissie's third foster home. From the very beginning, Mercy saw that Chrissie would much rather surround herself with the things that money can buy, rather than to have the money itself. As they got older and moved out on their own, Chrissie was proof that being a diva ain't got nothing to do with having money in the bank. Because even though she stayed in the company of men with money and more money, she, herself, had none. Chrissie was all about material possessions.

Mercy picked up a gold bracelet that Chrissie had dropped on her way out of the apartment and took it back into Chrissie's room. She looked around at all the stuff, strewn about the room as if a cyclone had hit, and thought that if Chrissie would sell some of those designer bags, jewelry, or televisions and stuff, then she would have a modest fortune going on. Mercy struggled and was the backbone of the two. Mercy kept the roof over their heads and made sure they had gas money and food in the fridge. Chrissie basically pitched in when she could. One thing for sure and two things for certain, when Chrissie had Mercy had. If Chrissie had a dollar, fifty cents was Mercy's, but if Mercy needed the whole dollar, it was hers. It wasn't no hateration, none of that, between the two of them. They both had made it through hell and nothing would ever come between them. Mercy was happy that Chrissie was having fun and getting what she wanted. She hoped that one day Chrissie would luck up and that one of the men would marry her.

Mercy thought about walking across the hall to Ms. Pat's house, but she saw her begging, junkie son over there and decided not to. Mercy plunked herself down on the leather living room sofa. She did not want to spend the night watching TV by herself, so she went through the phone book of her cell phone, looking to see if there was anybody she could call to kick it with, but there was no one. As bad as she wanted to call C-Note, she just couldn't bring herself to hit the *send* key. She was too embarrassed to call after witnessing him getting knocked out like Roy Jones, Jr. Then the way he snatched away from her like he had some ill feelings towards her just added to the reason she wouldn't, or couldn't, call.

Let me call that Herb dude, Mercy thought to herself. *Let me see what he's talking about.* She grabbed the phone and called up Herb.

"Yo," Herb said, answering the phone.

"Hey, Herb, it's Mercy," she said. "How are you?"

"Hey, Mercy," he said, all happy. "I'm chillin'. How are you?"

"Everything is good," she said as she picked up the remote, turned the television on, and started flipping through the channels. *Why the fuck do I even pay cable? It ain't ever a daggone thing on here. I could come up with better stories than they got on this thing. My life is way more interesting than this shit.*

"I didn't think you were going to call."

"I told you I was, didn't I?"

"Yeah, you did." He paused, then asked, "What you gettin' into?"

What was she getting into? She hadn't planned on getting into anything 'cept some more runs for Hyena, but now that old dream of hers, that dream of making something of herself, was surfacing in her mind.

"I'm just chillin', taking it easy," she said, "but later on I'm going to probably go out to the Literary Boutique. There's this book I need to pick up."

"What book you trying to get?" he asked.

"I want to get this book on how to write scripts and make movies."

"Word?" he said, sounding very surprised.

"Yup," she said, suddenly feeling excited.

"That's cool as shit. What made you decide that's what you wanted to do?" he said, trying to kick small talk, but at the same time sounding interested.

"Reading so many books and watching movies," Mercy replied. She felt her pulse quicken as she began to talk about her aspirations and dreams. "Whenever I go to the movies and watch them, I always feel like I could have done so much better with the project. So, why not do it? Oprah said follow your passion, and I'm about to make it happen."

"Look, let's do some lunch or something, and then maybe I can go to the bookstore with you."

"Okay. That sounds cool. Where you want to meet?" she asked, glad to be getting out of the house.

Mercy and Herb agreed to meet at the bookstore. After realizing they had lost track of time in the bookstore, lunch had come and gone. They decided to have dinner and catch a movie. After the movie Mercy was even more amped about turning her dream to write, direct, and produce films into reality. The whole time over dinner, she talked Herb's ears off about how she was going to make this come true. She couldn't think about anything but how bad she wanted to kick down the door of the film industry.

"You know, maybe I will do a DVD first and hope that someone will see my work and then want to take me to the big screen," Mercy said as they rode in the car.

"It's possible. Once your script is done, I know some people who could help you out."

"Fo' real?" Mercy said with excitement.

"Yup." He nodded, smiling at her. "And you know what?"

"What?" Mercy asked, focusing in on every word.

"I know you don't know me well, but I want you to know that I will support you in any way you need me to." Herb looked over at Mercy and licked his lips. "You seem for real about your shit. You might be a good investment."

"Oh, thank you so much!" Mercy said. She had never shared her dreams with anyone before. She might have mentioned it a time or two, but no one had really paid any mind to her seemingly far-fetched dreams.

"And I mean that shit, too."

Mercy reached over and gave Herb a hug, damn near making him wreck the car. His words comforted her and gave her that extra push she needed. Herb seemed genuine. Not for one minute did Mercy question what he might want in return. When Herb pulled up in front of Mercy's house to drop her off and didn't even try to worm his way inside, Mercy was even more convinced of his sincerity.

For the next couple of days, until she had to make her run, Mercy read the scriptwriting books she had just bought and began working on her first script, which she titled, *A Girl's Gotta Do What a Girl's Gotta Do.*

Once she returned from her run, she poured her all into her script, sometimes not leaving the house for days, most of the time barely taking a shower and changing out of her pajamas. She even slacked up on handling her business with Hyena. She printed out copies of the script and sent it to Raheem and Nayshawn to get their opinions and to help them both get their minds off of the jail time.

Raheem called her right away. "Boo, this here is really good. I can practically see it in my head as I'm reading it. You keep on keepin' on."

Nayshawn was just as encouraging.

Mercy would read excerpts to Chrissie when she was around, and Chrissie started planning the premiere party.

"Girl, we are gonna have famous rappers, and it'll be off the hook," Chrissie told her. "And you and I are gonna stroll up in our furs. We'll have a red carpet and everything."

Every day Herb would listen while she read her script to him either in person or on the phone. He seemed to be just as happy about her writing as she was. He encouraged her. Although it was obvious that Herb sold drugs, something about him made him seem so different from the other hustlers she had encountered.

CHAPTER 14

Everyone Is Suspect

After three months of working on her script, Mercy decided that she should take a course on script writing. She had been so caught up in her writing that her work wasn't consistent, which meant her cash flow wasn't either. She would have to figure out a way to pay for the class or get someone else to pay for it for her. She made a trip to the university to look into some screenwriting courses. Tution would be forty-five hundred dollars. She had been saving for it, but it was taking too long for her to get the full amount, so she filled out some financial aid papers. However, the school's intake person was not reassuring that she would get it.

Mercy was afraid that any day someone would produce a film similar to her idea and all of her hard work would be in vain. She wanted to perfect her game and get shit rolling now. As Mercy sat in front of her computer, she tried to figure out how she could cover her tuition for the courses plus keep a roof over her head. When Deonie left she never reported it to housing, so she was still on low income, paying next to no rent, but a sistah still had to live. She was too embarrassed to ask Hyena for an advance, because the reality was that she should have had enough money in her stash to be able to pay the forty-five hundred. How could she not? Hyena paid her a pretty penny for each run she made for him. It was just too bad that she had no control over it.

As Mercy sat on the round ottoman she had in the middle of her closet, she gazed over her designer shoe boxes, handbags, and clothes and began to sob. In her hands she held her latest bank statement. Her balance was seventeen dollars and eleven cents. After having to struggle and scrape for so long, once she'd gotten money, she had shopped as though she was ballin' out of control. Why shouldn't she treat herself? she'd thought. She had no man to surprise her with presents, so she'd showered herself with love. She'd spent like there was no tomorrow or if there was a tomorrow, she would have more work to bring in more money. In addition to wanting to treat herself to expensive clothes and jewelry, she'd wanted to be able to have something to show for it. Like most young people, Mercy hadn't thought about something to show for it being a nice fat savings account.

The reality set in that she had made many foolish decisions. She hadn't cut any corners, either. She did everything to pamper herself: manicures, pedicures, weekly facials, and hair fixed once, sometimes twice, a week. Clothes were always the best of the best. She rationalized her expenditures by telling herself, *I am a little thick, and I have to make sure my shit is ten times flyer than a little Jane Fonda bitch who can get away with that cheap shit.*

Although she was taking risks up and down the highway, she had the chance to take a bad situation and turn it around to something good. But now her pockets were on empty and she had no savings. All she had was some determination and her script, but from here on out, she knew that she wasn't splurging on anything. Her prime focus would be to make money to get her film out. She knew she would need some help, though.

Just then the phone rang. Mercy got up to answer it. She

looked at the caller ID and saw that it was just the person she had been thinking of. It was as if she had thought him up.

"Hello," Mercy said, clearing her throat, trying to pull herself together.

"Hey, lil' momma," Herb said.

"Hey," she said, sniffling a bit.

"What's wrong?" Herb said, concern in his voice.

"Nothing," Mercy lied, putting her head down.

"Come on. Now you know you can tell me."

Mercy paused. "It ain't nothing, just frustrated is all."

"About what?"

"My script," Mercy answered with a sigh. "I just want to be able to move forward and get it onto the screen. You have no idea how bad I want this. Before, it was just something I used to think about. But ever since I started talking about it to you and actually started to work on the script, I can taste it. I know you hear me talkin', but I'm sure those are just words to you. You can't imagine how strongly I feel about breaking into the film industry."

"Yes, I do," he said in such a sympathetic tone.

"I'm just feeling so overwhelmed right now, and I want this to happen more than anything." Mercy couldn't believe she was pouring her heart out like this.

"Look, you need to get out of the house," Herb said. "Why don't you come meet me somewhere? We can talk about it. You never know, we might be able to help each other out."

Mercy accepted Herb's invitation, and they decided to meet at a restaurant midway from where they each lived. She got herself together and headed out to meet him. The whole drive over to meet with Herb, Mercy just couldn't get his words out of her head. "We might be able to help each other out."

When Mercy arrived at the restaurant, Herb wasn't there yet.

She sat down anyway and waited eagerly to hear what Herb was going to say to ease her frustrations. *Is he going to turn me on to the folks he said he knew?* Mercy thought. *Is he going to spot me the money and become an investor? He might want to get legit, and this would be the perfect opportunity for him to clean up all of his dirty drug money. Or does he want to produce a little paper for a sexual favor? You never know with these types.*

"How long you been here?" Herb asked as he walked up to the table where Mercy was sitting.

"Oh, I just got here," Mercy said, looking up, catching a kiss in her left eye that was supposed to be for her forehead.

"You ordered yet?"

"No, not yet," Mercy answered.

"I'll send your waitress right over," the hostess said with a smile as she walked away.

"You look so down," Herb said, putting his hand on top of Mercy's. Mercy just sat there. "Look, baby, I understand how much you want this movie thing to happen, and I want it to happen for you. Remember that I'm that nigga that encourages you. I'm that nigga that held you afloat when you felt like you were sinking. Me, Herb."

"I know and appreciate that, fo' real," Mercy interrupted.

"Now remember when I told you in the beginning when you first started talking about your writing and stuff that I knew some people who could help you out?"

"Yup," Mercy answered, glad that he was getting to the point.

"I wasn't lying," Herb said sincerely.

"Fo' real?" Mercy replied, glad that Herb wasn't just selling her a dream.

He nodded in the affirmative. Mercy began to feel anxious. Just as she was getting ready to speak, the waitress came over to take their orders. Neither of them had even looked at their menus, so they asked her to come back in a few minutes. Just as soon as the waitress walked away, they went right back to the conversation at hand.

"Look, I'm finished with it. Now I just need it to be edited. My girl Chrissie was always the bomb in English class. She said she'll edit it for me. I want to throw her something. You know?" Mercy continued, not taking a breath. "I want to go to film school. It costs around forty-five hundred dollars, but with me paying for editing, buying these books to teach me how to write scripts, and whatnot, I ran through a lot of money, and now . . . ," Mercy paused. She took a deep breath. The last thing Mercy wanted to do, or any woman wanted to do with one of her male friends, was to let him know that she was broke. "I'm in a position to, and I want to, go to film school, but my money is all funny right now."

"That's what I'm talking about," Herb said, moving in closer to Mercy. "The people that I'm dealing with can put you in a good position."

"Okay, well, introduce me to them then," she said, but was wondering why he wouldn't just foot the bill himself. Forty-five hundred dollars shouldn't have been nothing but a drop in the bucket for a baller like him, balling out of control, flyest gear, tightest whip, and fat-ass bankroll. He knew her potential and had said it was good.

"Well, it's kinda tricky. That's why I wanted to meet with you face-to-face so that I could go into depth about everything."

"I'm listening," Mercy said eagerly.

Herb took a deep breath. "Well, first off, I have to confess something. I would like to come clean with you. My name isn't Herb."

Mercy snickered. "I kinda figured that. I figured it was something like Herbert and that they just call you Herb for short. No baller ever gives out his government, anyway."

"Not quite," Herb said, putting his head down. "It's Robert Cummings, and I'm . . . ," He paused for a moment and then continued. "I'm an FBI agent."

Those words went through Mercy like a sharp knife. She didn't know what to do. Her first instincts were to get up and run, but then she thought that perhaps the restaurant might be surrounded. She was in too much shock to even move.

He held out his hand to her. "Hold on to my hand. Take a few deep breaths and relax. Everything is going to be okay."

"What?" she screamed, attracting the attention of the other people in the restaurant. "What do you mean, 'Everything is going to be okay'?" Mercy then lowered her tone. "You're a fuckin' rat. You're a liar. What . . . what are you going to do, arrest me or something?" Mercy was starting to panic.

Once he saw that Mercy wasn't going to grab his hand, he withdrew it. "Let me finish," he said, trying to calm her down. "I know you're confused."

"Like a motherfucker. You got that right," Mercy said, thinking about how Herb had appeared so much like he was a big baller, getting money.

"Listen, Mercy, I don't want to arrest you for anything. I swear. As a matter of fact, we have something in common."

Mercy just sat there, listening to the agent. Looking at him now, he even looked like a fuckin' pig. "Oink, oink," she wanted to say to this hog. Listening to him, she noticed he was no longer using slang or some fake ghetto-ass accent. Now all of a sudden the way he talked was different, more professional and educated.

"I don't know what that could be," Mercy said, her thoughts running wild and stomach twisting in knots.

"A friend of yours," Agent Cummings said.

"A friend of mine?" she asked, with confusion written all over her face.

Just then the waitress came back over to the table. Mercy didn't say a word and just gave her the evil eye until she walked away.

"Yeah," Agent Cummings continued. "Your friend Raheem."

"What? What are you talking about?" She felt like vomiting, because she knew she was doomed and would be hauled off to the women's jail. Her ride sat right in front of her.

"Raheem sent us to you. He told us everything, Mercy, but don't worry. Like I said, it's not you we want to arrest."

Tears started to run down Mercy's face. She couldn't utter a word. Well, she knew better than to say anything, although Raheem had said it all.

Agent Cummings grabbed hold of Mercy's hand. He looked in her eyes and said, "Don't cry, Mercy."

Mercy closed her eyes. For a minute the feeling of having her hand held was comforting. It reminded her of when she would sit on her father's lap and he would sometimes put his hand over hers. The betrayal and pain she felt at that moment wasn't the same hurt that she'd felt when her father was cremated in front of her eyes, but it was damn sure close to it.

"Don't worry. You're not in any trouble."

Mercy opened her eyes and looked up at the deceitful man before her. She then looked down at her hand and snatched it away from Agent Cummings. "What do you mean by 'everything'?"

"He told us that you were his girl, that he had been down here living with you and that when he got knocked, he connected you with his friend Hyena." Mercy's heart was in her panties. "He told us that once he went to jail, Hyena took care of his lawyer and everything . . . and you."

"What do you mean by that?" Mercy snapped.

Agent Cummings continued as if Mercy hadn't even inter-

rupted him. "He told us that Hyena is the man behind the organization. Now, as you know, we could arrest you for taking
money—illegal money—and bring you in as a part of the whole
conspiracy. And you could be faced with a good twenty years." He
paused and looked into Mercy's eyes. "You were just doing what
you thought you needed to do to get by and to stand by your
man. You're just a girl doing what a girl's gotta do. Yeah, you
might seem a little rough around the edges, but you've got a good
heart. We know about what you did for your sister's kid and your
friend that's a prostitute, Chrissie, and all."

She interrupted, taking up for Chrissie. "She ain't no prostitute."

"Well, she might as well be the way she chases behind men
with the largest money sac in their pocket, but I didn't mean any
offense." He shifted the conversation. "As I was saying, you have
this natural ability to take care of others who you think need
you. That's what you were doing for Raheem. We know you were
just standing by him. We see young girls in your position every
day."

Mercy sat there listening to Agent Cummings talk as if he
could sympathize with her. *What does this six-figure-salary-making
pig know about a young black girl surviving the streets?* Mercy wondered. As far as Mercy was concerned, he was a liar, a joke. Just
someone trying to blow smoke up her ass, hoping she'd get high
off of it. Mercy looked around at the patrons of the restaurant and
wondered who was FBI and where the surveillance instruments
were set up.

"Mercy, do you know that Raheem would have taken any charge
that we might have had for you?" Agent Cummings continued,
now sounding sentimental.

Trust me, Mercy thought. *That nigga ain't taking no charge for
me. Shit, he done proved he can't do his own time.*

She didn't speak as he continued to pour what she assumed was his well-rehearsed bullshit speech on her.

"Raheem loved you so much that he didn't even have the heart to tell you that he needs your help."

"He needs *my* help?" Mercy asked.

"Yes, he needs your help. We need your help." He paused. "Help us get Hyena, Mercy. Otherwise we just waste time and money locking up people like Raheem and their runners."

Mercy shook her head at Agent Cummings's insinuation that if she didn't help, then she would perhaps find herself locked up, too.

"Getting Hyena would mean a sentence reduction for Raheem. He'd be able to get home to you a lot sooner."

"What? I don't understand," Mercy said.

"Yes, he's been working with us. Actually, he's been working with us for quite some time."

Mercy started to experience hot flashes as her hands got sweaty. She was beginning to feel dehydrated.

"I don't believe you. Raheem hated the law. He'd never join up with the fuckin' Feds."

"I know it's hard to believe, but believe it, Mercy."

"Stop saying my fuckin' name like you know me like that," Mercy snapped.

"I do know you, Mercy. I know your kind."

"Look, let me get this straight. So, you are police? They got you set up looking like and acting like a drug dealer?"

"Unh-hunh," he said.

"So, they got you balling big time. You got the car, the jewelry, and the lingo, and everything. Isn't that entrapment?"

"No, not really. Entrapment is only when a person does something that they normally wouldn't do. See, these hustlers, this is what they do: sell drugs."

"I can't believe you. I don't even know what to say." She shook her head.

"I know you are shocked right now. However, I want you to know that if you help us, not only would you be helping Raheem, you would be helping yourself also."

"Helping myself? I don't see how any of this can help me."

"See, the federal government is very powerful, and we know people everywhere in high and low places. We could get your script into the hands of the right people and guarantee your work would go on the big screen." He snapped his finger and said, "Just like that."

Mercy couldn't help but burst out laughing. "Just like that, huh? So the Feds and movie producers, y'all got it all on lock. Where's the hidden camera?"

"This is no joke, Mer—," Agent Cummings said, cutting himself off, as if he didn't want to patronize Mercy.

She let out a small chuckle.

"Share the laugh," he said.

"I'm just sitting here tripping off of how you waltz into my life pretending to be my friend and the whole time you had your own motives. Damn, do you police even have a conscience the way you play with people's emotions?"

"It's a very hard job; you have no idea. I really like you, Mercy, and wish that the circumstances were different."

"Well, they're not. You want me to snitch. Well, to be a snitch bitch!"

"Don't look at it like that. You're just helping a friend, that's all," he said soothingly.

"Look, my head is racing all over the place, as I'm sure you can imagine. I know this isn't the first time or the last time you have broken this kind of news. So let me get back to you," Mercy said, with no intention of ever addressing the situation again.

Agent Cummings replied, "Don't wait too long."

Mercy got up from the table and started to walk away.

"Yo, lil' mama," Agent Cummings said in his Herb tone. "You sho' you don't want nothing to eat?"

Mercy stopped in her tracks, turned around, stared him dead in his eyes, rolled her eyes, and then walked away. She got in her car and sat there feeling like she was going to have a nervous breakdown. Anxiety, hyperventilation, loss of breath all came and went. She didn't know who to talk to or confide in because everyone was suspect at this moment. On the ride home she looked around, and every single person she glanced at she wondered if they were a mole, informant, or FBI agent.

Real Chicks Do Real Things

Chrissie greeted her as soon as she walked in the door.

"Girl, I got this motherfucker you gots to meet," she said as she gave Mercy a hug. She had just gotten back from a rendezvous in LA, and shopping bags from Rodeo Drive cluttered the living room.

"I ain't in the right state of mind to meet nobody," Mercy said, brushing Chrissie off as she walked through the living room to her bedroom, almost tripping over one of the bags.

"Not meet him in person. Girl, he don't even live here. He live in Chicago. Just talk to this dude on the phone. He's cool with the dude I was just kickin' it with. Girl, he paid. He's a professional athlete. No, not the typical football or basketball player. He's a boxer. But he paid all the same. He gets about two fights a year and walks away with a check for four or five mill easy. And those fighters be fighting a good two times a year. You do the math, boo."

Chrissie was as excited as a priest among Boy Scouts. She just kept babbling on and on. Mercy couldn't muster up an ounce of excitement. She was still bugging out about Raheem being a snitch.

"I told him all about you. He said he's ready to meet a down-to-earth chick. He's tired of messing with all the girls he meets out at parties who can smell his green. Girl, and he up for one of the biggest fights ever, which means you need to hook up with him now before he get his purse—that way you won't be suspect. You know what I'm saying?"

"Yeah, girl, yeah," Mercy said, sighing and rubbing her forehead as she flopped her restless body down on her bed.

"Girl, what's wrong with you?" Chrissie said, sitting down on the chaise in Mercy's room. "I thought you'd be a little bit more excited than this. I mean, this dude ain't one of them thugs you usually fuckin' around with. Easy money come, easy money go. He got legit money, and lots of it, might I add, and by the time you add in the endorsement deals, that's more money."

Mercy was just staring off, not hearing a word Chrissie had just said.

"Hello. Is anybody in there?" Chrissie said, softy knocking on the side of Mercy's head.

"Girl, yeah, I hear you," Mercy lied, snapping out of her trance.

"So here it is." Chrissie pulled a phone number out of her pocket and handed it to Mercy like she was giving her the winning sweepstakes ticket.

"Here's what?" Mercy said, taking the number and looking down at it.

"His phone number, stupid," Chrissie said, getting up.

"I don't know what the boy even look like."

"The only face you need to worry about is those big faces on those hundred-dollar bills. He could look like Kermit the frog, but all money looks and spends the same," Chrissie put in her two cents.

"What's his name? Who is he?" Mercy asked with a puzzled look on her face.

"Were you not listening to a word I said? He's a world-ranked boxer, boo. Don't sleep on him. He went to the Olympics and everything. His name is Taymar. Call him, girl." Chrissie headed into the living room.

"Then why ain't you hook up with him?" Mercy questioned.

"If I could have, I would have. He's the friend of the dude I was with. They too cool for me to try to fuck with both of 'em. I was gonna put his ass on reserve, but I thought it would be nice to share for once." Chrissie winked at Mercy and then headed to the living room.

Mercy stared at the paper. For all she knew, this nigga was FBI, too. Everybody could be playing her, including Chrissie. She tossed the paper in a drawer and lay down to stare at her ceiling and try to figure out what to do.

Mercy lay in the bed tossing and turning. She was scheduled to make a run for Hyena in a couple of days. She needed the money, but she knew the Feds were watching him, and she couldn't subject herself to the brick wall that was sure to come crumbling down on him. If she did stop working for him suddenly, he would probably become suspicious of her, and any shit that did go down he would put on her. The last thing she wanted to do was to get caught in the cross fire, so she knew she would have to play dodgeball with Hyena, but she had no idea how in the hell she could get out of Dodge.

When the phone rang at nine o'clock the next morning, it didn't wake Mercy up from a deep sleep. She had spent the last few hours with her eyes closed, but she was anything but asleep.

"Hello," Mercy said.

"Mercy?" a male voice asked. She didn't recognize the voice.

"Yeah."

"It's good to know that you are a morning person. At least we know that we already have one thing in common."

"Who is this?" Mercy asked, sitting up in the bed. "You calling for Chrissie?"

"No, not right now," the caller said. "Right now I'm calling for you. Perhaps I'll be calling Chrissie later . . . to thank her."

"Who is this?" Mercy said, becoming slightly agitated. She wasn't in the mood to be playing any games on the phone.

"It's the next heavyweight champion of the world. I'm Taymar. Chrissie couldn't stop talking about you. I wanted to call you just as soon as she gave me your number, but I figured I had to wait at least twenty-four hours. I'm an impatient brotha, and want it when I want it. So I could only wait sixteen."

"Excuse me?" Mercy said, still not certain who this character was, trying to be so slick with his lines.

He laughed a conceited laugh. "I know, I know. I'm not used to this myself," Taymar said.

"Used to what?" Mercy snapped. "Calling women you don't even know the first thing in the morning, like you just woke up with a morning hard-on and gon' jack off to they voice on the phone or something?"

"Damn," he laughed. "Maybe I was wrong about you."

"You think?"

"Yeah, I think." He paused, thinking of some more slick shit to say. "You're not a morning person at all. But, it's cool. I think I can get past that."

Mercy couldn't help but let out a little chuckle. *This is one of them suckers who like to suck they own dick,* she said to herself.

"Was that laughter I heard?" Taymar asked.

Mercy didn't respond. She just shook her head.

"What, did I call you too soon? You want me to wait the eight more hours?"

Mercy laughed.

"Now, I know that was laughter."

"Do you ever stop?" Mercy asked.

"Nope, not until I get the W," he said smoothly.

"The W, huh?" Mercy asked.

"Yep, the W."

"Is that the win?"

"Normally. But in this case, it's the woman."

Mercy smiled from ear to ear as she blushed. Her initial re-action, to be a bitch and get rid of the ol' dude, disappeared as she found herself talking with Taymar for hours. He talked about his goals as a boxer, and she talked about her goals as a screenwriter. When she looked up at the clock, it was after one o'clock in the afternoon. She had lain in the bed like a teenager in high school, gabbing away on the phone about any- and everything. She needed to get her mind off of all the drama. She needed an escape. Perhaps Taymar was that escape in more ways than one.

"Do you realize that for what this phone call just cost me I could have bought you a plane ticket to come see me?" Taymar joked.

Mercy thought about the comment Taymar had just made. Maybe a trip to Chicago was just what she needed. It would be the perfect place to get out of Dodge, so to speak. Mercy thought up a quick comeback to Taymar's comment.

"Then next time you should just send me a plane ticket instead of calling me," Mercy said, chuckling, but so serious.

"Baby, you ain't said nothing," Taymar quickly responded. "I'm serious. Just say the word." He added, "See, I don't think you know who I am. I am the next heavyweight champion of the world. I make shit happen," he stressed.

She brushed off his last comment since she knew that he praised the ground that he walked on. "Show me. You keep talking 'bout it, show me the money, nigga!" Mercy teased.

"No, but seriously. I'm going to be training soon. I wouldn't mind taking these last few days before I commit my body to winning this fight to get to know you. My mind is already committed, but once I commit my body, I'll be living in the gym."

"When do you start training?"

"Next week," he answered.

"Next week!" Mercy said in shock. "Hell, that means I'd have to come tomorrow."

Taymar paused. "What do you say? Your ticket ain't nothing but a click away."

"And you still talking, huh?" Mercy played along.

"Look, I know you don't know me, but damn, I feel like you know more about me in the last four hours than my baby's mama knew about me in the last ten years."

"Why is that?" Mercy asked curiously.

"I don't know. I just felt like I was talking to one of my buddies. There wasn't anything I wanted to hold back from you. From the moment you said hello when you answered the phone, you didn't seem like a stranger. Maybe it was because Chrissie talked you up so much. She couldn't stop bragging about your scripts. Then to actually sit here and listen to you talk about it yourself. . . . Man, I'm just feeling everything about you."

"Do you rehearse the shit you say?" Mercy chuckled.

"Naw, baby. This is all real."

"It's all real?"

"Yes, it is."

Mercy closed her eyes and took in Taymar's voice, the sincerity of it. Taking off on a whim with someone she didn't even know wasn't something Mercy would have normally considered, but she figured if she could do it with Farmer John, then she could do it with Taymar.

"Then I guess I better get packing," Mercy said.

"For real, you coming tonight?"

Mercy thought for a minute. There was nothing more she wanted to do than to hop on a plane and get the fuck away, but there was something she had to do first. "No," she replied. She could hear Taymar's sigh of disappointment. "I've got to do a couple of things. I can come the day after tomorrow."

"Are you serious?" Taymar questioned. "The day after tomorrow?"

"Yes," Mercy assured him.

"You know I hate waiting. I'm used to people jumping to my beck and call."

"And me too," Mercy said.

"Well, I'm gonna go online right now. Give me your e-mail address, and I'll e-mail you your itinerary."

"It's havemercy@common.com."

"This is crazy," Taymar said, letting out a laugh.

"What?"

"Nothing," he said. "Since you're not a morning person I'm going to get you on the first afternoon flight available day after tomorrow."

Mercy laughed. "Sounds good."

"Then I'll talk to you tomorrow."

"I'll wait for your call," Mercy said in a sensual tone.

They ended the call, and Mercy threw herself back on the bed. She couldn't believe she was doing this, but she almost had to. Taymar was heaven-sent in more ways than one. Mercy closed her eyes, and before she knew it, she was sound asleep. She slept deeply for about an hour before she abruptly woke up and remembered why she couldn't leave tomorrow. There was something she had to do before even thinking about leaving town.

Mercy needed to go see Raheem. She had planned to go see him anyway, but now she needed an explanation as to what in the hell was going on with him supposedly working with the Feds. She needed to hear the bullshit from the horse's mouth. It was on her mind constantly, and she needed some kind of clarity as to why Raheem would sell out. He was her boy, no doubt. He had put her in a position to eat, but she'd been raised by two of the most crucial dudes in the game, and if she'd learned nothing at all, she'd learned that a rat was poison and spineless and could do no good to anyone.

If she obeyed traffic laws, the ride to the prison in Butner, North Carolina, was three hours away, so Mercy had to break a few. For the entire drive Mercy thought about what words could possibly come out of Raheem's mouth. What words could possibly make her want to fuck with him again?

When Mercy arrived at the prison she went through the typical procedures: showing ID, being searched before she was escorted to the visiting room. Although she only waited thirty minutes for Raheem to come to the visiting room, it seemed like an eternity. He walked in and gave Mercy a hug.

I wonder if this motherfucker is wearing a wire? Mercy thought, trying to inconspicuously pat him down his back and press her front tight against him as she returned the hug.

"Why you wait so late to get here?" he asked, looking at his watch. "I'm surprised they even let you in as shitty as they be acting."

"I don't know," Mercy said, sitting back down. "I haven't been able to sleep, so when I finally did fall asleep, I just slept."

"Why you ain't been sleeping?" Raheem asked with concern.

"You want to know why?" Mercy said.

"Yeah. Why?"

"Because I been thinking about you. I have been thinking about the person that I once was madly in love with. That person who taught me so much. That person who bailed me out of jail with a black eye—that dude. And now I'm wondering, Who is that dude, really? Who is he?"

Raheem grabbed Mercy's hand and said, "I'm still that dude. I'm still your friend, and I'm still your protector." He looked into her eyes and then continued. "And never would I let anything happen to you."

Mercy looked away from him. "I can't tell," she half mumbled. She took a deep breath. "You sent the police at me because you wasn't man enough to tell me that you was working with them. You could have told me yourself, Raheem. You should have told me yourself."

"Man, you don't understand," Raheem said, getting huffy. "Twenty years is a long time to be here in a cage around a whole bunch of niggas. Twenty years is a long time to be away from yo' family, loved ones, and kids. Twenty years is a long time to be here and never to touch a woman sexually. Mercy, baby, twenty years is a long time to be away from you. I can't stand having you out there by yourself." Tears began to roll down Raheem's face as he paused. "Twenty years is a long time."

Mercy had never seen Raheem cry before. The day he was sentenced he'd looked like he wanted to cry, but he'd just stuck his chest out and walked out of the courtroom with the deputy. Seeing him show his emotions to her for the first time made Mercy forget for a minute just how angry she was at him.

"Damn, baby." She rubbed his hand, and the tears rolled down her face. "I don't want us to be away from each other for that long either. I appreciate and miss a lot of the times we had, but when did we start working with the police?"

He took a deep breath and tried to make a joke. "Shit, we ain't working with the police. I basically told on niggas because niggas told on me, and as far as that Hyena nigga goes, they gon' pick that nigga up sooner or later and I ain't going to sit around and let them hear what he got to say about me. I'm going to beat that nigga to the punch."

"Damn, baby!" She sat staring off, wiping her tears away. "Damn," was all she could say.

"Don't worry, baby. Never will I do anything to jeopardize you or to put you in the line of fire," Raheem said. "You just gotta trust me."

"Just talking to them folks is putting me in the line of fire, Raheem," she said, trying to be selective about what she said because she didn't want to incriminate herself.

"All you gotta do is go cop from that nigga Hyena. The Feds will handle the rest. The less you know, the less you will expect; the less you'll look like you're in on it."

"I'm broke! Where am I going to get the money to cop anyway?"

"They gon' give it to you."

"They who?"

Raheem looked around and answered in a whisper. "You tell Hy that you know some people that want to buy some work from him. Act like you ain't nothing more than a middleman, someone who knows someone and who is just trying to help someone out. That's all."

"That's all, huh? Just play the role of the dumb little broad?"

Raheem paused as if he had intended to lie, but decided against it. "Naw, they gon' probably get you to do it a couple mo' times. Hyena had you deal with anybody else? We can get them, too. That's even better."

Mercy didn't comment. She couldn't believe her ears. Was the time really that much for Raheem to handle?

"Come here. Give me a kiss," Raheem instructed Mercy. "I love you, boo."

Mercy gave Raheem a kiss. As she looked in his eyes, she saw his desperation: the same look that a boxer gets in the last round of a fight. It was a look that said he couldn't go on and was willing to do almost anything to get out of the ring. Raheem had thrown in the towel. She couldn't believe how the system had torn him down and how weak he was to let those kinds of thoughts even set in his mind, let alone come out of his mouth. The Raheem she knew was a gangsta dude who had killed, robbed, and slung more drugs than a little bit. It was no doubt that he had done his crime, and twenty years wasn't nothing compared to all the things he had gotten away with for so many years. So why was it a problem for him to press that bunk and do his time? Mercy couldn't understand why Raheem had turned over and sold out to the Feds, but she knew one thing for certain: that she loved Raheem and deep down believed that if she had done the bit with him drama-free, when he came home, the two of them would have lived happily ever after. But on the same note, Mercy knew that there was no way she was going to sell her soul to the devil.

As the visit came to an end, Mercy gave Raheem a big hug and a long wet kiss as he walked her to the door.

"So do you got me, baby?" Raheem asked her. "You gon' hold me down and do what I need you to do to get me up out of here?"

As Mercy stood there, she could only think of one thing—the gambler's anthem that her daddy had told her was all she needed to survive: *You gotta know when to hold 'em, know when to fold 'em, know when to walk away, know when to run.*

Mercy looked up at Raheem, smiled, and kissed him good-bye. He smiled back. He took her gesture as a yes, but Mercy knew that she had to walk away from Raheem. She had to walk away forever. Raheem was playing a serious game, and she couldn't get caught up in the web.

"Baby, I can't take no stand against nobody. I love you and the whole nine and probably always will, but real bitches do real things."

She exited the prison in tears because she didn't know what hand would be dealt to her at this point. She wished she had never gotten caught up in that life in the first place. All she wanted to do was to continue to focus on her writing, which would lead her to honest money, an honest living. She thought about her script and how her newfound friend just might be her ticket to Hollywood. So Mercy hopped in her car and headed home to check her e-mail. Unless ol' dude was full of shit, Mercy was on her way to perhaps claim what was to be her meal ticket, and damn, was she starving!

CHAPTER 16

And in This Corner

Today was going to be the first day of Mercy's new life. Today would be the first day of her new beginning. She was turning over a new leaf. It all started right here as she waited patiently for the pilot to turn off the BUCKLE SEAT BELT sign. Never in all of her twenty-two years had she ever felt more confident, more secure, and more positive about her life.

I can't believe that I am taxiing the runway and butterflies are not fluttering around in my stomach. How crazy is that? This was the first time in three years that she had flown in a plane and didn't have some dope shoved up her pussy or some other kind of drugs stashed on her some kind of way. She wasn't even on her way to pick up any, either. *Wow, who'dda thought that the game would have totally changed for me?*

In less than fifteen minutes she would be greeted by Taymar "The Razor" Oliver. Although he was known to the entire world as The Razor, Mercy called him Tay. He said he liked the way she whispered his name through the phone receiver. He said her voice, her outlook on life, and the places she wanted to go in life were the sexiest things he'd ever heard. Mercy was starting to believe that she could truly fall for him. She had opened up to him and let him hear all of her ideas, goals, and aspirations. Reading and dreaming big had always been her therapy. This was her way of coping with all the abuse, all the agony and pain that she'd dealt with from foster home to foster home and then finally the group home. Her determination to make it in the world, each time she experienced some kind of abuse, had enabled her to run away from the different foster homes. She had no idea where the strength came from. Perhaps it came from her witnessing the desecration of her daddy at his funeral that gave her the spunk to do whatever she felt was best for her. She always reminded herself of the life that her daddy would have wanted for her: great success, lots of money, happiness, and a man who adored her. That's what she hoped she could find in Taymar.

Tay was also a heavyweight in every aspect of the word. As a matter of fact, that's how he'd gotten his nickname "The Razor." He was known for being razor sharp—not only in the boxing ring, but in the stock market as well. Five months ago he'd made boxing history. Not only did he knock the most undisputed boxer of our time the fuck out, but he did it in the first round of the fight. That alone would make him go down in the boxing history books as a legend, and Mercy felt that if she became his wifey boo and owned the key to his heart, it would be an opportunity in more ways than one.

From their long heartfelt conversations, Mercy felt she could finally be loved wholeheartedly the way that she knew her daddy always wanted her to be loved and the way she had always longed to be loved—genuinely loved for who she was inside and not for what she did for a dollar. The way those other men had her jeopardizing her life and freedom, there was no way possible they could love Mercy. But when it came to Taymar, Mercy felt that he would be different, that he saw her for who she was and what she desired to be.

Mercy couldn't help from looking towards the future with Tay. Becoming wifey to Tay was a way she could live her dream. It could be the key to her film career. Someone in his position definitely had to have the resources and connections to help her get her career off the ground. She had no interest whatsoever in being an actress on the big screen. She was a behind-the-scenes type of gal. After all, those kinds of people made the most money. They called the shots and had all the power. One way or another she intended to be one of those individuals, and with Tay by her side to love her first and foremost and then give her the necessary plugs, she couldn't go wrong.

As Mercy sat on the plane, her imagination ran wild as she thought of how crazy it was for her and Tay to be hooking up. Although they would have to have a long-distance relationship, him living in Chicago and her living in Richmond, Virginia, talking on the phone every single day would keep them on each other's mind.

Never having met him in person, Mercy hoped it was her mind and soul he was in love with. But that didn't mean that she couldn't wait for him to start loving her for other things as well. Mercy could hardly wait to get to his house. If everything went well, she was going to put it on him like Ja Rule talks about in that song with Lil' Mo.

"On behalf of the captain and the rest of the crew, we hope you enjoy your stay in the Chicago area. Thank you for traveling with United Airways," the flight attendant said over the intercom as the passengers jumped up to get their luggage from the overhead compartments.

Mercy grabbed her cute little Gucci carry-on and exited the plane. Her heart was racing as she entered the airport. Heading to the tram to ride it over to the baggage claim area, she reached in her bag and pulled out her cell phone to call Tay and let him know that her plane had landed, but she didn't have any service. As she rode the tram, she scanned it from left to right. Mercy always paid close attention to the people around her. It was a habit she got from running drugs. Living that kind of life, working that job, she never knew what or who was coming her way, so she had to be on point at all times. She noticed a lady in a business suit who looked as if she had a lot on her mind.

"Excuse me, do you have service on your cell phone?" the lady asked Mercy, noticing her phone in her hand. "Or is it just my crappy cell phone company?"

"My cell phone provider is just as crappy as yours," Mercy said as she looked at her cell phone. "Mine doesn't have any service either, but you know how these underground trams are."

"Yeah, with all this technology you would think that they would have the phones updated."

"I know," Mercy agreed. She could feel the tram slowing up to come to a complete stop. As she was walking off, she made eye contact with the lady and smiled.

"Have a good one," the lady said as Mercy headed to her designated carousel.

As her eyes swept the airport, Mercy was sure she would notice Tay from all of the flowers and balloons that he would probably have for her. He had already sent her "just because" flowers, a card, and some balloons, so she assumed he would have something for her in person. She had described the outfit she'd be wearing so that he would recognize her. She looked around at the gate but didn't see him anywhere.

Hmmm, this is strange. He must be running late, she thought. She looked down at her phone and saw that it now had service, so she dialed Tay's number. The phone rang three times and then went into his voice mail. She listened to his recorded message: "You have reached the voice mailbox of Taymar 'The Razor' Oliver. If you're calling to ask for money, to establish paternity, or some other drama, then hang up. But if your call is legit or it's my boo, then leave me a message at the beep."

"Hey, baby, it's me," Mercy said, speaking softly and sexily so that he wouldn't think she was pissed at him for not being there to pick her up on time or anything. She didn't want their little rendezvous to get off to a bad start. "I'm here. Where are you? I'm down here at baggage claim getting my luggage. It's baggage claim thirty-four, so you can meet me there. Can't wait to see you."

Knowing her phone would be ringing any minute now, she kept it in her hand as she took her luggage off the carousel. That's when she heard her phone's low-battery alert sounding.

"Oh, shit," she said to herself. When she was at the airport in Richmond waiting to board her flight to Chicago, she'd talked on the phone for a whole hour kicking the bo-bo with Tay, so now her phone was almost dead. The next thing she did was look around for a pay phone. She spotted one right by the restrooms. She didn't want to try to call him again with her phone's last bit of power, so she decided to use the pay phone to call Tay again just in case he tried to call her.

She dialed Tay's number again using a calling card that would bill the call to her home phone. This time he picked up on the first ring.

"Yo," Tay said in a dry tone. She thought he would sound more excited than that. After all, he was the one who insisted on the two of them getting together. There was definitely a connection. When she lay in bed at night with the phone to her ear, it felt like he was lying right there next to her. He had told her that he felt the same way. She assumed he would also be excited as hell to actually be next to each other in the flesh.

"Hey, baby, where you at?" she purred in a sexy manner.

"At the airport in traffic," he said, sounding very frustrated. She decided that she wasn't going to look into it, because she could only imagine how he felt about being caught up in traffic.

"You running late?" she asked.

"Naw, I'm good. Just got caught up in traffic," he stated.

"Well, I'm here," she said enthusiastically.

"I know," he replied, once again dryly.

"I'm still at baggage claim, so I'll just grab my bags and meet you outside."

"Oh, baby, it ain't no need for that," he was quick to say.

"You want me to wait inside?"

"Naw, you gotta decide what you want to do," he said, stressing the word *you*.

Mercy was caught off guard. "What you mean, baby?"

"I can either circle back around and pick you up and we can go and 'fuck out' the whole weekend, or you can change your ticket because it's fully refundable."

"Change my ticket?" she said puzzled.

"You can change your ticket, go back to where you came from, get a membership at somebody's gym, and run about thirty or forty pounds off. You can holla at me then. It's up to you."

Oooouuuch! That hand came out of nowhere and smacked Mercy right across the face. She could feel the tears in her eyes.

"Now, what's it going to be?" he snapped.

Mercy was speechless. She didn't know what to say or what to think at this point. This wasn't the Tay she had been communicating with, falling in huge infatuation with.

"I don't understand. Where's all this coming from?" she somehow managed to get out between silent tears.

"Mercy, look, I'm gonna be real with you like we have been with each other. I was already there, in the airport, and I saw you." He paused for a moment and then continued on. "You have everything I want in a wife except . . . except you are just a little thicker than the women I usually date. And as you know, image is everything to a nigga like me. We talkin' about the champ. I work out every day, and I can't have a plus-size, out-of-shape chick on my arm. I just can't. It's simply not a good look. Do you know what my publicist would say?"

Mercy immediately slammed down the pay phone. She felt that at this point there was no reason at all to even argue with the lame. He must have gotten his people mixed up, because a thick chick she was. But she knew she was cute and had enough male interest to confirm that for her. She knew she needed to lose a few pounds and had even considered liposuction. But first, she had to worry about film school. She'd had a total of forty-five hundred dollars that Hyena had sent her for a partial advance for a run—that really wasn't shit considering she had bills and she had to eat—until Tay had convinced her to come out and spend time with him before he went into training. She had used some of the money to get a couple of new outfits and some sexy lingerie. She hated to pinch her money, but she couldn't go nowhere broke, and by no means was she a freeloader either. Not to say that she wasn't hoping that Tay would treat her like a princess, wine her, dine her, and take her shopping. But since Tay had paid for the first-class round-trip ticket, she wanted to be able to at least treat him to a dinner or two to show him that it wasn't just about his money, that it was about him as a person.

"Ma'am, are you okay?" a woman asked Mercy, who had tears rolling down her face. Mercy looked up. It was that same lady who had asked her about the cell phone on the tram. She handed Mercy a tissue and put her arms around her. Once she did that, once Mercy felt the comfort of a caring individual, she let it all out and couldn't help but cry like a baby. Once again she'd had her heart broken, and this time by someone she hadn't even met in person. People were looking at her like she was crazy, but she didn't give a shit. She felt like cussing all of them out.

The lady placed Mercy's head on her shoulder. "Baby, it's going to be all right," she said as she helped her to the bathroom.

"What you looking at?" Mercy sobbed at a man who was staring at her. "You ain't never seen anybody cry before?"

Once they were in the bathroom, an airport employee who was in there cleaning the stalls asked, "Is everything okay?"

"Yes," the lady answered for Mercy, giving the employee a sharp look.

"Okay," the worker said as she continued cleaning the stalls.

Mercy couldn't believe how protective and comforting this stranger was, like she wished her mother had been to her. When Mercy was a child and needed comforting, instead of taking her in her arms to embrace her like a mother should, Mercy's mother was too busy running behind other niggas who were trying to conquer Nate's girl. Running behind them nothingness niggas, leaving her children in the house alone, led to those kids eventually getting snatched up by Social Services.

Mercy finally managed to get herself together. "Thank you so much," she said to the lady.

"No problem," she replied warmly.

"One favor deserves another. Let me buy you lunch?" Mercy asked.

She looked down at her watch and replied, "Okay. I'd like that." She smiled.

"What's your name?" Mercy asked her.

"Kathy, and yours?" she asked.

"Mercy."

"What a different, but lovely, name. How did you get it?"

"During labor my mother kept yelling 'Lord, have mercy' every time she got a labor pain. She said I gave her the most pain during delivery out of all her children. She screamed 'Lord have mercy' and 'mercy' so many times that they ended up naming me that."

They both laughed as Mercy looked her over for the first time.

I wonder what her story is, Mercy thought as she watched her chuckle.

The woman was an average-looking dark-skinned lady with salt-and-pepper hair, medium build, and about five feet, seven inches tall. She had on wire-framed glasses and braces on her teeth. She was dressed in a conservative but expensive business outfit.

"Kathy, where are you going? What's your destination, and what time does your flight leave?" Mercy inquired.

"Let's not talk about it. My flight doesn't leave for about three hours. They oversold my flight and rebooked me." She shook her head, saying, "But such is life. And yours?"

"Maybe that's what I need to do. I need to go and rebook my flight," Mercy suddenly thought and said out loud.

"Sure, we can do that first," Kathy said, "and then try to grab a bite to eat, depending upon when your flight leaves."

The next flight back to Richmond didn't leave for a while, so Kathy and Mercy had enough time to get something to eat. They got to know each other a bit over lunch. During lunch Mercy asked the waitress at the restaurant to plug in her phone so that it could charge while they sat and ate.

"What do you do for a living, if you don't mind my asking?" Mercy asked.

"I'm the vice president of a cosmetics company," Kathy answered.

"Oh," Mercy said, impressed. "How did you get such an important job?"

"I worked hard and didn't let a man ever stand in my way," Kathy told her. "I grew up in the projects, and we didn't have a pot to piss in. But I swore I would never let the past keep me down." She paused. "Now, I can tell some man is breaking your heart, but you have to look out for yourself. Men will come and go. Don't be fooling yourself into thinking that one of them is going to take care of you. You better take care of yourself and don't let anything or anyone stand in the way of your dreams."

"I won't."

"Make sure you call me once you get your film off the ground. I would love for my company to do some item placements in your film, and an endorsement deal could also be possible."

"I'm going to hold you to it," Mercy said.

"I just hope that this gives you the incentive to reach higher for your dreams."

After they finished their food, they exchanged numbers and promised to stay in touch. Finally, Mercy was on her way home, but as soon as she gave the flight attendant her ticket, her cell phone started to ring. She looked down and saw that it was a private number.

"Hello," Mercy answered as the flight attendant returned her boarding pass.

"Yo, what's up?" Tay's sexy voice said.

"What?" she immediately said with an attitude. *Damn this nigga got nerve.*

"What's the deal?" Tay said as if they were the best of friends.

"What?"

"I'm going to come and get you and give you some of this good dick."

"Nigga, keep that shit," Mercy said, removing the phone from her ear and looking at the phone like it was a foreign object.

"Naw, for real. I want to see you. I was mad for a minute, but I'm good. I'ma work with you. I'ma help you get a trainer, and when you do lose that weight, I'll showboat you then," he said. "Knowing I'm going to showboat you should be your inspiration."

Mercy sucked her teeth and chuckled just a little bit, although she was crying on the inside as he continued on. Kathy's words were still fresh in her ears. "You know you need me in your life. I can do a hell of a lot for your image, and I can make you into the person you want to be. Now, am I coming to get you or what?"

"Are you fucking crazy?" Mercy asked as she hesitated walking through the little tunnel leading to the aircraft.

"Naw, I'm trying to see you, so where you going to meet me at?"

A part of Mercy wanted to tell him to come and get her, but the words were stuck down in her throat. *You better take care of yourself.* She took a deep breath and sighed. "See you on the red carpet, motherfucker!" *Click.*

Mercy closed her cell phone and made her way onto the airplane. Once she sat down, Mercy tucked her boarding pass into her wallet, buckled up in her window seat, closed her eyes, and waited for takeoff.

In spite of everything, today was still the first day of her new life. The day she began to focus on herself and what she had to do for herself, not what anybody else needed her to do for them. If she did decide to make moves, it wasn't gonna be because that's what a motherfucker needed her to do. From here on out, what she did would have to coincide with what she was trying to do to better herself. Whether it be money or opportunity, it was going to have to benefit her. No more free favors. From this moment on, she vowed to always keep in mind that life wasn't about being the flyest chick in the neighborhood or getting the flyest car. It was about a bigger picture: her future. The things she wanted out of life—getting a career, a home, her credit and her shit right. And she knew that in order to get to the plateau where she needed to be, she had to start stacking her chips. It was as simple as that. And on everything she loved and on her daddy's grave, she was going to do the damn thing!

CHAPTER 17

Fun-chu Fooie's . . . Every Hood Has One

Cleezy was a changed man, and everybody could see it. In the streets it was often said that respect couldn't be bought. However, Cleezy not only toted a big pistol, the word was out that he wasn't scared to use it, which caused folks to fear him, and fear produced what seemed like respect. Only a matter of months ago, it was money that had gotten his dick hard, but nowadays, being feared got him off. Whenever someone violated any of the rules of the game that his brother had given him, they had to be dealt with.

Cleezy sat in his car, listening as the phone rang while he was trying to reach out and touch Paula.

"Look, this isn't right," he heard Paula say before she even said hello to him. "Hold on, baby," she spoke into the receiver before she went back to the matter she was handling. "I ordered a plain chicken breast, with nothing on it. I need you to fix this. . . . I'm sorry, boo," she said, now turning her attention to Cleezy. "I'm trying to get this food right."

"Where you at?" he asked.

"I'm over here at Fun-chu Fooie's. Where you at?"

"I'm 'bout to go handle this BI so I can make sure everything is in order before we leave out to go away in the morning."

"Yeah, make sure you handle everything," she instructed him, sounding excited about the next couple of days they would spend together, "because I can't wait to have you to myself." She paused, and he heard her tell someone, "I don't want this. You went in the back and just wiped off the mayo and lettuce. I said plain. Please cook me a fresh one." She then came back to her conversation with Cleezy. "Boo, I went to Priscilla's and got us some toys, and we are going to have some fun in that hotel room. Shit, we may not even leave it."

"Oh yeah?" Cleezy said, liking what he was hearing. "What we gon' do?"

Before she answered, Cleezy heard an Asian man's voice say, "$4.39 please."

"What's the $4.39 for?" Paula asked the man.

"You total," the Chinese man said in broken English.

"I already paid. I'm just waiting for a fresh one," Paula responded in a calm voice.

"You order new, have to pay for new," he said.

"No, my sandwich was made wrong, and not to mention that I had called it in to start with and had to wait when I got here. When I did get it, the sandwich was wrong. She goes in the back and wipes the dressing off and pulls the lettuce off and then tries to give it to me. I want a fresh sandwich, plain."

"No, you pay, you get new," the man insisted.

"I want what I paid for already," Paula said. "Boo, let me call you right back." She hung up, but a second later Cleezy's phone rang. He figured she had accidentally hit the redial. He got an earful of her conversation with the man. "Look, just give me my money back and I'll go somewhere else, because I've wasted thirty minutes in here and haven't even gotten my food."

"No, no money back. Take this and go," he said.

"I don't want that sandwich! I want my money back, and I'm

not going anywhere until I get my money back," Paula said, now damn near yelling.

"Get out of my store. Get out now, bitch. Get out now!"

"Motherfucker, have you lost your mind? Not until I get my fucking fo' dollars and thirty-nine cents back. Give me my shit and I'll leave."

"I call police," he shouted.

"Go ahead and call them. But before you do, you better make sure them illegal aliens is the fuck up out of here. Now give me my fucking money before I report yo' ass to immigration. You better have papers on all thirty of them motherfuckers living back there and upstairs and shit. Now, give me my damn money back before you get yo'self in trouble while trying to call them on me."

Cleezy could imagine Fun-chu Fooie pulling out that money so fast that it looked like a scene out of *The Matrix*. Then he heard the Chinese guy yell, "Bitch."

"You can throw the money all you want, but remember what the fuck I said," Paula said.

Cleezy was on the other end of the phone laughing his ass off. *I got me a real gangsta chick on my hands,* he thought.

"Get out, you ape," Cleezy heard the Chinese man scream at Paula. He laughed his butt off an hour later when he drove by and saw how the kinfolks of Fun-chu Fooie were vacating the premises with their belongings.

When Paula got home, she realized that in the midst of all the drama she had forgotten to call Cleezy back. She pulled out her cell phone and called up Cleezy.

"Hello," Cleezy answered.

"You ate?" Paula asked.

"Naw, not yet," Cleezy responded.

"Well what you want?"

"Whatever you feel like cooking. I'm on my way. I just gotta make one stop and handle one more thing. Then I'll be home in about thirty minutes," Cleezy said. "Yo, what time is it?"

"Time for you to come home and fuck the shit out of me," she informed him, and then answered the question. "It's about 9:25."

"I got to hurry up because the person I gotta meet is leaving at about nine-thirty, so I'll hit you back when I get back in the car."

"All right then, baby. Peace," Paula said, hanging up the phone.

Cleezy hopped out of his car and ran through the alley. He circled the block two times with his black Russell hooded sweatshirt on his head and pants to match. Anybody passing by could have easily mistaken him for a jogger. The second time he circled the block, he noticed that Fun-chu Fooie was about to come out of his restaurant. Cleezy crossed the street, and as soon as Fun-chu Fooie was about to pull the metal gate down over the front of the restaurant, Cleezy was at his back with a gun. "Get back in, you chee chee chong motherfucker," Cleezy said.

Automatically, the man began begging. "Please, just take all the money. Don't kill me," the Chinese man said as he went over to the cash register and hit the button to get the money out. "Here, take it all." He jerked the money frantically out of the register. "Just take it all." But Cleezy didn't move.

"I don't want your money," he told the man in an ice-cold tone.

"What you want?" the man asked, confused.

"I want your life, motherfucker."

Cleezy saw the look of terror on Fun-chu Fooie's face. Cleezy never looked down. He just smiled when he read the look. Fun-chu Fooie had shit in his pants. "You 'bout to die for a four dollars and thirty-nine cents sandwich. Fo' fucking dollars and thirty-nine cents. Fo' fucking dollars," Cleezy said, repeating himself.

Tears ran down the man's face.

"Remember the black ape bitch that came in here today?" Cleezy asked. Fun-chu dropped his head. "Look at me when I speak to you, you piece of shit." Cleezy jerked the man's head up by his chin. "Well, she belongs to me, and nobody disrespects what's mine. Nobody. See, you motherfuckers don't have shit when you get here, get a come-up over here in our world that we done fucking been raped of, beat, and slaved for." Fun-chu dropped his head again. "Didn't I tell you to look at me?" At that point Fun-chu looked up. "You motherfuckers get these lil' corner stores and you come here, step on our toes in our neighborhood, treat us like we shit and we the ones who put food in yo' mouth so you can eat and pay yo' bills to keep this shit here running." As if it was habit-forming, the man put his head down once again. "Didn't I tell you to look at me?"

Fun-chu started saying some prayer in his native language.

"Look, ain't no need in calling on Buddha. He can't help you, because the reaper spares no lives."

Fun-chu jumped at what he thought was the reaper in front of him with the black hood on his head, and when he did, Cleezy dumped three to his head and two to his heart. Cleezy pulled the gate down behind him and walked off like the avenger in an old Charles Bronson movie.

The next morning Cleezy did not show an ounce of emotion as he sat and ate his bowl of Wheaties and watched the reporter on the news announce Fun-chu Fooie's death. However, he did smile when the reporter said, "There are no leads in the case."

He lifted up his bowl to his mouth to slurp up the milk as the reporter said, "Crimestoppers would like your help." Cleezy put the cereal bowl down, stood up, and did a karate move. Then he went on about his day, knowing he was untouchable.

CHAPTER 18

A Pit Bull in a Skirt

After the ordeal with Taymar, Mercy knew that the fairy-tale life just wasn't for her. *Only bitches like Snow White and Cinderella are cut out for that shit.* So now it was back on the grind to make shit happen for herself. But being back home only reminded her that she had to take care of some things so that she could sleep at night.

Mercy took her bags up to her bedroom, sat down on her bed, and picked up the phone to check her messages. There were a few from Hyena sounding desperate. Leaving voice messages was something that Hyena just ordinarily didn't do. Mercy knew that Hyena needed her because she had been slacking since she started working on her script, and then she had run off in hopes of trying to establish a relationship with Taymar, which turned out not to be one of those whirlwind romances.

On her plane ride back home, Mercy had sworn that she would turn over a new leaf, and although she was broke she would close that door of being a player in the drug trade behind her. So she called Hyena and let him know that she was on her way to see him. He sounded so relieved to hear her voice, as if his main worker bee had just returned to the hive. Once she arrived at

Newark Airport, she was greeted as usual by luxury ground transportation and taken over to the XYZ hotel, where she was checked in by the same hotel clerk as usual.

"It's been a long time since we have seen you here, Miss Jiles," the handsome young clerk said to Mercy.

"I know, been swamped, handling a lot of business," Mercy replied.

"Business must be good. I see you still looking good." He complimented her just as he always did. "I like that new hairdo."

"Thank you," she said with a smile.

"How long will you be staying with us?" the clerk asked.

"Just one night."

"Just one night this visit?"

"Yup."

"How many keys?"

"Just one."

He issued Mercy one key as requested. "It's room 201, Miss Jiles. Take the elevators to the second floor, go right off the elevators, and your room is all the way at the end of the hall. The very last room."

"Oh, okay, thank you," Mercy said, taking the key and heading towards the elevators and up to her room.

Mercy put her overnight Gucci bag in the room, headed back downstairs, and was off to see Hyena. Her driver took her to a car wash where Hyena sat inside, acting as if he was waiting for his car to be finished.

When Mercy walked in, Hyena was reclining in a leather chair with a pit bull sitting next to him. He had a cigar in his mouth and wore dark shades, covering his eye patch. When Hyena looked up and saw Mercy, she could tell by the look on his face that he had missed her. He stood and hugged her tightly.

"Gal, I missed you," Hyena said as he continued hugging her

for longer than normal. "Don't stay away like that ever again. Just leaving out of town and not calling a cat," he said before he let her go. "What you Americans say? Never miss a good thing till it's gone." He made a joke.

Mercy was distracted by what seemed like a marble in a clear bowl of water on the table. Mercy didn't know if it was supposed to be some form of art or what, so she just came right out and asked.

"What's that?" Mercy said, pointing to the marble. "A piece of art you picked up somewhere?"

Hyena laughed and said with pride, "It's my eye."

"What?" Mercy asked. Her stomach began to turn.

"Yeah, it's my eye." He took his shades off and put them in his jacket pocket. He then walked over and picked up the bowl. He took his index finger and his thumb, lifted the eyeball out of the bowl, and popped that sucker into his socket like it was a contact lens. Mercy was stunned.

"Well, put a fork in me, because I am outdone with the stun gun!"

"See, we family. I wouldn't feel comfortable doing that in front of just anybody, you know. You my family, Mercy." Hyena walked back over to the chair and sat down while Mercy tried to keep down the peanuts she had eaten on the plane.

"My eye got shot out," Hyena started to explain. "I know you been wanting to ask me. I ain't ashamed of my one good eye. I'm blessed to have that. That's all a man need to be able to look in another man's eye and decipher whether he's friend or foe. You know what I mean?"

At that moment Mercy felt as though her heart had stopped beating, but she knew it hadn't because she heard it thumping loud and clear. It sounded like the police knocking on a door. In no way did Mercy ever want Hyena to think that she was foe, so she figured she'd get right to the reason she was really there.

"Hyena, I need to talk to you." Mercy walked over to Hyena. *God, I wish he'd put those damn sunglasses back on,* Mercy thought as she tried not to cringe at the sight of his glass eye.

"You know I look at you like you are my big brother, right?" Mercy said, closing her eyes, wishing that Hyena would close his.

Hyena nodded. "Of course I know," he said.

"And you know I would do anything for you. I would climb the Golden Gate Bridge for you if your life depended on it. I would walk across the Sahara Desert in a mink coat if you needed me to. That's how much I care for you and appreciate how you brought me up on the come-up. I may be out of touch with you for a minute, but never ever would I or have I ever betrayed your trust in me."

"I know, my Mercy. If I ever thought that for one minute, you wouldn't be sitting here talking to me right now." Hyena pulled his jacket back so his pistol could be seen. When he did that, Mercy didn't blink or bitch up. She had seen bigger guns than that.

"Well, I've got to keep it real with you, because from day one you've always kept it real with me. When I told you what Raheem was paying me, you said that that wasn't even minimum wage, when you could have easily been selfish and continued paying me those pennies that he was."

"Right, right," Hyena said, closing his eyes, rocking his head back and forth, agreeing with her.

Finally, Mercy thought, *a few seconds of not having to stare into that lifeless glass eye.*

"Well, I know you might find it hard to believe, but one of your so-called soldiers just deserted the army," Mercy said, sighing. All of a sudden she felt as though she were in a catch-22. She didn't want to play snitch for Raheem, but now she was snitching on him, so to speak.

"Who?" Hyena asked, looking like a kid who had just found out that the Grinch had stolen Christmas.

She took a deep breath and replied, "Raheem."

Hyena was speechless. Had they been acting in a movie, that's when the opera music would have begun, because the twisted expression on Hyena's face was not a Kodak moment, that's for sure. He shook his head and only uttered one word, "Damn."

Mercy kept talking, although she knew that Hyena was stunned by the information she had just given him. "I know you love the work I do for you, and nobody can, has, or will do what I do better; but, baby, this is going to have to be our last time meeting." He looked up with an expression on his face as if asking her why, so she continued. "They are probably watching me."

"They who?"

"The Feds. They want me to help." Although Hyena didn't budge, he listened attentively as Mercy went on. "But you know that ain't happening, because I'm a pit bull in a skirt."

Hyena let out a small chuckle when his pit bull barked after Mercy's comment.

"You know why I keep me a pit bull around?" Hyena asked, stroking his rednose pit bull.

She shook her head no as he proceeded to tell her. "Because once they bite, then they get in the do-or-die mentality, and they can stand the highest threshold of pain. So they won't turn on me under any circumstance. That's how they are trained."

"I know," Mercy said as she decided to give Hyena her own insight on the treacherous breed. "See, originally, it wasn't Ray-Ray and them training no pit bulls in their backyard or alleys. That's some shit they just started recently. I read somewhere that pit bulls were used over in some foreign country, where they were overpopulated with rats. They specifically used pit bulls to kill them. That's how they were bred, to seek out rats and kill them."

"So I see you've done your homework," Hyena said as he patted his dog's head. "You know I hate rats."

"Don't we all?"

They both sat there for a moment in complete silence and let the dialogue they had just exchanged marinate. Then Hyena stood up and said, "Wait here. I'll be back in a few minutes." He disappeared and returned with a Jimmy Jams plastic bag and passed it to Mercy. "Here, take this."

She accepted it and asked, "What's this?"

"It's like twenty grand, so you can eat while you play the low until this shit blows over."

"Thank you, Hyena," she said as she hugged him.

Damn, twenty fucking grand, Mercy thought. *That's all I get for risking my life, my freedom, putting up with the bullshit. Twenty grand is all the retirement money I can get. Twenty measly g's is all he feels his freedom is worth.*

Mercy felt like someone at a steel plant who had put in years of dedicated work at the plant only to arrive at work one day to find that the plant was closing down and all he would get out of the deal was some insulting pittance of severance pay. However, when she looked at the big picture, she realized that she could have walked away with nothing, *nada,* zip, zero, diddly-squat, and not a got-damn thing. So she gladly accepted the twenty g's, hugged Hyena, and thanked him. She gave him Ms. Pat's number in case he ever needed to get in touch with her. "You should get your number changed. Maybe get rid of your phone, period. Oh yeah, and don't leave any more messages."

"I think that's a good idea." Hyena smiled as he embraced her tightly.

Hyena got his driver to drop Mercy off back at the hotel. Mercy stuck the twenty grand into a secret compartment in her suitcase. Although it was still early in the evening, around eight o'clock, she was tired from all the action of the day. Mercy went into her room and jumped directly in the shower. She thought about the events in her life, thought about her hopes for her script, and was enjoying a nice erotic massage with the water. Over the water and the shower radio, she couldn't hear anything else until suddenly the bathroom door was kicked open. She was so frightened she couldn't even scream.

Just then a guy wearing a black hoodie and a George Bush Halloween mask yelled, "Bitch, you know what's up?" He grabbed her arm and pulled her out of the shower butt-ass naked. The coldness of his voice put fear in her heart, especially when he threw her down on the floor and got on top of her. He put his hand around her throat and slowly tightened his grip. "Bitch, where is the fucking yeo at?" He was so close to her she could smell the Hennessy on his breath.

"Give it up, the fucking shit. I need all of it," he said in a tone that meant business.

Mercy stared at him in shock and fear, but she didn't say a word.

He smacked the cowboy shit out of her and then punched her in the face. "Bitch, don't fucking play with me. Tell me where the shit is at before I kill you."

"It ain't none." Mercy gagged. "Nothing is here."

"Bitch, don't you know I will kill you?" he asked as his spit hit her in the face.

Just then his partner, who was wearing a Richard Nixon Halloween mask, entered the bathroom and said, "Ain't shit out there." He then focused in on his partner and Mercy. "Be easy, man," he said. "She ain't gon' be able to tell us shit if you choke her to death." He then addressed his words to Mercy. "Hey, hey, look, baby. Listen, get up and put this on." He handed her the hotel's plush robe that was hanging on the back of the door. His voice was familiar to Mercy, but she couldn't place it. She put the robe on and tied the sash in a knot. The two men then escorted her into the hotel room and sat her down at the head of the bed.

The guy with the Richard Nixon Halloween mask looked at Mercy and said, "Listen, I don't want to kill you. You're too beautiful to die, so just tell us where the shit is."

For a split second she thought that Hyena had sent some guys to kill her and make it look like a robbery or a drug deal gone bad. However, that last statement was a dead giveaway. Mercy clearly recognized his voice: the guy behind the Richard Nixon mask was the clerk at the hotel.

"Look, baby, I promise you I don't want to hurt you, so just give up the pack and we'll leave quietly," the clerk said.

"It ain't no pack. I swear on everything I love, it ain't no pack. I ain't got nothing," Mercy screamed through tears.

The guy in the George Bush mask walked up. "You lying bitch," he yelled, and smacked Mercy's eye with the butt of his gun, knocking her off the bed so that she fell backwards and hit her head on the night table. He hit her again and again with the gun. From that point on everything else became a huge blur as she went into shock. Barely conscious, Mercy could hear everything that was going on, but she was paralyzed and couldn't move. She wanted to try to fight, but there was no fight in her as the guy in the George Bush mask mercilessly laid a hellacious pistol-whippin' on her. She just lay there and took it.

"I'll stop anytime you want me to. Just let me know where the money is," he said.

"That bitch ain't lying; it ain't nothing here," his partner said, dumping the contents of the suitcase on the floor.

The one in the George Bush mask paused a minute from Mercy's beat-down and redirected his attention to his partner. "What da fuck you mean, nigga, 'it ain't shit'? You been watching this, beyatch," he said, kicking Mercy in the face. "You been watching this bitch for all this time, knowing she been moving all this fucking weight, and now when the shit goes down you say the shit ain't here. I thought you checked the room before she left," he said, shaking his head.

"I knew she was checking out tomorrow and knew she would be bringing the shit back with her," he said.

They were a day late and a few dollars short.

"Let's get the fuck out of here," the guy in the George Bush mask said angrily.

His partner looked down on the floor at Mercy's almost lifeless body bleeding. "Hold tight," he said, unbuckling his belt buckle. "I'm about to hit this right quick. Nigga gotta get something out of this shit."

"Nigga, if you pull your dick out, you and this bitch gon' die. I'm going to slump you for being stupid and that bitch for seeing it."

"Go ahead. We boys. You know we better than that. I know you ain't going to front on me 'bout no pussy."

The guy in the Bush mask stared at his partner straight in the eyes through the mask and said with a cold dry voice, "Try me."

Nixon changed his whole demeanor and replied, "Man, let's roll the fuck out," leaving Mercy holding on for dear life as she fell into unconsciousness.

CHAPTER 19

The Knocking at the Door

"**B**ooooommm! Boooommm!" It only took two hits before the hinges fell off of the door, and the police officers wearing all black with the bulletproof vests on top of their uniforms stormed into Cleezy's apartment like they owned the place.

"Get on the ground!" a few of the police yelled out as they approached Cleezy with their guns pulled.

"Conrad Fargo, we have a warrant for your arrest," another officer said.

Cleezy didn't utter a word or show one ounce of fear even though this was his first time being arrested. The police put him facedown on the floor of his two-bedroom apartment. The lead detective walked in with a huge rhino's butt, throwing it around, and headed straight to the bedroom where the police had Cleezy. He got all in Cleezy's face. He was so close to him that although he was in Cleezy's ear, Cleezy could smell the tobacco on his breath. "You have the right to remain silent, and anything you say can and will be held against you."

It didn't take long for Cleezy to realize that the lead detective was none other than Columbo, the same detective that had been on his brother's butt like a wedgie for years. Now the family curse had been passed on to Cleezy. Columbo was the legal nightmare from hell. He had stalked Lynx for many years, and now he was determined to get Cleezy since he was Lynx's brother. Columbo's total existence revolved around trapping the two brothers, and he wanted them in the worst way.

It was like the detective had been holding a secret for years and was just now able to tell it as he began reading Cleezy his rights. After doing so, he took Cleezy into his living room and sat him down on the cream faux-leather sofa while the other officers searched the apartment.

"So, this is how your kind lives, huh?" Columbo said as he walked around Cleezy's living room inspecting everything, the fifty-inch big-screen television and then the thirty-one-inch television that sat on a black stand right beside it with his video games hooked up to it. "I'm not impressed."

Cleezy ignored Columbo's comment, which annoyed the detective a great deal. Columbo had been hoping that he could get a rise out of him and possibly get an obstruction charge or resisting arrest out of Cleezy to add to the charges that they already had pending. He was even more bothered that with a major charge like this, murder in the first degree, he couldn't get any sort of a reaction out of Cleezy. Even in handcuffs Cleezy had gotten comfortable on the sofa. Columbo stared at him, searching his face, and could not find an ounce of fear in his eyes, even though he had to know he might go to jail for the rest of his life.

"They say you was theeeee man," Columbo said with his back to Cleezy. He then took a brief tour of Cleezy's very plain, undecorated apartment. His bedroom was furnished with an average mahogany bedroom set. However, his exquisite, expensive bedding would reveal to a blind man that Cleezy was no slouch. He had no television in his bedroom, but a stereo system with surround-sound speakers. His closet was running over with clothes and sneakers. The second bedroom had clothes everywhere, including on the Soloflex workout system. His kitchen set was nothing out of the ordinary.

"The man, huh?" Columbo sighed. "But the informants must not be reliable, judging by the way you live. Where is the plush furniture? Where's the safe? Oh, I get it. All you want is to sell dope so you can get the new Air Jordans, because that's the only thing you got in here worthwhile. You dumb motherfuckers kill me—all you want out of the hustle game is a pair of sneakers or a big-screen TV."

Cleezy didn't let that crap the detective was talking get to him. He knew the real deal as to what his paper was looking like. He was certain that he was irking Columbo by not paying him any attention, so to annoy him even more, he only started singing over Columbo's riff-raff chitter-chat a Biggie Smalls song, word for word. Before he could get to the chorus, one of the police had called Columbo into the back room.

"Columbo," the officer called. "I think you should see this. We may have won the lottery."

Cleezy never stopped singing his song; nor was he alarmed. He knew that they were just like a man who thought he had hit the lottery but had played his number for the wrong drawing. They were just that close; so they thought, anyway. Columbo came waltzing back in the living room and said, "So are you going to tell me how to open up that gun cabinet, or am I going to have to blow it off for my evidence?"

"Work to get your evidence, because I damn sure ain't going to help you," Cleezy spat.

Another officer came in with a drill in his hand, and Cleezy still didn't bust a sweat. He knew that a cabinet full of guns was the closest thing that any street hustler would get to the hand grenade. However, he was a U.S. citizen and could exercise his

constitutional right to bear firearms because he was not a con-
victed felon. Besides, Cleezy wasn't stupid enough to keep any
dirty guns in his possession. None of his shit had bodies on it.
Whenever he was done with a gun, he took it straight to James
and let James dispose of it at the bottom of the river.

"Package them up and get them over to the lab. I want the re-
sults back yesterday," Columbo said. "Let's get him downtown."
Then he added, "I'll ride in the front of the paddy wagon with
this piece of shit."

Cleezy paid him no never mind and continued quoting Biggie
Smalls word for word as they took him out of the apartment to face
his neighbors, who by now had gathered around to see what all the
commotion was about. The police took Cleezy to the Richmond
City lockup, where he was booked on the charge of first-degree
murder and was not given a bond.

After he sat out a couple of weeks at the city jail, Cleezy's attorney informed him that his murder trial for the bouncer was flimsy
and that they had an informant who had confirmed the events
surrounding the bouncer's death. Although the case was weak, he
had no bond and would have to sit until the trial was over. Await-
ing trial for any person is always hard. Not knowing one's own
fate, which is in the hands of twelve strangers, is enough to make
any man crazy. However, Cleezy just rolled with the punches and
made himself comfortable, since he was going to be there for
longer than a hot minute.

Cleezy tried not to ride the phones and attempted not to
get too accustomed to Paula's weekly visits. How could he not,
though? He received at least two pieces of mail from her every single day. She was always available to take his calls and never complained when the majority of the calls consisted of her making
three-way calls. The part that spoiled him the most was that every

single visiting day, if she wasn't the first one through the doors of the Richmond City Jail, then she was one of the first.

"What's wrong with you today, baby? You okay?" Paula asked softly through the bulletproof glass that separated the two of them.

"I'm a'ight," Cleezy said in an unconvincing tone.

"You know I'm going to be there on the front row on Tuesday when you go to court, right?"

"Ain't no need because they probably going to continue that shit. You know that motherfucker Columbo is going to come up with some kind of shit so I can sit in this cage as long as possible."

"I know that they are probably going to continue it, but I am still going to be there for you. You know this is until death do us part."

"You mean until the time do us part," he said, not believing she meant what she said.

"You know what, Cleezy?" She looked into his eyes, and tears began to form. "It doesn't matter if you get twenty or thirty years, I am going to be here for you. I love you, and I ain't going nowhere."

"You say that now, but once the days start turning into months, the months turn into years, the years turn into decades, you ain't gon' be singing the same tune." Cleezy chuckled at his next thought. "And I ain't gon' be there to fuck you, either. . . . Jake will slip into my side of the bed and then the visits will slow up. Then the next thing I know you only taking my calls when Jake is at work or on the block."

"You got me all wrong. I love you and I plan to be with you—bad, good, happy, or sad," Paula pleaded.

Cleezy dropped his head down and didn't say a word. As bad as he wanted to believe Paula, he just couldn't. He had been warned long ago, ever since he could walk, to be careful of women, and that warning had stuck with him. But except for the reputation that she had acquired years ago, Paula had never given him any reason not to trust her.

"Cleezy," she said, putting her hand on the glass. He didn't respond. "Cleezy," she called out to him again. The person in the booth beside her looked over at her, but Paula didn't care. Cleezy finally looked up at her. "Baby, what do I have to do to prove my love for you? Tell me. What? When you were home, I cooked, cleaned, and played wifey to you and never have you ever caught me doing anything other than that. Nothing changes because you are in here." She pointed to her heart. Cleezy turned up his lips. "What is it? Oh, I get it. I understand." Cleezy looked at her as if he was trying to figure out what it was that she understood. "I understand now; it's because of my past with other niggas that make it so you can't trust me."

"Hold on, shorty," he said, but she cut him off.

"I might have carried it like that with them other niggas, but never have I disrespected you or myself since we have been together," she said, breaking into tears, but Cleezy was completely unaffected. "What I got to do, Cleezy, to show you? To prove my love? What? Just fucking tell me. Or will I ever be able to?"

"Look, just calm down. Just pull yourself together," Cleezy said, starting to feel sorry for Paula, sitting there before him in tears. Even if her feelings were short-term, wasn't nobody else coming up there to visit him or sending him letters. Cleezy just thought it might be easier if he pushed her away now before she even got the chance to leave him hanging. But sitting there looking at her, maybe it wasn't the right thing to do. "Look, give my mother the phone and pull yo'self together."

Lolly had been sitting about fifty feet away on the bench gossiping with another visitor. Paula put the phone down, wiped her eyes, and walked over to Cleezy's mom. "Ms. Lolly, Cleezy want you," she said, wiping her eyes. Lolly got up and walked over to talk to Cleezy. Paula stayed there and sat down in her seat in order to give them some privacy. After about five minutes, Lolly called Paula back over and handed her the phone as she just stood there next to Paula.

"Look, I apologize for making you feel a certain way," Cleezy said. "You say you love me, right?" Paula nodded. "Well, I would feel better if you give up your apartment and move in with my momma."

"Okay," Paula said without hesitation or deliberation.

"You know you and my momma are my favorite girls. I took care of both of y'all, and I want y'all to help each other and take care of one another while I'm in here."

"Okay," she said again easily. "I'll give notice to my landlord. My lease isn't up for three months, but I'll stay at your mom's as soon as she'll have me."

Just like that Paula moved in with Lolly. She was home every night at a respectable time. Lolly kept close tabs on Paula, but Paula didn't mind. Anything to please her man . . . anything to prove her love. Hopefully it would be enough.

CHAPTER 20

Bermuda Triangle

A nurse assisted Mercy in adjusting the hospital bed. She'd been the first nurse to see Mercy when she had arrived at the hospital four days ago. She had taken a special interest in her, wanting to protect her from the police, the press, and the ambulance-chasing attorneys who had practically been camped outside of her room. This was the first day that Mercy had opened her eyes. Although she was completely out of it and on medication, she was well aware that Nurse Allen had been there for her and acted as a mother would even though she was only a nurse.

Mercy looked around the hospital room for a moment and then closed her eyes to rest them. The ringing of the phone startled her. As she started to stretch and answer it, she saw Nurse Allen putting down the flowers.

"I'll get it for you, sweetie," Nurse Allen said as she picked up the phone. "Hello." After telling the caller to hold on, she passed Mercy the phone. "It's your sister. She's been up here around the clock. She had said she was only going back to the hotel to shower and change clothes."

"All the way up here in Jersey?" Mercy asked Nurse Allen, assuming it was Zurri as she took the phone from her and then gave a groggy "hello" into the receiver.

"Hey, baby girl," the voice said.

"Who is this?" Mercy asked, not recognizing the voice.

"This Tallya," the caller said.

"Who?" Mercy asked. She heard what the caller said, but this had to be a prank.

"Your sister Natallya."

Mercy was shocked and couldn't believe her ears. Natallya was her oldest sister, who had been estranged for many years. Mercy had not seen her since her father's funeral. When he was alive, Tallya was bitter that Nate had married Mercy's mother, Pearl, and not her own; however, she wasn't disrespectful nor did she fall out of line. Once Nate died, Tallya's mother moved on with her life and refused to stay in touch with any of Nate's other women or children. Her famous line that she would tell Tallya was, "Mother made 'em, mother fuck 'em!"

"Oh my God! I have been up there around the clock. I saw what happened to you on the news when this first happened. I heard the name Mercy Jiles on the TV, and I was, like, wait a minute, that's my sister's name. Honey, I dropped everything and drove over to that hospital like a bat out of hell."

"Last I heard, you were living in DC with your mother," Mercy groggily said, still confused from the medication and even more so by this call.

"Nope. I live here in the Hamptons with my man. But like I said, I couldn't believe it. I had to come up there and see for myself if it was you."

Mercy smiled. "Thank you," she said, but it hurt her to speak.

"I was so worried about you, especially when they said you were bleeding internally. You were in critical condition, and we didn't know if you'd make it."

"Thanks, girl, by the grace of God, I'm okay."

Nurse Allen brought the card from the flowers over to Mercy. As she listened to Tallya, Mercy read the card: "Always know you are truly loved, Your Big Brother Forever, Death B4 Dishonor." She smiled at the gesture from Hyena.

"I'm up and on my way over there."

Tallya visited Mercy at the hospital faithfully every day. When Mercy first saw Tallya, she couldn't believe how pretty she was.

They both had that walnut-brown complexion. They were about the same height, but Tallya was a lot thinner than Mercy and a lot more polished. While Mercy was laid up in the hospital bed bruised and broken, she checked out Tallya. Tallya looked like money: Her skin was flawless, and her clothes were top of the line. Her whole package made Mercy proud of her sister, including the implants that she confessed she had gotten. Whatever she had become in her life, it was clear that she had somehow come into some money. Mercy was happy for her, because she'd heard that Tallya's mother was always lying about how Nate left money to Pearl and her kids but nothing for her. If Nate had left any money, Mercy sure didn't see a dime of it.

Mercy's suitcase from the hotel had been brought to the hospital. When she was able to move around, she checked her secret compartment, but it was empty. She figured the hotel clerk and his partner must have taken the money as their consolation prize. When the police asked Mercy what had happened, she clammed up. She told them she couldn't remember a thing. But the police had found the ID of one of the guys on the floor of her hotel room, so they'd get caught eventually. Either way, that money was gone.

Once the time came for her to be discharged, Tallya drove Mercy in her SLK Mercedes-Benz to the mansion that she shared with her sugar daddy, Benjamin Arlow. Benjamin Arlow was a dirty old man hitting his sixties or possibly his seventies, although he tried to maintain his youthfulness by staying fit and keeping a bald head to camouflage his gray hairs. A suave, debonair, jazzy man who loved women, young women especially, he was just a few notches down from being the black Hugh Hefner of the hip-hop world. He had never been married, but fathered one daughter—and a week after her birth he had a vasectomy so he would never get trapped again. He paid the mother of his child a healthy sum and kept up with child support until his daughter turned eighteen. She still came around, and when she needed something, he doled it out to her just as if she were one of "his girls."

He had wined and dined countless women in his day. Not only did he have a way with women, but he knew his way around a boardroom table, having his hands in a few urban companies making him a mega money bank.

Mercy had heard of Benjamin Arlow but didn't know much about him until Tallya showed her all of the articles he was mentioned or featured in. Mercy read up on him while she recuperated, and she stumbled upon this one tabloid talking about him and Tallya. *Is she another Anna Nicole Smith?* Mercy thought as she read the article. According to the gossip rag, Benjamin had really fallen for Tallya, because she was the first woman he ever took in to reside with him in his twelve-million-dollar house along with his butler, maid, cook, and chauffeur. Benjamin was nice to Mercy and treated her like royalty while she visited. He persuaded Mercy to work out with his trainer, utilize the pool and tennis courts. Just like any good houseguest, she did, but she didn't want Tallya to think that she was getting too comfortable.

She was well on her feet before she decided to go home. She and Tallya had been enjoying each other's company so well that she didn't mind hanging out. Although she and Tallya were cool, she didn't want to wear out her welcome. About a week before Mercy was planning to go back home, she and Tallya were out having lunch poolside.

"Girl, thank you so much for taking care of me," Mercy said as she ate a forkful of the albacore tuna salad that the cook had prepared.

"That's what family for," Tallya replied. "Especially big sisters. It gave me a chance to be the sister to you I never thought I would be."

"Well, you're surely making up for it now," Mercy said. "Thanks for never leaving my side and then having me into your home with your man. Not to mention buying me clothes and whatever else I needed. I truly appreciate it. I never had a sister to really hold me down. I mean, I see Zurri, but only when she needs a few dollars or for me to babysit. So I truly appreciate this." Mercy gave her a hug.

"Look," Tallya said, wiping her eyes, "you're going to make me get all teary-eyed." She then changed the subject. "When I was in the hospital and you were all drugged up, they gave me your stuff from the hotel and I saw your screenplay. I don't want you to think I was being nosy all in your stuff, but I read it."

"No, no problem, you're my sister."

"Girl, I read it and—"

Mercy cut her off and asked, "And . . . ?" like any artist would when they were about to hear someone address their work.

"It was sooo good!"

"For real?"

"Yup," Tallya said, nodding. Tallya's smile then faded away. Something was troubling her. "Once I brought you home from the hospital, I noticed Benjamin's been keeping late hours, which probably means he's fucking some bitch behind my back and think I don't know. Like I was so busy caught up into you that I wouldn't pay it any mind."

"You think so?" Mercy said, genuinely concerned.

"It's all good, because it ain't nothing I ain't know would happen eventually."

Mercy grabbed her hand. "Girl, I'm so sorry you gotta deal with this."

"Oh, I got a plan, don't worry."

"Do you need any help? You know I got you. You want to beat that bitch. What?"

"I got something else in mind for his old ass. But I do need you for real. We need each other. Fuck all dem niggas. It's about us. I know we were separated, but we can never lose each other again. We've got to be there for each other no matter what. We got to make sure we okay, because when the dust settles, we gotta be the last two standing. You know that's how Daddy would have wanted it."

"I feel you. Now let a sister in on the plan. But can I ask you something first?" Mercy said with a puzzled look on her face.

"Go 'head."

"What does any of this have to do with my script?"

"Look, your script is hot. Let's take that shit straight to DVD. You don't even need to waste your time with no big distributors like Miramax, Sony, and shit. Shit gets bootlegged to DVD anyway before it even hits its second week at the box office. I'm going to get the money from Benjamin, start my own straight-to-DVD production company, and we gonna Thelma and Louise this shit. Get us some real money so if Benjamin or any other nigga want to fuck around, we can roll out!"

Mercy was starting to get high off of the excitement and determination in Tallya's voice. "Let's do this shit, then," Mercy said as she reached out to shake Tallya's hand.

Over the next few days, Tallya incorporated her company, Bermuda Triangle Entertainment. She had a contract drafted to purchase Mercy's script, and before Mercy got on her plane to go home she had in her hand a check for fifteen thousand dollars of the thirty-five-thousand-dollar advance. Mercy felt good knowing that she had money in her pocket and had found someone who believed in her work enough to buy it from her. She thought she would never come down off the cloud she was on. Her dream was finally turning into a reality; her script was going to be produced.

Making a movie was harder work than Mercy could ever have imagined, but it was fun, too, and she learned from the pros. The professor at the school where she had wanted to take classes had looked over Mercy's script for her. He even offered to put her in touch with a director who could give her some pointers. Mercy soaked up every bit of information she could about the movie industry. She learned how a writing credit alone sometimes isn't enough. It's always good if directing and producing credits can be incorporated—that way, there is a paycheck for writing the script, a paycheck for directing, and a paycheck for producing. Now Mercy understood why actors always fought so hard to get producer credits. It didn't mean that they necessarily produced anything, but it did mean they got another check.

In order to put everything she was learning to work, Mercy started out assisting the folks that Tallya had put on payroll. Mercy was amazed at how helpful everyone she met was. It seemed like they all wanted to be known for helping this unknown talent get on her feet. It was as if they knew she was going to be something big.

The director who was giving her pointers gave her the phone number of Pete, a retired line producer in New York, who said he'd come out of retirement for one more job. Mercy didn't even know what a line producer was, but pretty soon Pete had helped her hire a camera operator, lighting director, sound crew, and an editor. A local assistant director came on board and brought some production assistants with her.

The crew was pretty easy to find. Once they all read the script, they couldn't wait to put their skills to work, but casting was another story. Mercy wanted to use unknown talents, because Tallya said they didn't even have enough money to pay for D-list actors. Mercy knew that there were plenty of unknowns out there with a raw unearthed talent, just waiting to be given a chance, just like her. All she had to do was find them.

Tallya, Mercy, and Chrissie, who had volunteered to help out with the casting calls, traveled from Richmond to Atlanta, finding just the right actors for the parts. They found a beautiful young woman named BoNita Numeya to play the lead female. She was so eager to have the part that she offered to do it for free, but Mercy insisted on paying her even though Tallya was willing to take the girl up on the offer.

"If we don't pay her something, we'll regret it in the long run," Mercy told Tallya. "I don't want to get known for being too cheap to pay my actors!"

"And I don't want to get known for being too broke to pay actors!" Tallya argued, but Mercy prevailed, paying BoNita a modest stipend.

Finally they were able to start shooting. Mercy read every book she could find on the ins and outs of shooting a movie. She still continued to absorb every piece of advice she could get from the film director she had first contacted as well as every member of her crew.

"It's your vision," the camera guy said to Mercy. "You tell us what you want and we'll get it for you."

They put in fourteen-hour days and worked six days a week,

and at the end of four weeks, shooting was over. They couldn't have been more lucky that BoNita Numeya wasn't a diva, but just a hardworking girl who needed a break. She didn't mind the crazy long hours and the short pay. One actress tried getting out of hand, and Mercy fired her on the spot. That may have had something to do with Ms. Numeya's humble obedience.

"I don't have the time or patience for people who can't act like professionals," Mercy shouted indirectly so that the other actors would take the girl she had fired as an example. Easy come, easy go. The same way that chick would be replaced, they could be replaced too.

In just a couple of months, Mercy had gone from being a dope runner to a scriptwriter and film director. She wished they had more time, but every day of shooting cost money, and fortunately they were able to shoot the whole thing right in Richmond, straight in the hood, which enabled Mercy to easily find plenty of extras. Although the film was done on a tightly tied shoestring budget, Mercy pulled it off just like she always did.

Then the big night came. The editors had finished doing their job, and Mercy, Tallya, Benjamin, and Chrissie watched the rough cut in Benjamin's media room.

At the last fade to black, the four of them sat quietly for a moment. Then Chrissie screamed and Tallya jumped up in excitement and Benjamin pulled out a bottle of Dom Pérignon while the girls danced around.

"Ms. Jiles," Benjamin said as he proceeded to pop the cork, "I think you have a hit on your hands." The champagne cork shot across the room.

"Benjamin, I think you're wrong," Mercy said. "We have a hit on our hands."

"Hear! hear!" Benjamin said as he poured them each a glass.

Mercy sat back and indulged in the taste of the Dom. It was official—she was on her way. For so long she had fought her way through the jungle trying to find a path to lead her out of it. Finally, she had located the path. The only thing was, was it the path leading her out of the jungle, or deeper into it?

CHAPTER 21

G-2

The Richmond jail was a city within itself. Just like the streets of Richmond, it was split up into sections. There were three main housing units within the jail: E, F, and G tiers, each occupying three separate floors. E pod was for the kitchen, school, trustees, and a few others. F pod was mostly for the guys north of the James River, and G pod was for the fellas from the south side. The open dormitory-style G-2 housing unit had eighty beds, but 140 bodies resided within its walls. There was one television, at best two working clock radios, five telephones—one of which was almost always guaranteed to be out of order—and one community shower with three spigots.

G-2 reeked of a foul indescribable odor: a combination of sweat, musky balls, armpit odor, feces, and other unidentifiable scents. It was basically hell on earth. As soon as a man walked through the door, it was survival of the fittest. If he wasn't strong physically or if he didn't have some street credibility or know someone who did, if he was lucky, he might get to sleep on the floor and keep his commissary. If he was unlucky, he got his stuff taken and the shit beat out of him. Or even worse. Some would rather check themselves into solitary confinement than go to F and especially G units.

The characters residing on G-2 were even worse than the living conditions. It was basically five kinds of guys residing on G-2. There were guys that were "no-hope" cases: guys usually sentenced to forty years to life whose next stop was to live among the living dead for the rest of their lives in the penitentiary. Their only way out was in a coffin. Then there were the "doomed" cases: the ones who were simply doomed for their own foolish reasons. They were too comfortable in their present situation, as if the jail was home to them, and they depended on what their bullshit-ass court-appointed attorney said was law. That kind would never take a trip to the law library to see if they were being sold out or what the actual guidelines were on his case. Instead, they spent their time playing cards, fucking faggots, wrestling, joking, making wine, and getting high like it was all good. Then there were the "penny guys" who had a small bond but no one would bail out because they'd burnt so many bridges. The fourth kind were the timid guys who feared for their lives and would do anything for protection. Last was the minority, who were sharp in all dimensions: the streets and the penal system. These were the ones who wanted to understand their case and wanted to prepare themselves for their defense or whatever their hand called for.

Cleezy sat at the stainless-steel table on the G-2 housing tier kicking it with his man, Ty. They appeared to be homeboys since the sandbox, but in all actuality they had just met only a month ago while both were doing time down at the city jail. A lot of bonds and relationships are made and formed behind prison walls. Cleezy's and Ty's was just one.

"Man, I hope this fucking lawyer comes to see me and lets me know who the motherfucking snitch is on that motion of discovery," Cleezy said.

"When did he file it?" Ty asked, so that he could calculate how long it should be from the date of the filing to when Cleezy's lawyer should be visiting him.

"Shit." Cleezy paused to think. "It's been 'bout a month now."

"Yeah, that nigga should be coming down here, because it takes 'bout that long to get them back. I think it takes 'bout twenty-one days, plus he's got to get it in his hands and look it over. He should be down here any day now."

"I'm going to call my girl and see if she heard anything from him." Cleezy got up to walk over to the phone to dial Paula. A lame on the phone saw Cleezy waiting for the phone and didn't recognize that he needed to get the fuck off. See, Cleezy and his clique on the tier had a phone open at all times for them. No one was to touch that phone unless they got permission from someone in the clique to use it. Permission was only given for important calls, a lawyer call, or someone trying to make bond—and that was decided on a case-by-case basis.

"Yo, who let you on this phone?" Cleezy shouted.

He waited for a few seconds, and when he had just about decided to bust the lame across the head, he was distracted by a loud voice screaming, "Laundry." It was the CO.

Cleezy called out to Ty, "Yo, get my shit, too," as Ty headed for the catwalk—the space between the cage and the window where the guards make their rounds—so they could switch out their laundry without the fear of being attacked by the inmates.

Once Cleezy put his clean linen on his bunk, he and Ty sat at the back in the cut and jawboned about who had fucked the baddest bitches until chow was called. Cleezy ran and grabbed his knife and headed for the door. Some of the other inmates had the homemade shanks—a metal spoon with the top broken off and filed down—but Cleezy had a six-inch fold-out buck knife. Although the jail officials had it set up where each pod was supposed to go to chow separately, the deputies sometimes fucked up. And when they did, Cleezy had to be good and ready for beef. So just as most people never left home without their American Express cards, he never left out of G-2 without his shank.

In most jails, correctional centers, prisons, or penitentiaries, the chow hall was usually the place where fights went down. The other place was the rec yard. Before Cleezy walked to the chow hall, he ran upstairs to holla at a few brothers on G-3.

"Yo, Cleeeezzzy," one of his homeboys called out to him.

"What up?" Cleezy said.

"Man, niggas up here saying that one of yo' niggas giving you up and shit."

"What?" Cleezy said, stopping in his tracks.

"That's my word, my nigga."

"Naw, not none of mine. Niggas just talking because I ain't got nothing but straight soldiers on my squad."

"I just wanted to put you up on coversations those jokers putting down. Get P to come and see you tomorrow, because my people coming."

"Just tell yo' people to call Paula so they can work that shit out, but I got you, partner," Cleezy said, knowing what time it was. That was another thing about the beefs. The visiting rooms were the only place where guys from all the buildings were not segregated, so most of the time guys from the same set tripled up in the visiting room, having their family come at the same time so they wouldn't be in the v-room alone, left to get jumped by another set.

Although this was Cleezy's first bid, his brother had been in and out of jail and had always been deep into the game. Silently observing how Lynx did his, Cleezy pretty much handled the prison politics like a seasoned vet. However, on the inside it bothered him that he didn't know his destiny or who the snitch controlling his destiny was.

As Cleezy exited the chow hall, he saw a guy carrying his gear and mattresses. The guy had just gotten processed into the jail. He looked kind of familiar. Cleezy knew that the guy was probably snitching because he was coming back from the federal penitentiary. Cleezy hoped and prayed that the clown came to G-2.

Once they were all settled back in from chow, there were four programs that were a must on the G-2 television set: any sporting game, *Showtime at the Apollo* on Saturday nights, *The Young and the Restless,* and the local news at noon, six, and eleven. They all were watching the six o'clock news when the news anchor said, "There's a local screenwriter taking urban films to the next level, and we are here to get the inside scoop on her movie, *A Girl's Gotta Do What a Girl's Gotta Do.*

"So, Mercy, tell me," the reporter asked, "how does a girl who grew up in eleven foster homes, who was assaulted by armed robbers, and who has endured so many struggles find herself on the path of becoming a recognized celebrity?"

It was obvious that Mercy hadn't yet polished up her interview skills as she sat in the studio fidgeting.

"My life has been filled with turmoil and obstacles. But like Tallya, my sister, who believed enough in my screenwriting gift that she single-handedly financed its production, God is a restorer. He restored my life, and now look at all he has blessed me with." Mercy spoke from her heart, so everything flowed naturally.

"What do you say to people who call you an overnight success?"

"I'm not an overnight success," Mercy said with sincerity. "My script might be an overnight success, but me, Mercy the person, is no overnight success."

Cleezy sat on the top of the table dumbfounded. He could not believe Mercy was doing the damn thing and doing it big. Suddenly the guard popped the door and the guy Cleezy had seen earlier in the hall with the mattresses walked through, smiling like he was somebody.

"Man, this got to be my lucky day," Cleezy said, rubbing his hands together as he turned his attention away from Mercy's interview on TV.

"What up?" Ty asked, thinking he was talking about the news because Cleezy had told him about the past encounters he'd had with Mercy. Through their hours of jawboning, Cleezy had told him that she was more or less the one who got away, the one he wished he could have made his.

Cleezy looked at the newcomer, toting his mattress in his hands. "It can't be," he said, as he got up for further inspection. He noticed the five-percenter tattoo on the newcomer's right hand. He recognized the tattoo and the face. There was no doubt he was standing face to face with one of the two guys that had robbed him of his brother's chain in Miami. Indeed the world was small.

"Yo, man, that's da clown that stuck me up down in Miami," Cleezy informed Ty.

"Who? That New York nigga you was spittin' about?" Ty replied.

"Fa' certain, this shit crazy."

"You want to go get that nigga now?"

"Naw, let that motherfucker get comfortable first."

"A'ight," Ty said. "This world is small as shit. Motherfuckers traveling I-95 need to understand this here Richmond City Jail is a fucking stop-off point at one time or another. And a nigga shit better be right when he come through. Especially dem New York jokers who go from state to state, hustling."

The whole clique was notified as to what was up as the word spread around the tier. The New Yorker had three whammies against him. First, he was from New York and didn't belong there, next he had robbed Cleezy, but most important, he was a snitch.

"Motherfuckers need to understand that all guns are left at the quartermaster," Cleezy said. "It ain't no guns allowed in here. If a nigga's knuckle game ain't airtight he better check himself into solitary."

Ty laughed and cosigned. "Many niggas done got their head smashed. They don't understand that behind these walls they got to give account for that shit they do with a gun," he said, laughing while eating a Twinkie.

Once Raheem got far enough from the door and deep enough in the terror dome, someone he knew from the streets let him know that he needed to set up his bed in the back of the tier. Once he was all comfortable, out of nowhere came a powerful blow to his eye. The Styrofoam slippers he wore made him slip on the floor, which was one of the reasons why he couldn't fight back. However, the main reason he couldn't fight back was because there were about twenty niggas on him. Fists and feet were raining down on him from all directions. Before it was all over, damn near the whole tier got a piece of his ass. Some he knew and some he didn't. That's how it went down on G-2. If one fought, then they all basically fought. By the time all the guards and backup arrived, the fight was over and Raheem had been pounded to within inches of his life. The tier went on lock because nobody would reveal who was fighting, and Raheem was rushed off to MCV.

By the time the tier had calmed down, it was almost eight o'clock at night, and that's about the time Cleezy's lawyer finally came to visit him. His lawyer wanted to do the small-talk thing, asking him how he was doing. Cleezy cut to the chase.

"Man, what's the deal? Whose name is on them papers?" Cleezy asked anxiously.

The attorney looked down at his paper although he had the name memorized in his head. "Uh, Shawn Justice," the attorney muttered.

Cleezy was quiet for a minute. "What? Let me see it with my own eyes."

The attorney adjusted his glasses on his nose before handing Cleezy the papers. He then added, "He said he was there the night in question." The lawyer carefully thought before he said each word. "And if he testifies this could be detrimental to our case."

"Look, just do your job," Cleezy said, smacking his lips. "This nigga is lying. He ain't seen shit, because it wasn't nothing to see."

"He's your homeboy, so why would he lie?"

"I don't know why, but I know he ain't going to be able to look me in the face. Naw, that nigga ain't taking no stand. Trust me."

The attorney was quiet as he packed his briefcase up. "Stay strong, man."

"No doubt."

Cleezy realized that this wasn't his lucky day after all, and to put the icing on the cake, G-2 was locked down and they couldn't get any visits or use the phone. So he had to "tier hop" to another tier and make a phone call to put all this madness to bed.

"Man, look, I ain't got but a minute because we on lock. That nigga Jus is on my paperwork. I need you to—"

"Say no more, my nigga." Cook'em-up cut him off. "Say no more. No need to worry. I got you."

As Cleezy made his way back over to G-2, tears filled his eyes, and his stomach was balled up in a knot. His right-hand man had rolled over on him. Jus, his best friend since the sandbox, was the prosecution's key witness for this murder charge. It hurt him to his heart. What scared Cleezy most—all he would be able to think about for the next few days—was what else Jus had told. They had sold so much drugs and done so much dirt together. . . . what else had he told? What else? He wondered over and over when the Feds would come.

CHAPTER 22

The $hit Rolls Downhill

Mercy sat by the pool at Tallya's house, drinking a vodka and tonic. She looked down at her perfectly painted toenails and admired the pedicure she had gotten the day before. She finally felt like she was living the life she was born to live. Her straight-to-DVD script was a blockbuster.

"It's a good thing, girl, that we went straight to DVD," Tallya said.

"Why is that?"

" 'Cause most bootleggers spend more time pushing films that's slated for the big screen. Their whole hustle is based on providing consumers with something that ain't available yet for home viewing," Tallya explained.

That made sense to Mercy. People always found pleasure in getting things they weren't supposed to have, even if it did mean taking money from an artist. But since Mercy's joint skipped that entire process and was immediately accessible to the public, her work didn't get hit as hard.

No store on the East Coast could keep copies of her movie on the shelves. Her name was ringing all over the country; reporters from magazines and television alike wanted interviews with her.

People were amazed by how successful she was becoming, but even more so, they were moved by her story of the road she had traveled before becoming such a success. Everybody roots for the underdog, so when they learned that Mercy had been a foster child, was only twenty-three years old, had barely finished high school, had taken no formal writing courses, and yet despite all that had written one hell of a screenplay, that made them love her that much more. She was an inspiration to every young black girl in the hood and was labeled "a diamond in the rough." Even schools were soliciting Mercy to come talk about her success. At first Tallya forwarded all of the inquiries she received on Mercy's behalf directly to Mercy. But it seemed like lately she was trying to screen who had access to Mercy, so Mercy finally asked her about it.

"I just don't think it's good PR to have you on TV and going to schools and stuff doing those interviews," Tallya said, setting her drink down on the table between them.

"Why do you say that?" Mercy asked. She was just starting to accept the fame that promised a financial fortune.

"Because, you know, image is everything."

"Okay, so what are you trying to say? My image ain't up to par? I think I dress cute whenever I am in front of the camera."

"Yeah, but I looked at the repeat of you on *106 and Park* and you was looking like a stuffed turkey. Benjamin even said something to me about you being fat." Oooohhh, that hurt Mercy. First Taymar with his mean comments about her weight issues and now this.

"What does my weight have to do with anything?" Mercy snapped.

"People just view you different when you are not fit and in shape. Makes you seem lazy, like you just sittin' around eating steak and lobster all day, collecting the money from what they spend on your work."

Mercy looked down at herself in her new bathing suit. She wasn't fat, maybe a little thick, but Tallya had carried it too far. This was not how sisters should treat each other.

A day later she left Tallya's house and flew back to Richmond. As she flew the friendly skies she thought about the way Tallya had been treating her. In the beginning, Mercy had had no idea that Tallya would turn jealous of her. After all, Tallya was making much more off of Mercy's work than Mercy was. But Mercy was too new to the game to realize that different players played the game for different reasons. Some want the money more than they want the fame. Others get orgasms off of name recognition alone and couldn't care less whether they are broke just as long as people know who they are. Then there are those, the real players, who want it all.

Mercy realized that Tallya wasn't jealous that Mercy was the one getting all the attention. Tallya was all about the money, but she was small-time compared to the major film and distribution companies out there. She knew it would only be a matter of time before all of the attention and press that Mercy was getting would land Mercy an offer she wouldn't be able to refuse. Tallya was tearing Mercy down in any way she could to convince her that nobody else wanted to work with her in spite of what seemed like overnight success.

"They all want screenwriters with experience," Tallya had said to Mercy. "You're still rough. No one will take your script like we did and work with it. The story was good, but it wasn't well written."

"Well, the same way you thought it was good enough to work with, someone else will," Mercy replied.

"Do you know how many scripts they get from experienced people? They come a dime a dozen, girl. Do you think they want to spend as much time as we did cleaning up your scratch when they have someone who already knows what the hell they are doing?"

Mercy didn't know what to say. She had never thought about it like that before. She was just going to let it go because she didn't want to keep going back and forth with Tallya, but Tallya wasn't that quick to let things go. She didn't stop tearing down the house just at the roof; she wanted to see that sucker crumble to the ground and then light a match to it.

"Besides," Tallya continued, "I don't think you have another good script in you, not as good as this, so you should just milk this project for everything it's worth. This will probably be the most money you'll ever get out of a deal. We could have taken our money and put anybody on, but no, we chose you. Not that your script was the best out there, but because you are my peoples."

Mercy was starting to feel as if Bermuda Triangle had done her a favor and she hadn't done shit for them, but once Mercy really had time to sit and think about it, Tallya had basically stolen her screenplay. Although neither was sure of the going price for a script such as Mercy's, they agreed to pay her $35,000. Somehow they managed to chicken-feed her the money. Mercy had only received $15,000 upon signing the contract and was promised the rest when the film came out. Tallya told her that she needed a few weeks to make the money back she'd spent on the project and then she would pay her. As bad as Mercy needed the money, she tried to understand the big picture and believe in the growth of Bermuda Triangle. She wanted it to succeed so bad that she even directed the film—working with the actors and the crew, spending long hours in the editing room with the editor and not charging Tallya anything because she wanted her project to be done the right way. Most important, she understood the struggle. But Mercy struggled financially in her own life while Tallya still lived the glamorous life, never giving a damn about compensating Mercy.

Mercy never complained about the way Tallya nickel-and-dimed her by paying her the balance of her money five hundred dollars here and a thousand dollars there when her project was moving like uncut dope at the first of the month.

A few days after she made the comment about Mercy's weight, Tallya sent her a check for $3,000. Mercy was so grateful for the money, she decided to forgive Tallya for her unkind comments. She had that money spent on bills before she even walked into the bank to cash it. But when the clerk pointed out to Mercy that the check was postdated, Mercy could have cried. She had to hold on to it for two more weeks before she could deposit it, which meant two more weeks of being broke. Two weeks later Mercy was back at the bank depositing the check into her account. She wrote checks to pay off her overdue bills. Who'dda thought the person the media was starting to call the Urban Princess was behind on her bills? A few days later Mercy started getting notices from her bank that checks were being returned because her account had insufficient funds. In the midst of the notices was the one informing Mercy that Tallya's check had bounced. Tallya's bank had returned the check for $3,000 like a broke chick returns an outfit the day after she done sweated it out at the club. To top it all off, this was the third check Tallya had written Mercy that had bounced. Mercy was starting to think that she was stuck in a game of dodgeball. The freaking checks were the rubber balls, and Tallya was dodging the fuck out of making good on them.

After reading the notices, Mercy had to come down off of her damn-near anxiety attack before calling Tallya to find out what the deal was.

"Hey, girl," Mercy said, trying to make general conversation.

"What's up?" Tallya said, acting like she didn't know why the hell Mercy was calling.

"Nothing, sitting here going through my mail. I just got a notice that the check you wrote me for $3,000 wasn't any good." Mercy paused, then continued, "I got all kinds of checks out there for bills. I don't know what could have happened, but I was wondering if you could just send me another one."

"Okay, I will," Tallya said, not adding any further explanation as to why the checked had bounced. Mercy didn't really care as long as she was going to make good on the sucker.

"I'd prefer a money order so that I don't have to wait for it to clear. You think you can overnight it to me?"

Tallya sighed as if Mercy was asking to borrow money instead of trying to collect what was legitimately owed to her. "Damn, I'm going to send it when I get around to it."

"Well, Tallya, keep it real now," Mercy said, trippin' off the fact that Tallya was snappin' on her about a check she had bounced. "You bounced me a check, and this is the third one. Just play fair. I've been working with you on the money thing, and it's, like, I got bills and need my money."

Tallya completely went off. Something about the talk of money just put her on edge. It was all good if the talk was about her getting money, but when it was about her giving it, she went crazy. "Look, we just sent you a thousand dollars last month. What are you doing with all your money? Are you going to be like Mike Tyson and be broke?"

"No, but what is one thousand dollars when you owe several thousand? Shit, that ain't even ten percent."

"I'm just trying to look out for you and do you a favor," Tallya shouted at the top of her lungs.

Mercy remained calm. She wasn't trying to get into no shouting match. She just wanted her money. "Honestly speaking, it doesn't matter if I want to smoke crack all day and jerk off all my money. It's mine, so if I am broke then so be it. I don't need no-body to hold mines."

"Whatever," Tallya said, sucking her teeth. "Look, I'm going to be frank with you. So what, we bounced you a couple of checks. *So the fuck what!*" Tallya's tone suddenly changed into a raging scream. "So what, the money be fucked up. Your shit is moving, ain't it? Selling like crazy? So what? But guess what? You can't get shit until I give it to you. So the more you worry me for *your money,* the longer I am going to drag my fucking feet to give it to you. See Bermuda Triangle Productions, I own this shit. This ain't yours. Not you. You ain't no CEO or president. You ain't even a shareholder. I run this shit, not you. I write checks and make final decisions. If you don't like it, carry yo' ass on." After getting slick out of the mouth Tallya hung up the phone.

See, this bitch don't know who the fuck she dealing with, Mercy thought as she hung up the phone in disbelief. And the reality of it was that Tallya really didn't know who she was dealing with. Mercy had just been excited and grateful that she had a relation-ship with her sister and that someone had given her first project a chance, so she'd never complained about much of anything. Be-cause of Mercy's grateful demeanor, Tallya thought Mercy was weak. Tallya looked at herself as the strong, authoritative one. Like she was God and Mercy was a peasant at her feet—only Tallya had no intention of using Mercy for good. Tallya couldn't care less about benefiting man. All she cared about was herself.

The day after Tallya displayed her nasty temperament and greedy nature, Mercy received a phone call from an agent named Davey Donk in LA, who promised to negotiate huge deals on her behalf. He wasn't the first one to call her, but up till now her loy-alty had been to Bermuda Triangle. Now that Tallya had made it clear that Mercy wasn't nothing more than a 1099 for her company, Mercy had to start looking out for herself. Mercy asked the agent to let her think about it. As soon as she hung up with him, her phone rang.

"Hey, girl," she heard Tallya say as if they were not just sisters, but best friends, too. Mercy couldn't believe her ears.

"What?" Mercy said as she rolled her eyes.

"Look, you know I love you, right? But this company just got me stressed. There's all the orders that are coming in that I can't fill because I'm waiting to be paid by these distributors. When I do do a print run, the orders are gone before the DVDs even get here. Since my company is doing so well, Benjamin been acting funny. I think he thought that my company wasn't going to be hitting on jackshit, that it was just a little hobby for me. He took me for a joke."

"So what that got to do with me, Tallya?" Mercy was quick to say.

"I mean, you understand how it goes, and I know I hurt your feelings and I'm sorry." Tallya tried to sound sincere, but Mercy knew what was up so she just listened. "I'm so sorry that I take you for granted. It's like you are always there for me. You believe in my company like it's your own."

Mercy knew all these things, but she knew that she couldn't do this anymore; she had to look out for her own best interests because Tallya was only looking out for *numero uno*. It was funny how Tallya never said one thing about sending Mercy another check or any money at all for that matter.

The only way Mercy was able to make ends meet while she waited for her checks was by buying DVDs from the distributor and selling them out of the trunk of her car.

Tallya changed the subject. "Are you writing?"

"Yup," Mercy said nonchalantly.

"You know, you need to let me see your script so we can come up with a plan to get it into motion," Tallya said.

Mercy took in Tallya's words, paused for a minute, and then said, "Look, Tallya, I ain't ever been no fake chick. I try to keep it real. At one time I looked at you as my long-lost sister. We've both been there before. Now understand that I am a hustler in every aspect of the word. So, when you came to me and was like 'Let's Thelma and Louise this shit,' I thought about what Biggie said about keeping friends and family and business completely separated. However, I am never a hater and I love you. I would rather for you to do my DVD than somebody I don't know to make money off of it." Tallya listened as Mercy continued. "I played fair with you from the gate, and you shitted on me time and time again with my money, which is cool. I'm not mad at you, because I understand who you really are. You're a selfish bitch, and you'll never be a team player."

"What?" Tallya said in surprise.

"I don't understand how you want a company, but it's all about you. It should be about the team, because you can only be as good as your team."

"Listen, Mercy, you are probably right. But understand I ain't never had nobody to play fair with me, so if I do stuff you have to pull my coat for me," Tallya said, whining. " 'Cause if you remember, I didn't have a daddy who loved me the way he loved you."

"That was a long time ago, Tallya. So, look, this is how it's going to go down. I am a writer, and I need to be focused on writing."

"You're right, you are a writer and we want you to focus."

"My point exactly," Mercy said. "I can't be preoccupied, focusing on money, and since the only thing we seem to fight about is money, I'm going to get an agent to handle the money-aspect part of our relationship."

"Oh, that's some real snake shit," Tallya immediately huffed. "What the fuck do you need an agent for? You know an agent will take you away from me to a much larger company."

"Look, I'm not interested in going to another company," Mercy assured her. "I'm only interested in making sure you pay me. I have no intentions of going to another company just because they are bigger."

"How about can't a motherfucker on God's green Earth make sure I pay you," Tallya retaliated with a slight chuckle. "I pays a motherfucker when the fuck I—that's right, when I—get ready. And just for the record, and just so that you know—hoes come and go in this pimp game. So you may be the first to leave, but you won't be the last. What you need to understand is I, Tallya, AKA Bermuda Triangle Productions—that's me, me Natallya—that's right, I own yo' shit. I can do whatever I want to do because your DVD is mine. Understand? As a matter fact, since you want to bring in another motherfucker to try to be a mediator, shit rolls downhill from here, boo. Because I ain't paying you shit!" Tallya screamed at the top of her lungs. "Have your attorney contact mine," she yelled as she slammed the phone down.

Mercy stood there with her mouth open, holding the phone.

"No, this bitch just didn't . . . ," she said, shaking her head.

Although Mercy wanted to break down and cry, she could only laugh. She thought about all of the checks she had written that were bouncing from one end of Richmond to the next. She wondered how she was going to pay the bills this month, next month, and the month after that and she wanted to cry, but instead she laughed. She wasn't about to give Tallya the satisfaction of bringing her to tears.

Mercy had overcome adversity since she was seven years old.

Just for a minute there she'd finally thought God was shining a little light on her. Now suddenly Tallya had cut off the electricity, leaving her in darkness. It didn't seem fair, but maybe God had no choice but to show her Tallya's hand, so that she would quit eating from it. Now she wondered where in the hell her next meal was going to come from. But one thing for sure two things for certain, God always provided.

CHAPTER 23

Where da Money?

"**M**ailllll calllll!!!" The loudmouthed guard called out. "Fargo!" He called Cleezy's name a few times. Paula made sure he had plenty of mail. Cleezy put his magazines to the side to read another time. He looked at all of his cards that Paula had sent him and then opened the lastest letter from her.

Hey Boo,

First, I love you. Next, I miss you more than I could ever express to you in a letter, in any words, which I am sure that deep down in your heart you already know these things.

Ms. Lolly told me that I missed your call the other day. I'm sorry, baby. I got off work late because I had two walk-ins. I took those because you know I hate using your money for things other than what you need me to do for you. So, they delayed me in two hours getting off. That's why I wasn't home when you called the house. And when you called my cell phone, I had left it in the car when I was pumping gas. Ever since that man's car caught on fire, I don't be talking on nobody's phone when I am pumping gas.

Anyway, I went to pay your storage bill, which was two

hundred thirty nine dollars. I got your momma her birthday
present, the dining room set, like you asked me to. I went ahead
and got the two extra chairs because if I got the eight chairs
instead of the six, we got twenty percent off, which made it lower
than we anticipated. With the delivery charges and taxes, it
totaled up to be $4,262. I paid the phone bill, which was $254,
so I have $107,000 dollars of your money left. However,
Cook'em-up called and said that you said to give him a G, but I
had not spoken to you, so I wasn't giving him any money out of
yours. So, I only gave him what I could afford to spare of my own
money. I know he's your boy and all, but at the same time, I don't
give nobody nothing of yours unless you approve it. Anyway, he
told me to let you know to stay up and that everything is real in
the field as far as he's concerned, and said that you knew what he
meant. Other than that, by the time you get this we would have
talked, but always know that I love you and I am praying that
everything works out for us in court.

Loving you Forever and Ever,
Until Death Do Us Part,
Paula

He smiled at Paula's letter, and for the first time the thought
crossed his mind that he could possibly make Paula his wifey, his
Bonnie, maybe even his Whitney.

The next day Cleezy went to court and Jus did not show up to
take the stand.

Cleezy turned to look at Paula, who was sitting in the second
row of the courtroom. As she gazed in his eyes, he knew that his
heart was safe with her.

"Your Honor," the prosecutor stood up and said, "I would like to request a continuance from the court."

"Your Honor," Cleezy's attorney jumped in, "it's clear that the prosecution does not have his witness, and he is not only trying to string my client along, but the whole judicial system as well."

"Counsel, you need to proceed now with your case."

The commonwealth attorney took a deep breath and sighed. "Your Honor, I'm asking for a continuance because our witness, Shawn Justice, seems to be no longer available."

"What do you mean 'no longer available'?" the irritated judge asked.

"Your Honor, may we have a sidebar?"

The judge nodded his head. The attorneys approached the bench and began to speak in hushed voices. Cleezy was able to hear a little. He heard the prosecutor say something about somebody being murdered in North Carolina and "genitals in his mouth."

The judge nodded. As the prosecutor turned his back to the judge to walk back over to his table, Cleezy glanced behind him and saw Columbo sitting there looking smug. He obviously hadn't heard what Cleezy had heard. Columbo whispered to one of his fellow officers. They sat there and carried on a conversation, happy as a lark that they finally had Cleezy where they wanted him. "There is no talking in my courtroom, Officers. If you want to have a conversation, you take it outside my courtroom," the judge said to Columbo and his companions.

"And, Counsel"—the judge redirected his attention to the prosecuting attorney—"this case should have been dismissed as soon as you found out your witness was dead."

Cleezy saw Columbo's mouth drop open and his eyes harden. "You have people here sitting in this courtroom on this beautiful afternoon as you pray for a genie to make your witness reappear. I don't beleive in genies, and this court has better things to do."

The judge then turned to look at Cleezy. "Mr. Fargo, I am dismissing all charges against you, and you are free to go."

Of course Cleezy had to go back to jail and get processed out, but once he was finally released, Paula was waiting in her car for him just as soon as he walked out of the prison doors.

He smiled and got into the car. "Damn, baby, you love this nigga, don't you?" he said, leaning in and giving her a kiss.

"You know I do," she said as she embraced him.

"You must do. How long you been waitin' on me?"

"Umm, since court."

He looked at his watch. "It's six o'clock, and court was over at two."

"I know. I just didn't want you to come out here and have to wait for me."

"It didn't take but a few minutes for them to slap the cuffs on me and drag me in that mothafucka, but it took hours for them to let me go."

"I know, baby, but at least you're out," Paula said, looking into Cleezy's eyes as his eyes swept her body.

"So you gon' give me some of that?" he said as he began rubbing her thighs.

"You know it, but we need to get a room, because I am not going to feel right fucking in your momma's house."

"Then drive to the Marriott," Cleezy said with a wink as Paula smiled, pumped the gas pedal, and then sped off.

Cleezy could barely keep his composure until they got to the hotel. He rubbed and kissed on Paula the entire drive, telling her how he couldn't wait to be inside of her. Once they got to the hotel, the door to their room barely closed behind them before Cleezy spun Paula around and began tonguing her as he lifted the little Ralph Lauren tennis dress she was wearing over her head.

"Baby, don't you want to slow down?" Paula asked him in a sensuous tone. "You might miss a spot."

"Trust, I'm gon' hit every spot."

Cleezy picked up Paula, and she wrapped her legs tight around his waist. He carried her over to the king-sized bed and laid her down. She watched as he took off his shirt and undid his pants. Once he was butt naked, he just stood there for a minute, allowing Paula to recollect what she had been forced to live without. Paula quivered at the sight of her well-hung buck. Cleezy removed her panties, then lay on top of her.

Paula lay there looking at the ceiling, feeling a little awkward. A minute ago her man was rushing her out of her clothes, and now he was just lying there on top of her.

"Something wrong?" she asked.

Cleezy shook his head. "Couldn't be more right. I just want to lay here and feel you for a minute. I mean really feel you."

And that's what he did. His body was so warm on hers. He could keep her warm in an igloo. She put her arms around Cleezy and closed her eyes. It felt good just holding him, too.

Cleezy lifted his head and looked down at Paula. She opened her eyes and smiled. In sync they reached to kiss one another, not with their tongues either—just a soft kiss on the lips. Slowly Cleezy started to grind himself against Paula. Just his dick touching her gave her chills, creating a creamy wetness that was icing his dick with every stroke against her. Paula began grinding herself hard against Cleezy, and after only a few brushes of her throbbing clit against him, she came.

"Oh, Cleezy," she said, almost embarrassed. But before the embarrassment set in, Cleezy was inside of her, stroking her vigorously and passionately like it was the last pussy he'd ever get.

It was evident to Paula that Cleezy must have been jackin' off while locked up, because he should have been the one to cum quickly. Instead she was the one who couldn't prevent the sudden climax. But it would only be a few deep strokes before Cleezy would release his juices into Paula.

"You feel so good," Cleezy said, still up inside of Paula. Before he could even start to soften up, Cleezy quickly rolled over and pulled Paula on top of him, using his hand to keep himself inside of her. "Ride it," he ordered her.

Paula began to move up and down on Cleezy, the sound of her wetness driving him crazy. "Faster." She sped up. "Faster." In no time at all Paula looked like she was riding a mechanical bull. Cleezy was in control, pumping faster and faster with each stroke, forcing Paula to keep up. Up and down she went, her titties flopping. Cleezy lifted his head and looked down to see the cream settling in Paula's jungle. He then grabbed hold of Paula and stood up. He leaned her against the wall and just started pumping as deep as he could.

He began to moan and groan as both he and Paula came at the same time. Cleezy was right when he'd told Paula that he was going to hit every spot. That is exactly what he did.

Just as the two were coming down off of their high, Paula's cell phone began ringing. Caught up in the moment, she didn't dare have Cleezy move so that she could answer her phone. It then began ringing again.

"Just answer it," Cleezy demanded as he pulled himself out of her and unpinned her from the wall. Paula quickly got the phone.

"Hello," she said. She paused and waited on a response, but there was none. She sucked her teeth and threw the phone down on the bed after she turned it off.

"Who was that?" Cleezy asked as he lay down on the bed, still trying to catch his breath.

"I don't know. They didn't say anything, and they blocked the number." Paula picked up her panties and her dress. "I'm going to go take a shower real quick."

As Paula got into the shower, Cleezy called Cook'em-up and told him to meet him in the lobby of the hotel in fifteen minutes. Cleezy wanted him to bring him up to speed on everything that was going on.

In fifteen minutes, Cook'em-up was there waiting in the lobby when Cleezy got off the elevator. "Good looking, man," Cleezy said as he greeted Cook'em-up with a brotherly hug.

"Oh, anything for you, pad'na'," he replied.

"So what did that nigga have to say when you went to see him?"

"At first he kept denying it all, said he hadn't ratted on you. Then he finally broke down and told me that he couldn't do the time. He caught a case and was faced with thirty years. It was either you or him."

"When did he catch a case?" Cleezy said curiously.

"He ain't tell nobody. He kept it hush."

"But me and dat nigga go way back to fat shoelaces in sneakers."

"Niggas don't give a fuck, and especially when it's some bitches involved."

"Bitches?" Cleezy asked. "What you mean bitches?"

"I ain't want to say nothing to you, my nigga. When I went to see that nigga he was harpin' on some shit about you stole Paula from him."

"I stole Paula?" Cleezy had a baffled look on his face.

"Yup, that nigga said you knew Paula was always his 'girl' back in the day, some 'bout you always wanted to fuck her."

"What dat got to do with anything? All dem years, why he ain't never get at her?"

"Let him tell it, he did," Cook'em-up said, then switched the subject. "All I could think about is it was either going to be him or us, and it wasn't going to be us, so I rocked that nigga"— Cook'em-up smiled—"straight to sleep."

When he extended his hand to give Cleezy a brotherly shake and hug, Cleezy said, "Well, my man, thanks for putting him to sleep for me. I couldn't have handled the shit any better."

"So, what's up with your peoples? They gon' hit you up or what?"

"They gon' throw me something. I'm going to have to dump and reup again as quick as I can. They going away for two months to Colombia. I know the motherfucker they gon' put me wit' ain't goin' to look out for me as decent as my man do. So I'm just trying to stack as much work as I can. So in the next two days, when that shit arrives, I'm buying as much as I can and getting fronted as much as I can. Nigga, I'm using stash money and everything."

"Once the shipment get here, your president of defense is here at your convenience," Cook'em-up said as he flashed a big smile.

The rest of the night seemed to fly by for Cleezy as he enjoyed the pleasure that Paula poured onto him. Ms. Lolly had been blowing Paula's phone up with messages, but she never did turn her phone back on that night. The next morning Paula went to work late. Cleezy dropped her off and then went to his mom's.

His mom wasn't there when he got in. The first thing Cleezy did was go to the place in the closet where Paula told him his money was. He immediately put the money on the bed and started counting it. According to Paula's calculations, there should be around one hundred and seven thousand dollars. To his surprise, there was only forty thousand dollars. A wave of fire flushed through Cleezy's being. He took a couple of deep breaths and then recounted the money. Once again, he counted only forty thousand dollars.

"What the fuck!" he shouted as he threw the money. Bills fluttered down all over the room. "Ain't this a bitch," he yelled as he punched his fist down on the bed. "That bitch!"

Cleezy couldn't even think straight. Never in a million years did he ever imagine that he would slip up bad enough to the point where a bitch would stick him for his paper. Just when he had serious thoughts about making Paula his wifey, his paper comes up short. Not only had she taken his money, but on top of that she didn't even bother to let him know that Jus had been trying to holler at her. After seeing over half of his money vanish into thin air, now he was wondering if indeed she had really fucked Jus and maybe they were just trying to get him out of the picture. Cleezy angrily paced the floor, contemplating his next move. How was he going to stay up on his feet with thousands missing? Now his plan had been completely messed up.

I knew this bitch was a fucking fraud, he thought. *And to actually think that I loved this ho. Damn, I knew from day motherfucking one that you just can't under any circumstances turn no ho into no motherfucking housewife.*

Paula saw Cleezy pull up as she was finishing locking up the shop. A huge smile covered her face. She had been all day waiting to be with him, like they were new lovers. It was just something about Cleezy that made her feel brand-new, like she didn't have a past because he loved her for who she was now. Paula walked out of the shop and locked the door behind her. When she turned around, Cleezy was standing there leaning against the building.

"Hey, you startled me," she said. She hadn't noticed that he had gotten out of the car.

"I startled you, huh?" He moved in closer.

She nodded her head, knowing that something was wrong. "Yeah, you surprised me. I didn't see you standing there like that."

"And you surprised me, too," he said in a bitter tone.

"What are you talking about, Cleezy?"

"You stole my fucking money." Cleezy looked at her dead in her eyes. His eyes watered with tears of anger.

"What?" Paula shot him a look that could have killed him. The stare was filled with hurt, confusion, and anger.

"Yup, you just told me not even a month ago that I had one hundred seven thousand dollars, and now I only got forty. What? Was you hoping the prosecutor's star witness would keep my ass behind bars so you could spend up the rest of my shit?"

"Yo, don't even come at me like that," Paula said, walking off.

"Fuck you going, bitch?"

"You know what, Cleezy, fuck you!" she screamed. "I'm so tired of this fucking bullshit. Tryin' to prove my love to you. Over and over again. It's all bullshit. I do everything, and it ain't ever enough."

"Look, Paula, I would have given you whatever you wanted. Anything, but you ain't ever ask for shit, and now my money is gone. The whole time you masquerading like you hit the number, and you got all these new clients and that's how you going to Gucci and Louis Vuitton. But the whole time you jerking my money off."

"Think whatever. I don't owe you an explanation. Fuck you, motherfucker. I done did all I can to show you where we at. As a matter of fact, I would've been better off hollering at your boy when he was at me hard while you were fighting your case. But I ain't even want to tell you about how that nigga was some shit and how he was straight begging to pay me to eat my pussy. I ain't even want to bring that shit to you while you were locked up. You had enough shit to worry about." Cleezy never responded because he wanted to believe what she was saying, but then out of anger, she hit him with the ultimate blow. "And from what I hear, that nigga had a way bigger dick than yours," she added, just to insult his manhood so that he would feel less than a man the same way he was making her feel less than a woman.

Cleezy's heart broke at that moment, and he snapped. He pulled out his pistol and without even taking a deep breath he pulled the trigger and put three to her heart.

CHAPTER 24

Nobody's Snitch Bitch

"Your Honor, the prosecution and the defendant have agreed on a plea," the prosecutor on Mercy's assault case said as the bitch-ass hotel clerk sat at the defense table and sniffled.

Mercy was relieved that the hotel clerk had pled guilty, because she didn't want to take the stand on anybody. Not even her worst enemy. She just wasn't raised to be nobody's snitch bitch, not even against the person who had the gun to her head and left her for dead. Being a snitch bitch was not in her genes.

The court-appointed lawyer got up out of his seat, buttoned his jacket, and began to speak. "The defendant, Andrew Long, has agreed that the facts supporting his guilty plea are as follows: that he, along with his alleged accomplice, Mr. Samuels, force-fully entered into Ms. Jiles's hotel room with the intent to rob her. They assaulted her with a deadly weapon, that weapon being a stolen gun. They held her against her will, resulting in the charges of attempted murder, abduction, and aggravated assault. Mr. Long understands that the victim in this case, Mercy Jiles, suf-fered serious injury. As a part of the plea agreement, my client promises to pay restitution as well as cooperate with the authorities to provide information about other serious criminal acts."

A lame motherfucker, Mercy thought as she sat in the court-room. *He ain't no big man now. He could beat me up and play Mr. Bad-Ass when it came to me, but now this motherfucker wanna be a prostitute and turn snitch and puppet to the police.*

The judge sat up in his chair and looked at the former hotel clerk. "Mr. Long, is this correct?"

"Yes, sir," Andrew replied, with his head down.

"Has anyone forced you to enter into this plea?" the judge asked.

"No, sir," he answered.

The judge wrote something on the case file sitting before him before speaking. "Mr. Long, your plea of guilty has been entered and is accepted by the court. Sentencing will be set for a later date."

Mercy listened as the attorney and prosecutor went through their calendars to come up with a date. Once the date was set, court was adjourned and Mercy and Chrissie, who had been there for support, strolled out of court not believing that ol' dude had just rolled over on his man.

"That stupid motherfucker was the one who dropped his ID," Mercy said. "They didn't know nothing about his man being there until he said something. How he just gonna snitch on his man like that?"

"That nigga is weak," Chrissie added.

"Don't get me wrong. I'm glad that they got both of them coward-ass rat bastards."

"Me too, but Mer, if we ever did some ol' wild shit, you gon' hold yours, right?"

"You know I would."

"Damn, Mer, you were just worrying about having to take the stand on a motherfucker who damn near killed you."

"I mean, even though I had been subpoenaed, I still felt bad. But hey, that nigga made it so I wouldn't have to."

"Girl, you really are a real mothafuckin' gangsta bitch and straight up true to the game," Chrissie said as they exited the courthouse and prepared to hail a taxi.

Mercy was distracted with her cell phone. "I wonder who this is calling me from up top," she said as she looked down at the phone and saw that someone with a 646 area code had called a couple of times under her missed calls.

"Girl, it ain't no tellin' like Pete told Helen," Chrissie joked as she flagged down a cabbie. The girls got into the taxi, instructing the cabbie where to take them.

In the taxi, Mercy tried calling the 646 number but only got a voice mail. Once the cab dropped her and Chrissie off at their hotel, they stopped into the hotel restaurant to get something to eat and then headed up to their room. Mercy's cell phone rang as they entered the hotel room. She looked down at the caller ID and saw that it was the mysterious 646 number again.

"Hello," Mercy answered.

"Hello to you, too," the voice on the other end said.

"Heeeeyyyy, Baaayyyybeeee." Mercy was all smiles, happy to hear Hyena's voice.

"Congrats are in order. Both on the outcome of the trial and your new projects."

"Thank you!"

"I saw the video, and I must say you are very talented. I am proud of you."

"Thank you so much!"

"I see everything is good for you."

"You know what, Hy?" Mercy said as her voice declined. "I'ma keep it real. I'm doing dirt-ball bad. I need some help bad. That deal with that company was no good."

"Don't worry," Hyena said in a consoling tone. He must have missed her as much as she had missed him. "I need some help like you. I'm going to wire you some money, and I need you to bring your bathing suits. Is it cool for me to have Uncle Chris pick you up at Granny Smith's tomorrow?"

Mercy knew that he was talking in code. He was asking if he could send the money in Chrissie's name and that he needed her to meet him in the Big Apple. She chuckled a bit and then replied, "Yeah, that's cool."

"All right. So I'ma knock that out, and then we're headed to the beach for the family reunion when you get to Grandma's."

Hyena's call was right on time. Although a part of Mercy told her to hang in there, try to stay legit, and let things work themselves out, Mercy now had a little bit of hope. She could see a flickering light at the end of the tunnel—she just hoped it wasn't the train headed straight for her. This time, just like the last, she told herself it would be her final run. She slept well that night before she and Chrissie headed back home the next morning.

When Mercy got home, she was greeted by a warrant in debt, a court notice that she had not paid her rent. Yeah, Hyena's call was definitely on time. At first she was reluctant about making the run for him, but once the reality set in, the call from Hyena was a godsend, and one job was what she needed to catch up on her bills. So she prepared herself mentally to do the damn thing. Everything went as planned as Mercy arrived in New York. She hopped in the rig with Farmer John just as she had done before, and this time headed to Miami.

CHAPTER 25

Get Yo' Mind Right

Since Paula's death, Cleezy had gone on with his life as if the time he'd spent with Paula never existed. At least he tried to pretend that it hadn't. He stayed focused on stacking as much paper as he could. As he got ready for his biweekly trip to Miami, he stopped by his mother's house to get the new Triple A card that she had been worrying him to come and get for the past three weeks. It would be his luck that just as soon as he didn't go by there and get it, he would end up needing it.

As he went through the mail on the new dining table, he couldn't find the card anywhere. He went into his mother's office and began looking in the drawers of her new cherrywood desk. Cleezy just happened to stumble upon his mother's bank statements. Ordinarily, he wouldn't care less about what his moms was holding, but for some reason, this little voice inside his head kept nagging him to take a look at them.

Cleezy couldn't believe his eyes as he flipped through the past bank statements only to find that each month the balance was growing increasingly larger. He knew that her factory job wasn't kicking out for that kind of money. No way could his mom just have that kind of money at her fingertips. If that was the case,

Cleezy should have been joining her at Bingo a long time ago. Cleezy did a double take when he saw plain as day that there was over forty thousand dollars in his mother's account. He stood there stunned.

"Ain't this a motherfucking bitch?" he screamed. He thought about Paula, and a rush of rage came over him. He threw the bank statements across the room, kicked the desk chair into the wall, and knocked the computer on the floor.

Why was he surprised that his mother had played him just like she had played every other man that she'd ever had in her life? The writing had been on the wall for many years, especially the past few months since he had come home from jail. The new living room suite, the nice Cartier watch, the fine jewelry, clothes, the expensive trips, and all of the things that she claimed she got from working overtime, winning at Bingo, and using her good credit to finance. Never had the thought crossed Cleezy's mind that his mother would have robbed him of his riches, an act that he blamed Paula for and made her pay for with her life. It was a low blow, and he could not understand why his own mother would steal from him. He had given her everything that she wanted, spoiled her better than any of the women that he had ever fucked.

Cleezy made his way downstairs in a zombielike daze. His limp body collapsed in the new sectional furniture in the den. Almost robotic, he turned on the stereo. Listening to the surround sound of Jay-Z's tune "Song Cry," he thought about Paula and he cried like a baby. For the next couple of hours, he drank one Heineken after another as he waited for his mother to arrive home. By the time she did, Cleezy was all cried out. He heard the automatic garage door open and Lolly's car pull up into the garage.

"Cllllleeeeezzzzyyyy," she called out, after spotting his car parked out front. "Hey, baby," she shouted. As she was bringing in her shopping bags, he appeared and just stood across the room. "Boy, you better help yo' momma with these bags."

"For what? It looks like you done helped yo'self," he said dryly.

"Baby, what's wrong? You look like some woman done broke your heart," his mother said as she got closer.

"Yeah." He nodded with tears in his eyes.

"Come here and tell Momma all about it." Lolly reached out to him as if she wanted to embrace him with a hug, but he refused her gesture.

"Momma, stop faking," Cleezy said as he pushed her away.

"What?"

"Why the fuck you take my motherfuckin' scratch?" he yelled, blatantly accusing her.

Lolly looked like she had seen a ghost and then quickly pulled herself together. "You better get out of here with that nonsense," Lolly said.

"You know it ain't no nonsense," he said, reaching into his back pocket and pulling out her latest bank statement. "Where the fuck you get this kind of money from? That bullshit-ass assembly-line job ain't paying like this, even with overtime. And I'm sure if yo' ass had hit the jackpot at Bingo, you would have told me by now. If you ain't pinch off my loot then explain this shit. Explain this shit right here!" Cleezy screamed, as saliva flew with every word. Cleezy reached down and felt the cold steel of his gun brush up against his side.

Lolly swallowed, still sticking to her guns. "I work," she answered, but not meeting his eyes.

"It ain't that much work in the motherfuckin' world." Cleezy then reached in his front pocket and pulled out her pay stub and moved in closer to her, backing her into the corner. "Ma, you don't make shit. And I don't see no goddamn overtime." Lolly shook as Cleezy continued. "You don't make but ten dollars a motherfucking hour but yet you got sixty thousand g's in your account. Sixty fucking thousand dollars?"

Lolly had tears in her eyes. For the first time in her life, one of her underhanded scandals hadn't played out the way she thought it would. She was cold busted. She looked into her son's eyes and saw a side of him that she had never seen before. Hurt, pain, and confusion crossed his face. He was turning into a monster right in front of her eyes. He was no longer the son that she had nurtured and raised from a boy to a man. Never thinking that she would see the day that she would fear her own son, Lolly stood there petrified.

Cleezy looked capable of doing the unthinkable. He put his fingers in her face as he continued to roar in anger. "Just fucking admit it! That's all I want you to do is fucking confess," he screamed at the top of his lungs. Then he just lost it; his mind was in another place.

"Cleezy, stop, baby. I love you," she said, looking into her son's eyes, trying to reach him somehow. "I love you, baby."

In Cleezy's mind he was in a place that he'd never thought he'd return to again: Paula's murder scene. Though he saw his mother's lips saying she loved him, it was Paula's voice that came out. It was Paula's voice that he heard echoing through his head. At that moment he saw Paula's almost lifeless body on the ground, and as he was taking her life, her last words were, "I love you, Cleezy, till death do us part."

Never had he regretted taking a life or sparing one, but his heart was heavy with Paula's laughs, smiles, and cries. No amount of money could ever take it away. There had only been two people on the face of the earth that could surprise Cleezy by crossing him: his mother and Paula. His mother had crossed him. He was dealing with a double-edged sword because he had killed the only woman who had ever been genuine and loved him wholeheartedly. In this case, blood was not thicker than water.

"I want you to know that the sixty g's got blood all over it," Cleezy said as he backed up off of his mother to let her out of the corner.

Silent tears rolled down her face. "Cleezy, please, I'm sorry. I'm sorry. I do love you. Please, I'll give you all the money back tomorrow just as soon as the bank opens."

"Keep it, because it's cost you. It cost you your son. From this day forward you are minus a son." Cleezy turned his back to his mother and headed towards the door. Before leaving the house he called out from the door, "I mean that shit from the bottom of my heart." He looked into his mother's eyes and then closed the door behind him as he exited the house to hit I-95.

Cleezy listened to Jay-Z's song about how he needed a gangsta girl to ride in his passenger seat in the song "Get Yo Mind Right Mami." As he rolled down I-95, he asked for forgiveness and vowed to himself that if he ever encountered a real chick again, he wouldn't let anyone or anything tear them apart. This time it would be until death do them part!

Ms. Celebrity

The road trip to Miami with Farmer John wore Mercy out. Tired and irritable, all she wanted was a hot shower, something to eat, and to get in the bed. After checking in and getting settled into her hotel room, she picked up the phone and called room service.

"Hi, I would like a grilled chicken sandwich, plain with Swiss cheese only and a side of honey mustard," Mercy said.

The attendant read the order back to Mercy, and then she informed her that it would be brought to her room in about thirty minutes. Mercy hung up the phone and hopped in the shower. No sooner had she slipped into her silk lavender pajama short set than there was a knock at the door. The timing was perfect. It was room service with her meal. She was so famished that she didn't even wait for the guy to wheel her food into her room. She lifted her tray right off of the cart herself, handed him a five-dollar tip, and sent him on his way.

Mercy bit into her grilled chicken sandwich. Hungry or not, it was not what she expected.

"What the fuck?" Mercy said as she looked down at the sandwich. "Mayonnaise?"

Immediately Mercy picked up the phone and called downstairs.

"Room service," the voice on the other end of the phone answered. Mercy could tell that it was the same attendant who had taken her order in the first place.

"Yes, this is room 311, and I just ordered room service," Mercy said, struggling to be polite, although her patience was quickly wearing thin.

"Yes?"

"Well, I asked for a plain grilled chicken sandwich with honey mustard on the side and instead you put mayonnaise on it."

"First off, I didn't put anything on it. I'm not the cook; I just take the orders," the attendant said in a joking tone, but Mercy could tell she was serious. *Oh no, this chick didn't disrespect me,* Mercy said to herself. "Secondly, I'm sorry about that. If you like we can bring you another sandwich."

"You're not the cook, but now you deliver the food?" Mercy shot back. "I thought you just took the orders." The attendant was about to respond, but Mercy cut her off. "Anyway, I would like very much if you would deliver another sandwich, and I'm certain that for my inconvenience there won't be a charge to my room." Once again the attendant tried to say something, and once again Mercy cut her off. "Yes, I thought so."

Click! Mercy slammed the phone down.

About fifteen minutes later there was a knock on Mercy's hotel room door. It was room service. Mercy opened the door, and this time it was a different man delivering her order. Mercy took the tray, and the man stood there for a minute.

"I know you don't think you're about to get a tip," Mercy huffed. "Here's a tip for you: Tell the broad taking orders to get it right the first time."

Mercy sent the attendant on his way. She bit into the chicken sandwich they had just brought her—and again it had mayon-naise.

That trifling funny-sounding beyatch done this shit to deliberately get under my skin. Mercy's first instincts were to call that bitch up and check her, but she decided to do her one better. Mercy slipped on a pair of jogging pants over her pajama shorts and her lavender spa flip-flops with the silk flowers on them. She then grabbed both the chicken sandwiches and made her way down to the hotel restaurant.

This simple bitch don't know who the fuck she playing with and the type of day I done had, Mercy said angrily to herself the entire way down to the restaurant. She even rehearsed in the elevator mirrored doors what she was going to say to the waitress. "I hope your ass is hungry, you minimum-wage beyatch," Mercy said, pointing to her reflection in the mirror, imagining herself shoving the sandwiches down the girl's throat and making her eat it.

Unfortunately for Mercy, 'cause she wanted to tear into that ass, but fortunately for the attendant who took the order, the woman's shift had just ended. Mercy missed her by less than a minute. The new guy on duty had to bear the brunt of Mercy's complaint. As Mercy stood at the end of the bar raising holy hell about the food, she didn't pay attention to who was sitting at the other end of the bar.

"Damn if ain't Ms. Celebrity," she heard a male voice say.

"Oh, my God," Mercy said, surprised to see who the voice belonged to. Although she hadn't seen him in two years, she ran over and gave him a hug. "Hey, how are you?"

"I'm good, now that I see you," he said, as smooth as Billy Dee Williams.

Mercy couldn't help but blush. "Stop trying to play me, C-Note." She smiled.

He looked deeply into her eyes and said, "I'm serious, and call me Cleezy. The last time I saw you shit was crazy, and due to circumstances beyond my control, I pushed you away; C-Note pushed you away. However, I'm a new man, and Cleezy will never let a good woman like you get away." He winked at Mercy and took a sip of his drink.

"I hear you," Mercy said, impressed by his words. He looked the same, but there was something different about him. She couldn't put her finger on it, but she liked it.

"Don't just hear me, believe me."

The attraction between the two of them was magnetic. Mercy had only had those feelings three times in her life, and none of them was with him—until now.

The dominating aura that hung over his head like a halo just swallowed Mercy up. He seemed to encircle her in an unspoken comfort zone. It was almost uneasy for Mercy, because it was a feeling like that of a father figure, like he could be her protector, the same way her daddy used to be. But then again, what little girl from the ghetto wasn't on a quest for daddy?

She didn't know how to take Cleezy's last comment, so she changed the topic of the conversation. "So what you doing in Miami?"

"Business," he quickly said. "And you?"

She smiled and replied, "Business."

They continued the small talk, but the lust between them was thick.

"Are you taking your food back up to your room, or will you stay down here?" the bartender asked Mercy.

"Excuse me?" Mercy said, forgetting why she had come down-stairs in the first place.

"Your chicken sandwich?" the bartender asked.

"Oh, yeah. I'll take it to my room, so please give it to me to go."

"Yes, ma'am," the bartender said, turning away to oblige Mercy's request.

"My man," Cleezy called to him. "Please let me get my check."

By the time Cleezy settled up his tab, the bartender had handed Mercy's food to her. "Again, I'm sorry for the mix-up," he said sincerely.

"No problem," she said to the bartender and turned to Cleezy. "Are you staying at this hotel?"

"Are you?"

"I am, but we ain't talking about me."

"Do you like this hotel?"

"Yes, it's cool. Why, where are you staying?"

"With you. Wherever you want to stay. If you want to stay here, we can go up to my suite. If you want to go somewhere else, we can do that."

Mercy didn't want to seem like a skeezer, but she wanted more than anything at that moment to go with Cleezy. What she didn't want, though, was to be just another Miami fling, so she went with her first instincts. "I am not trying to go with you."

Sensing Mercy's lips saying no but her eyes meaning yes, Cleezy said, "Look, bottom line is this, shawdy: Life is too short and time is too precious a commodity to waste another minute without you, or better yet, for you or I to not be us."

That comment was as smooth as silk to her ears. *Damn, this nigga game is airtight,* Mercy thought.

"Yo, I know you think it's game, right? But it ain't. I am dead-ass serious. We've been trying to make this shit happen for longer than a minute. I know a good girl when I see one, and I am not letting you get away from me again."

She looked him over, searching his face, hoping for something to show her whether he was just trying to get his fuck on or if he could possibly want her for her. Did he know her reputation for being one of the best and most loyal mules to ever leave her mark on I-95? And if so, was he looking to recruit her?

Mercy sighed. "Look, I'm hungry and tired. Let's just do breakfast in the morning, all right?" Mercy started out of the restaurant, and Cleezy walked beside her.

"Yo, you think I'm playing? I ain't letting you get away from me."

"Stop playing."

"Look, three strikes and you're out, and this is our third encounter and I ain't trying to be out." They stopped in front of the elevator. "So we like glue now, baby. We stuck." He pressed the button to go up. "We like shoes, a pair." The elevator door opened, and he motioned for her to get in. She did. He put his key card into the slot so he could gain access to the presidential floor where his suite was located. "We like those Gucci jeans you had on that night—tight."

"Damn, it's like that," Mercy chuckled. She knew right then and there that she wasn't about to push button number three. Room 311 would remain vacant that night as the elevator rode to the top floor.

CHAPTER 27

Me Plus You Equals Us

They stepped off of the elevator and into Cleezy's suite. It was the largest hotel room she had ever seen. Even bigger than her three-bedroom apartment. It looked like Cleezy had made this room his home away from home. Mercy looked around at all of the shopping bags with items still in them and the clothes all over that place that still had tags on them. Hassim had put Cleezy on hold for the last five days because his people had him on hold, so Cleezy had made himself at home. He did all the things that Miami offered ballers like himself. He had been living like a king, shopping every day, funning out of control, Jet Skiing, windsurfing, partying on yachts, eating and drinking the best money could buy. Being able to splurge in Miami came with lots of perks, including the occasional ménage à trois with some of the baddest bitches in the city that didn't cost him an iron dime because he looked and played the part. The broads had the disease to please, hoping to luck up and cash out on him as one of his long-term bitches. They felt like their pussy was crack. Their scheme was to give it away at first, just to hook a nigga, but then he'd have to pay. Too bad broads had it all fucked up, because Cleezy wasn't taking none of them hoes home.

Cleezy and Mercy rented a couple of pay-per-view movies and kicked it about this and that while catching up. Mercy took off her jogging pants and sat next to Cleezy on the couch, then got up to get herself something to drink and turned and asked, "C-Note, what you want to drink?"

"Look, baby, come here for a minute," he said softly.

She walked over to him. She could tell something was wrong by the look on his face. "What's wrong?" she asked.

He grabbed her and put his arms around her. "Come here," he said, embracing her with a warm hug.

She could tell that something was on his mind by the way he chose his words. "Look, baby. Please don't call me C-Note. I feel it's a form of disrespect when people call me that name." He took a deep breath.

Mercy was surprised. She felt uneasy, but she tried to play it off. "I apologize, but when I met you that was your name."

"Cleezy is my name now, and everybody calls me that, even my momma."

Downstairs she hadn't really paid it that much attention. But this time the way he called himself Cleezy, with such strength and conviction, got her panties wet. It dawned on her right then and there: She had heard talk all over Richmond how Cleezy's name was ringing, but she'd had no idea that C-Note was the person they were talking about and that C-Note or Cleezy or whoever he was had been living a double life.

"Okay. I really didn't know, but if I am so special why I gotta call you what everybody else does?"

"As a matter of fact, you can call me Conrad. That's my government name, and nobody calls me that. Nobody."

"Wooowww!" she said, trying to be funny. "I feel so important."

"You should always feel important when I'm concerned." He leaned in to kiss her. Mercy couldn't help but to kiss him back.

Before she knew it his hand was down her shorts. At first, when he touched her private place, Mercy was almost embarrassed. She didn't want him to know how wet she was, how wet he had made her just by being him. He looked up at her.

"Damn, baby," he said.

Mercy leaned in and began tonguing him to get his mind off of her wetness, but that was to no avail as he continued to play in it, only making her wetter.

"Take these off," Cleezy whispered as he helped her slide her shorts down her legs and off of her ankles. Still fully dressed, he got on top of her and continued kissing her, his hand separating the two of them as he began fingering her. The faster he plunged his fingers in and out of her, the more Mercy groaned and ground herself against his hand.

Cleezy knew Mercy was on the verge of coming, but he wanted to be in her so she could come on his dick. He undid his pants and pushed them down just enough to pull himself from out of his pants and place it against Mercy's wetness.

"No, no," Mercy said, pressing her hands against Cleezy's chest and softly pushing.

"What's wrong?"

"This. I don't want it to be like this."

Cleezy sighed. "I feel you, ma," he said as he got off of Mercy and zipped his pants up.

"You mad?" Mercy asked, afraid he would think of her as a tease.

"Hell, no. I ain't trippin' like that, ma," Cleezy said.

"You sure?"

Cleezy looked down at Mercy, who was sliding her shorts back on. He then extended his hand to her to help her up off the couch. "Come on. Let's just go to bed."

He turned the television off, then led Mercy into his bedroom, where the two just lay in each other's arms. Mercy had her back to Cleezy's chest, and he had his arms around her. It was dark. Their eyes were closed. Neither spoke, but neither of them was asleep. They were too busy thinking about being intimate with one another. It was a feeling neither of them could seem to control.

Softly and slowly, Cleezy began rubbing his hand up and down Mercy's leg, causing chills to run all over her body. Just his touch made her want to come. She moaned and squirmed against him. She felt his nature rising. His hardening dick against her ass only made her wet all over again. Cleezy's hand managed to find its way down Mercy's pants again to her crotch. Once again, her wetness only made him horny.

"No, don't," Mercy panted as Cleezy began to remove her pajama shorts.

"Come on, I ain't going nowhere. I promise, this ain't no hit-and-run."

"I hear you, but whatever," Mercy said doubtfully.

"It ain't about no whatever," Cleezy assured her, pulling her face around gently, then reaching over to kiss her softly on the lips. The kiss put her over the edge, and it was as if that was the kiss that sealed the deal. Mercy turned over on her back and opened herself up to Cleezy. He dove deep inside her, drowning in her wetness.

"Oh, Cleezy," Mercy moaned.

Cleezy paused briefly. He quickly rammed himself in and out of Mercy. She tried to throw her hips at him, but couldn't seem to keep up. She still felt good, though, good enough for Cleezy to explode inside of her.

Although the sex wasn't mind-blowing like it was with Paula, nor did Mercy have shit on the freaks of the week that he had encountered in Miami, Cleezy didn't care, because he and Mercy had something else. She was smart and funny, and he knew he had found his true equal in Mercy. He wouldn't make a mistake again. The physical could come later, but it was the mental Cleezy was wrapped up in. They had great chemistry in every other way, and it was a meeting of the minds—a meeting that, if he could help it, would never be adjourned.

CHAPTER 28

Hugging the Block

The next morning Mercy and Cleezy lay in each other's arms. Right in the middle of their pillow talk Mercy's cell phone rang. She looked at the clock and knew that it was Hyena.

"Daggone, I forgot I got to go this meeting," Mercy said, pressing a button rejecting Hyena's phone call. She wasn't about to talk about work in front of Cleezy—not the work she was doing for Hyena.

"Let's get up and get dressed and go to the meeting, then. I'll roll with you," Cleezy said in a scratchy morning voice.

Mercy didn't know what to say. Cleezy was pleasure. This was business. "Ummm, you can't go," Mercy said straight out, not bothering to fumble for words.

"Why? I could just sit in the waiting room," Cleezy said.

She slowly said, "It ain't that type of party."

"What do you mean?"

"Look, I want to keep it real with you, but I can't right now," Mercy said, getting up and going for her jogging pants.

"Mercy, you made me jump through hoops to make you understand how I want to be with you and now you tell me you can't keep it real. Who's gettin' played here?" He sat up in the bed and looked at her. "This is some real bullshit, you know that, right?" He got up and slipped his boxers on and proceeded to the bathroom.

"No," Mercy said, feeling bad, following behind him. The last thing she wanted him to think was that she was trying to play him, that she had somebody else she was kickin' it with that she had to get shit straight with.

Not realizing that Mercy was following him, Cleezy went into the bathroom, pushed the door behind him and proceeded to sit down on the toilet and use the bathroom.

"Listen, boo," Mercy said as she barged into the bathroom.

"It's cool. Keep your little secrets and I'll keep mine. I know how I'ma carry it. It's cool."

"Nooo . . . ," she whined.

"Shut the door, so I can shit in peace," Cleezy ordered, and shot her an evil look.

She didn't follow his cold orders. She stood there as tears came to her eyes. She could hear the frustration in his voice, a feeling that was mirrored in her heart. "Look, my story ain't pretty, but I'll share it with you."

"I'm listening," he said. He looked up at her. "You know what? Wait a minute, let me finish this here."

Mercy waved her hand across her nose, then exited the bathroom, closing the door behind her. She went back into the bedroom and sat down on the bed to try to gather her thoughts.

Her heart started beating fast when she heard the toilet flush and even faster when she heard him washing his hands. She didn't know if she should walk away and let their night together be just that, one night together, or if she should just come clean about who Mercy Jiles really was. That she wasn't the superstar success he thought she was, but that she was a broke bitch getting raped by some broad, her sister at that, who'd sold her a dream. A dream that she'd bought. That she wasn't a strong stallion at all, but instead some fuckin' mule, a workhorse. It had been a long time since Mercy had given herself to a man, not just physically but emotionally as well, and Cleezy was indeed a mind trip. Did she really want to risk having him think that she was just another chick hiding a shovel behind her back, ready to go diggin' for gold? Mercy decided that she was going to have to tell him the truth. If Cleezy wasn't all talk and really wanted a real relationship with a down-ass chick—not just any chick, but her—then she was about to call his bluff.

Cleezy came out of the bathroom and sat down beside Mercy on the bed. She took a deep breath, then started her unrehearsed, from-the-hip spiel.

"Look, my daddy always told me to never confess to anything in this lifetime," Mercy spoke.

Cleezy chuckled. "Word?" Mercy nodded. "That's the same shit my daddy told me."

"For real?"

Cleezy nodded. "Okay, so continue."

"Well, first let me say this: My daddy was my everything. He died when I was little, and my whole life changed."

"I feel you," Cleezy interrupted. "Mine was too. He passed on when I was little, but I remember everything—every single thing he ever told me."

"Me too. That's sometimes what keeps me going. I know he's watching over me." Mercy knew she had to change the subject because she was already on an emotional roller coaster. "Like I said, I don't confess to a damn thing. But since I'm trying to build something with you, I guess there can't be any secrets, right? But at the same time I don't want you to take what I'm saying to you and try to use it to your advantage."

"Come on now, be real!"

"No, I'm just saying."

"A'ight, well, just say it then."

"Look, the people I signed the deal with, my script and all, they just basically fucked me. I'm broke. It's plain and simple. The fame always comes before the fortune. And with that being said, I had to do some things that I had no business doing in order to eat, you know." A weird look passed across Cleezy's face. Mercy sucked her teeth and said, "No, nothing like that, nasty." Cleezy let out a sigh of relief. He wasn't trying to get caught up in no déjà vu mess that would make him reminisce over Paula.

Mercy continued to speak, telling Cleezy the story about her dealings with Tallya and Benjamin from start to finish. He listened attentively as Mercy told him everything from the hotel scene with Raheem and him snitching, to the whole hotel episode when they tried to rob her.

Cleezy sat for a minute trying to take everything in. Mercy didn't know what to think. She didn't know what was running through his mind about her. After she was done, to Mercy's surprise, Cleezy took her into his arms. His embrace seemed to say: "Don't worry about it, ma, I'm going to take authority over the situation" and let her know he had her back.

"Look, baby," Cleezy said, releasing her and looking in her eyes. "This is how it's got to go down. Both of us can't be on I-95. If anybody is going to get their hands dirty, it's going to be me. Not you. You have a dream, you have a career, a way out. That's what I need you to focus on, your craft. Your talent. I need you to be legit—if not for you, then for us."

"I know, but I-95 has been my only means of survival for so long. I finally thought I was going to be able to leave that life behind when I hooked up with Tallya, but then when she did that shit to me, I had no choice."

"I feel you, but peace this, you throwing in the towel." She tried to speak, but he cut her off. "You got me now, and I'm going to make sho' you a'ight. That's on everything I love," Cleezy said sincerely.

Mercy didn't know what to think. Everything Cleezy said sounded good. She felt the chemistry—she knew there was something there—but was it enough for her to cut off the hand that was feeding her, the hand that had seemed to come swoop her up just when she was about to fall? She really didn't want to break off the relationship with Hyena. Although her work was done, she had been waiting around to see if she could pick up another job on the way back. But instead she called Hyena right there in front of Cleezy. She told him that she had a family emergency and had to go back home so that the meeting had to be canceled. After Mercy hung up with Hyena she flopped down on the bed, not knowing what her next move would be, realizing that she had taken her fate out of the hands of one man only to give it to yet another. It seemed to be a cycle Mercy had no control over.

"Look, I want you to focus on your new movie and continue to create larger-than-life scripts, a'ight," Cleezy said. "The public loves you, and you have to be able to be in the public eye."

"Without a doubt, I am going to always write, but I'm not going to be in the public eye no more."

"Why?"

She didn't answer at first, but then Cleezy gave her a look and reminded her to "keep it real."

"Because I'm just not what people are expecting. I mean, look at me. Do I look like the success story everybody kept hearing about at first? Look at me. I mean really look at me. I'm too damn fat to be on anybody's red carpet, and image is everything," Mercy admitted.

Cleezy looked her up and down for a minute. Yeah, she was thick, but for some reason, until she'd pointed it out, he had never thought twice about it. She was phat but not fat, and very sexy to him. It didn't matter to him. "Well, we gotta get a trainer then, and we'll work out together. Me drinking and eating good got me getting a little pudgy." He patted his stomach.

"I been damn near working out for years and it don't work. I need a quick fix."

"Like what?"

"I need some plastic surgery."

"I don't really agree with that mess. That's white people's shit."

"Well, I do, and that's what I want."

"Look, I don't want you cutting on yourself." He took her hands and continued. "You cool just the way you are, and for real, don't nobody want no skinny broad."

"I ain't trying to be skinny. I just want to be happy with my body and my weight. I have been struggling with my weight for so long."

"I understand."

"Really, do you?"

"Yeah, I do. Are you sure this is going to make you happy, though?"

"Yes, I am really, really sure. A flat stomach and a small waist would be great for my self-image."

"A'ight, well, we'll make an appointment and see what the doctor is talking about."

Mercy was shocked. "Are you serious?"

"Why not?"

"But I told you I ain't got no money for that. The money I have is for paying my bills."

"Don't worry. Didn't I tell you I got you? I got that. I'm serious, Mercy. I ain't about talk. I'm a man who knows what he wants off the bat. I don't have to go through all the pleasantries of dating and all that bullshit. I just know."

"You just know, huh?" Mercy said, feeling good as she heard the sincerity in Cleezy's voice.

"Yeah. And if this is going to make my baby happy and help enhance your image, then it's done. Look, don't worry about the money—just focus on your career."

Although Cleezy had never been the type to take care of any woman besides his scandalous mother, he was willing to have Mercy's back without a doubt.

"Okay," she agreed, and gave Cleezy a hug. "Just promise me something: Don't leave me."

"Just don't ever cross me."

CHAPTER 29

Pretty Woman

When Mercy and Cleezy returned to Richmond they found themselves in a whirlwind romance. When Cleezy wasn't grindin', he was taking Mercy out to the movies. This might not have been a big deal for most, but Cleezy wasn't the "going out to the movies" type of guy. If he wanted to watch a flick, he just copped the movie bootleg; but the first time he went out and bought a bootleg DVD Mercy clowned. After breaking it down to him how she felt about someone else making money off of something she put her blood, sweat, and tears into while she didn't see a penny of the profit, he had a new opinion about buying bootleg shit. He simply didn't do it. Other than that little incident, Cleezy and Mercy rarely had disagreements about anything.

They never imagined that they could have so much in common. Within a month, Mercy had used all her movie contract as financial leverge to purchase a nice $500,000 spec home. Cleezy would give her the cash to buy the home outright later, so no questions would be asked about the source of the funds. That sucker was nice, too. The couple who'd originally had it custom-built ended up separating between the time the hole was dug and the time the carpet was laid. Luckily for Mercy and Cleezy, the couple had excellent taste, and since it was a spec home, they were able to move in right away.

The 5,000-square-foot, five-level split home had two master suites, both equipped with Jacuzzis in the corner of the room. The suite that Mercy and Cleezy shared had a marble shower area that was the size of a walk-in closet. Over their bed was a five-by-eight skylight with an electric shade. Although Mercy couldn't do that much damage in the kitchen, it was full of state-of-the-art stainless-steel appliances. The main attraction was the lower-level entertainment center that had the perfect theater screen they would use one day to view Mercy's movies.

For the first time ever, Mercy truly felt like she was living the life she was supposed to. Everything seemed to happen so fast. Cleezy deliberately tried not to keep long hours in the streets, but on nights when he came in at the wee hours of the morning, Mercy didn't argue with him about it. Most arguments between drug dealers and their girls were because of the late nights, but Mercy understood that hustlers could actually be out hustling and chasing the block all night long. But Mercy hugged the block herself. It wasn't literally the drug block, but she kept late hours on her computer perfecting her craft, chasing dollars. Then there were his business trips, which she didn't care about either as long as she could reach him. After all, she did the long nights on the computer and traveled herself to promote her project. Their relationship had an easy rhythm, and the communication was on point.

Other than Cleezy leaving to make that money and her time spent working on her scripts, they spent the majority of their time with each other. They had the same tastes. They could be driving down the street and if an old hip-hop song came on the radio, they both would sing the song word for word. Their theme songs were "Sunshine" by Jay-Z and Foxy Brown, and "All I Need" by

Mary J. Blige and Method Man. When "Me and My Bitch" came on by Biggie, he sang the words to her. Sometimes people in the cars alongside them would look at them and shake their heads.

Cleezy catered to Mercy in every way. He rubbed her feet and always treated her like nothing less than a queen. Cleezy never claimed to be a huge romantic, but he would leave notes for her all the time. One morning she woke up and found a note on Cleezy's pillow that read "I'm downstairs fixing you breakfast in bed." If they went out and Mercy picked up something to look at twice, Cleezy would often make it his business to go back and get it for her, no matter what the cost.

If there was one weak spot in the relationship, it was the sex. Mercy had a hard time relaxing around the more experienced Cleezy. It was as if now that she found true love, the sex meant more and she worried she couldn't please him. And although Cleezy couldn't have asked for a more perfect relationship, he knew that he had to do something to help Mercy get her hips and back into the sex. He ended up paying for her to go to belly dancing classes. He told her that it was in order to tighten her stomach muscles, but really he wanted her to get the rhythm and learn to move her hips the way he needed her to. The sex got better and better each time.

Mercy had found her prince, she lived in a castle, she had the career of her dreams. She and Cleezy were on their way to happily ever after.

CHAPTER 30

Cut the Check

Three months later, Mercy flew to Los Angeles to meet with her agent, Davey, and pick up her check. Although he had told her he would overnight the check from the movie company to her, she was so excited to finally get her first huge check that she flew to LA to pick it up and to thank her agent in person. Not only did her agent give her a check, but he also gave her the date when her next movie would be shown on the big screen. Unlike her first, Mercy wouldn't be directing this film, and she was thankful for that. Directing had been fun, but she didn't want to take all that time away from Cleezy or from her writing. However, it was written in her contract that they would call her in as a consultant and she would get an associate producer credit. Davey explained to her that whatever she had experienced with Bermuda Triangle, that was small change and this was big-time.

"You are about to be larger than life," Davey said. "And so is this project. You have no idea what kind of press you are about to receive." Mercy smiled as Davey continued talking. "So you have to prepare your guest lists for your premieres. The studio needs that within the next month or so, so start thinking about that."

"I will," Mercy said as she sat at the table across from Davey in a trendy LA restaurant, getting a glimpse of the paparazzi who flashed their cameras at whichever star they could spot dining.

"It's only a matter of months before they know who you are, and your life is never going to be the same."

"You really think so?"

Davey smiled. "I know so."

Mercy smiled from ear to ear. Davey and she had a great relationship; and from day one, he'd always been intrigued with Mercy, where she came from and her thoughts. It made Mercy feel good that he wasn't just concerned about the money she could make him, but about her as a person. As Davey slid in another comment, Mercy's smile got cut short. "You know we are going to have to really get your situation with Tallya taken care of."

"I know." Mercy frowned. Just hearing Tallya's name made her blood boil.

"I know she's your sister and all but—"

"You know what I just found out?" Mercy jumped in.

"What?"

"My uncle Roland, who is in the clinker—," Mercy began, and looked at Davey.

"Unh-hunh," he said, nodding.

"Well, I spoke to him right before I left to come out here."

"He called you collect?"

"Davey, how the hell else you think I am going to speak to him?" she joked, because at times Davey could be so clueless about life outside of Hollywood.

"I didn't know, maybe you went to visit him or something. Anyway, continue, continue," he said.

"Well, he told me that the bitch might not even be my real sister! That she has always been suspect from day one. My daddy was not the type to get no blood test or none of that done. He believed if he slept with a woman and she said the baby was his, then it was. But in my heart I know that bitch ain't no sister of mine. My daddy didn't raise us up like that."

"Well, sister, mother, or brother, she's going to have to cough up your money. I am going to have my attorney look over your contracts to see if he can find a loophole."

"I have my attorney working on it too, but all this legal stuff is taking too much time," she said with a frustrated look on her face.

"I know. Just be patient," he looked at her and said. "So, next week I am going to meet with your friend Kathy. She said she met you in the airport and promised you an endorsement deal."

"Oh, yeah, she got in touch with me and told me she had tried to contact me through Tallya and Tallya wouldn't give her any info. After a few months she finally got in touch with me, and I gave her your number."

"She's probably going to want to do something soon, so that you can wear her cosmetics for the premiere. She knows she's going to have to move fast, because if she doesn't, someone else will."

"I really want to deal with her because she kept her word."

"And she wants to deal with you, too. Here. Enjoy all this success and know that you are going to make a lot of money," he said as he handed Mercy a check. As she pulled it out of the envelope, Davey could see the awe written all over her face. "And there's more where that came from. You know that's only part of it."

She felt like jumping up and doing the holy ghost dance, but she kept her composure until Davey was gone.

After lunch, when she was alone, she looked at her check. She had never had that much money in her life. She immediately called Cleezy.

"Baby, I need a Brink's truck to help me carry this big-ass check," Mercy exclaimed.

"For real?" Cleezy responded.

"It's weighing me down."

Cleezy laughed. "Congratulations, baby. I wish I was there with you so we could celebrate together."

"Me too, but I'll be home tomorrow and we can celebrate then."

"You know that. Just hold on tight to that check. When you get home, deposit that shit right in the bank."

"Boo, you know I got you if there's anything you need to do with this money."

"Naw, just save it all for a rainy day. You know I take care of you, and just because you got a fat-ass check, I'm still your provider."

"I know, but just so you know that this is our money, not just mine."

Cleezy switched up the conversation a bit. "Use that money I gave you before you left and buy something nice. You in LA, baby!"

"I know, and you know they got some good shops out here."

"Yeah, so just go splurge with my money and keep yours in the bank, just like you always do."

"Boo, honestly, I probably can't wear nothing in those shops and especially the extra-high-end boutiques. That stuff is made for petite women."

Cleezy tried to be comforting. "Look, baby, it's a whole bunch of shops out there and a lot of shoe stores."

"Boo, I can't wait for my lipo. I'm tired of all this fat I'm carrying around."

"I told you before, baby, and I meant what I said. If it makes you happy, then we just gon' cut him the check. It's just that simple. For the record, I don't see nothing wrong with you. Big or small, I love you, and that shit right there ain't going to ever change. But I'll support your decision."

As the date of Mercy's movie premiere grew closer, she nailed down a date with the doctor to perform her plastic surgery so that she would have enough time to heal fully. Mercy decided on a tummy tuck and some lipo. She was scared of going under, but with Cleezy by her side the whole way, she proceeded with her surgery. She needed a whole month just to walk upright and another month to get back into the groove of things, and still she had to take it easy. As she healed, she lay in the bed and tried to think about all the important people who had impacted her life to invite to the premiere. She couldn't wait for everybody to see the new Mercy. Nurse Allen, the nurse who took care of her after she was beaten in the hotel, was one of the folks she invited. Mercy wasn't sure if she still worked at the hospital, so she decided to call and see.

"Hi, I'm calling to speak with a Nurse Allen," Mercy said into the phone.

"May I ask who's calling?" the operator asked.

"This is Mercy Jiles. I was a patient of Nurse Allen's."

"Hold please, and I'll connect you to her unit."

Mercy sat on hold for a few minutes listening to what sounded like elevator music until a voice picked up on the other end of the phone.

"Nurse Allen speaking," she said.

"Hi, Nurse Allen. I don't know if you remember me or not, but my name is Mercy Jil—"

Nurse Allen cut her off. "Ohhh . . . I can't believe it. Mercy Jiles. My gosh, girl. I am so proud of you and your accomplishments."

"Thank you so much," Mercy said, humbled.

"You know you were my favorite patient."

"And you know you were my favorite nurse."

"I don't believe you."

"You were."

"Get out of here," she said, surprised.

"I heard all about and saw how you took care of me."

"I tried to do my best to protect you. As soon as you came in, I took your things and put them away so the police wouldn't get them. I didn't know if you were doing something you had no business to be doing or not, but I did know that you were too pretty to be caught up in that madness."

"Thank you so much!"

"No problem, baby. I'm just glad that your sister showed up and I was able to give her your money to hold."

"Money?" Mercy said, confused.

"Yeah, all that money in your suitcase. It had to be over twenty thousand dollars. I know you got knocked up pretty bad, but don't nobody forget no twenty thousand dollars. Lucky for you that your sister—God bless her little heart for staying at your bedside day and night—was able to hold on to it for you."

Mercy's temperature rose. Tallya had stung her again. Mercy didn't want Nurse Allen to pick up on her boiling anger, so she played it off and continued with her reason for calling.

"Yes, and I truly thank you so much! Look, I want you to come to my movie premiere."

"I wouldn't miss it for nothing in the world."

"Well, I need to get your mailing address so we can get the special passes out to you."

Mercy could not wait to hang up the phone to call Cleezy to let him know about Tallya's larceny-hearted behind. Once she wrote down Nurse Allen's address and they said their good-byes, Mercy hung up the phone. She was piping mad, and picked the phone right back up to call Cleezy.

"Boo, I can't believe this hating-ass no-good beyatch!" Mercy yelled into the phone. "That ho Tallya not only tried to cock block me from getting a cosmetic endorsement deal with my friend Kathy, the one I told you about that I met at the airport—"

"Umm-hmm," Cleezy said, waiting for Mercy to get to the point.

"—well, that bitch had the nerve to keep my twenty fuckin' grand. Them dudes never even got me for my paper; that bitch got me. The bitch straight up robbed me. When I see that bitch I swear I'ma beat her ass. I promise you that. So just have the bail money in the stash."

"Calm down," Cleezy said in a relaxed tone. "Baby, listen. Don't focus on that negative shit. Focus on the positive."

"I just hate that bitch not only won't pay me for my work, but the little bit of money that she did pay me"—Mercy's voice got louder as she stopped pacing the floor and emphasized—"she paid me from my own shit. That bitch paid me with my own goddamn money. How about that? She over there eating bon-bons, sippin' on latte, and ain't write shit. And the only finger she lifts is to spread the Grey Poupon and count my money."

"I know, baby," Cleezy said, still in a relaxed tone. "I'm on my way home and we gon' talk about it then. Just calm down."

Cleezy's cool tone made Mercy feel less upset. "I'm sorry, baby. I know you are working, but I just had to vent, and who better than to my knight in shining armor?"

"I know, baby. I know, but check this; I'll be home in a little while and we'll talk then."

"Okay, baby," Mercy said as she hung up the phone. If Mercy only knew that her Prince Charming wasn't always charming when someone violated anything that was his, and without a doubt, Mercy was his and Tallya was in violation.

CHAPTER 31

It's a Wrap

It was during the wee hours in the morning when Cook'em-up and Cleezy crept down the wide foyer leading to the master bedroom of Benjamin Arlow's Hamptons mansion. The security wasn't as airtight as the owners thought it was. In the forty seconds the alarm system allowed for the homeowner to punch in their security code, Cook'em-up had already disarmed the system. If they had known that it was going to be that easy, then the task at hand would have been completed days ago.

"Get the fuck up, bitch," Cleezy yelled as he stood over Tallya, who had been sleeping like a princess, probably counting money in her sleep. "Bitch, get the fuck up."

Tallya jumped up in surprise and woke up Benjamin, who saw what looked like two black ninjas at their bedside.

"Don't try nothing stupid, Grandpa, because my man ain't rocked nobody in a hot down-south minute," Cook'em-up warned him.

"W-What's wrong? T-Take whatever you want," a nervous Benjamin said.

"Get the fuck up out of the bed, bitch! Your beauty rest is over," Cleezy said, pulling Tallya up out of the bed by the arm.

"Bitch, move faster. I ain't never been no woman beater, but I will beat the shit out of you and kill you just on GP after I get what I want."

"What is it that you want?" Benjamin said in a calm tone, making it clear that he wanted peace. His old butt wasn't on no Superman shit, trying to save the day. "Money? Is it money that you want? I can get you money."

"Shut the fuck up and just listen," Cook'em-up said, and turned to Cleezy. "Yo, man, you deal with Gramps and I'll handle her."

Cleezy released Tallya with a push into Cook'em-up's hands. Cook'em-up then ordered Tallya to take him to where she kept her books. Tallya led him into her office.

"Sit the fuck down," Cook'em-up said as he pushed her down onto the expensive brown leather couch in her office.

"Please, just tell me what you want? I'll do whatever you want," Tallya said, insinuating that she'd do anything, even if it meant sex.

"Bitch, please." He laughed.

"Please, just don't hurt me," she sobbed.

"Oh, now you want to cry like a bitch, huh?"

Cleezy was in the bedroom with Benjamin, who was terrified and yet tried to remain calm while getting to the bottom of things.

"I don't understand," Benjamin pleaded. "What is it that's going on here?"

"Look, old man, it's like this," Cleezy started. "Your bitch ain't playing fair with you or with her affiliates in her little bullshit-ass company that you fronted. And as you know, what your bitch does reflects on you. I've followed your career. You've always seemed to be a pretty respectable player in the game. I got a lot of respect for you, so that's why I'm talking to you man to man. I didn't come in here to make this place a massacre or tie you up or none of that. A nigga like you, I know your kind and I know you ain't trying to die for no bitch. Or are you?"

Benjamin shook his head. "Hell no. Die for a broad . . . I got too many of them to die for just one."

"Okay then, playa, we're on the same page." Cleezy didn't raise his voice as he continued schooling Benjamin. "My man got the broad in the other room. I need you to go in there and get all of the contracts that she has signed with her artists. I need copies of them all." Cleezy began to run down his list of demands. "The contracts need to be not only burned, but I need documentation that she is releasing each and every artist out of their contracts and that their rights will revert back to each and every one of them. Just in case you try some shit."

"No problem," Benjamin said without hesitation.

"I want the documents faxed and e-mailed. But first I want you to call your attorney right now and let him know that you want the company dismantled because you and Tallya had a fight. Say something like you caught her fucking a nigga in your shit and the bitch is done." Cleezy handed him the phone, and Benjamin did as he was told. Then Cleezy had him follow up in an e-mail to his attorney. Benjamin looked up from the computer, shaking. Cleezy thought he was going to fall over into convulsions.

"What is it? You all right, old man?"

"I need a smoke," Benjamin said, nodding towards the drawer on the credenza behind him.

Cleezy gave him a Cuban cigar, and they sat and had a drink together like two old college buddies as they waited for the attorney to call Benjamin to tell him that the release documents had been drawn up.

"I swear, man," Benjamin said. "I didn't know she wasn't paying her people."

"Well, she wasn't," Cleezy informed him. "If she was, I wouldn't be here now."

"I believe you. It's just that there have been times when she came to me for the money she needed to pay them."

"Well, the joke was on you, huh?"

Eventually the attorney phoned Benjamin to let him know that he was faxing the documents. Once they arrived, Cleezy had Benjamin take him to the office where Cook'em-up and Tallya were. Benjamin walked into the room with his cigar in his mouth, placed the documents and a nice Montblanc ink pen in front of her, and said, "Sign right here."

Tallya skimmed over the documents. "Baby, what's this? Why are you doing this? My company?"

"My company," Benjamin corrected her. "Just sign them."

Tears filled Tallya's eyes as she began signing on the dotted line. Benjamin might as well have been pouring gasoline on every dollar she ever got and lighting a match to it. The life she had been living was over.

"There's one more thing you guys forgot about," Benjamin said.

Cleezy looked at him with a puzzled look on his face. "Pardon me?" Cleezy looked over at Cook'em-up as if saying, "Is this nigga stupid or something? Damn, I know we were drinking together, but I know he ain't about to help us out."

"You nice fellas need to go into her purse and get her checkbook so that she can pay the artists whatever they are due from her own personal checking account. I'm sure she has it there. I mean, it has to be somewhere," Benjamin said, turning his attention to Tallya, "since there isn't any money in the company account and the only thing that has been paid out of that account are bills to Louis Vuitton, Chanel, and Saks."

Cleezy watched as Tallya damn near had a nervous breakdown coming off all of those ducats that she had hidden away in her own personal account.

"And don't even think about trying to stop payment on those fuckin' checks, either. You stop payment, bitch, you stop breathing," Cleezy sharply and coldly reminded her. Tallya looked up at him, and his eyes confirmed to her that he meant business.

Cook'em-up suddenly intervened, as if having an epiphany. "You's a smart little bitch." He then looked up at Cleezy. "It was in the name. It was all in the name."

Tallya stopped whimpering for a minute and looked at him. "It was in the name, only motherfuckers just didn't get it," Cook'em-up continued. The room was silent. "Bermuda Triangle. Motherfuckers don't never know what they getting into when they go into the Bermuda Triangle. I should kill you for being a bold bitch!"

"Package that shit up," Cleezy said, turning his attention back to the release documents. "Put them in the FedEx envelopes and address them out. This is the last mail run for Bermuda Triangle." Tallya did as she was told. "And it's like this. All that shit that you sold, talking that gangsta shit, that's what the fuck I live every motherfucking day. Every time you think you want to talk about this night, think about the worst killing ever done gangsta style, and that's what you are going to get."

"And that's a promise, you greedy beyatcchhh," Cook'em-up added.

"I'll make the drop of those packages for you." Cleezy grabbed the packages and exited the house.

They went to the nearest FedEx drop box and put the envelopes in them. The next morning the packages were delivered to each of the artists. Some were greeted by letters from Tallya on their fax machines and e-mail accounts letting them know that their rights had reverted back to them. The next day, the coroner announced that Benjamin Arlow had died in his Hamptons mansion of cardiac arrest.

CHAPTER 32

Lights, Camera, Action

It was three days before the premiere of Mercy's movie. The front-page story on every newspaper stand as well as the top story on every news broadcast were all the same. "In a sad and bizzare turn, noted billionaire entrepreneur Benjamin Arlow died recently from a heart attack in his mansion in the Hamptons. It has been speculated that this was precipitated by an argument with his girlfriend, Tallya Daniels, whom he caught in a compromising position with two men in the home they shared. Daniels is currently on suicide watch in the county jail after being arrested for embezzling funds from Bermuda Triangle, the film distribution company that she and Arlow founded, and which Arlow recently dissolved.

"Immediately after the death, Arlow's daughter, Monique Arlow, pressed embezzlement charges against Daniels. When the authorities finally caught up with Daniels, she was on the Brooklyn Bridge about to jump." On BET news, Monique Arlow provided the following comment: "My father had plenty of gold diggers in his life, but never has one ever got away with his riches." She then looked into the camera and added, "And this goes for Ms. Daniels. I never liked the *bleep* anyway."

As Mercy tried to digest the news about Tallya, the entertainment reporter came on, and she heard another anchor say, "That brings us to Mercy Jiles's new movie, *A Snitch's Life,* which is about a drug dealer's girlfriend who kills a snitch to save him. The movie hits the big screen this week. Her first film was produced by Bermuda Triangle, but her new work was produced and distributed by Paramount Pictures—and the inside scoop is that the film is a winner! Two thumbs-up for Mercy Jiles."

Mercy was overwhelmed by all the free publicity for her new movie as the gossip papers and shows called her for a comment on the "Bermuda Triangle tragedy," as they called it. She spoke to any and all and pushed her new project each time. The day of the movie premiere, the response was overwhelming. Everybody who was anybody in the entertainment industry was at her premiere. There were major openings all over the country, and people came out of the woodwork to see her movie.

But her hometown premiere was the best of all. Ms. Pat showed up with all of her old cronies from the projects. Even Brianna was there, acting like she was one of the dang stars, but all in all she was cheering from the sideline.

"You look beautiful, baby," Cleezy said as he removed her long mink coat that she endorsed for Alan Furs. He proudly escorted her into the lobby of the theater where they were showing the Richmond premiere. Mercy sat on the edge of her seat, listening to the reactions of the audience. They laughed and cried at all the right parts. When the movie was over, people applauded and the compliments flowed.

As she and Cleezy came out of the theater, Mercy saw so many people who wanted to meet her. It seemed like everyone wanted a job from her, including a very forgetful Farrah, who acted as if she and Mercy were old friends. Her mouth started hurting from all the smiling she felt she had to do. Mercy noticed a local reporter interviewing a woman in a long black dress outside the theater. It was her momma! *Guyd damn people crawl from all under rocks when you make it.* She hadn't seen her since that day at the Ambassador Hotel. Her mother was still a good-looking woman, and now she was out here talking about "my baby girl . . . always knew she had talent. She takes after her daddy."

Mercy stood there with her mouth open. Her mother looked over at her with proud tears in her eyes, and in that instant Mercy forgave her and released any hatred she had in her heart. After all, you only get one momma.

"You done so good, Mercy, baby," her mother said. "I hope you can forgive me for not being the kind of momma you wanted me to be. I guess I lost my head after your daddy died. I know I can't take back the past; I can only move forward. I have God in my life now, and I am a changed woman."

Mercy didn't know what to say. She might be able to forgive her momma, but she would never forget the way her momma ran around and desecrated her daddy's memory.

"I'll call you sometime," Mercy said. "I have other events to go to, but when I get back and I'm not so busy maybe we can see each other."

Her mother nodded as if that was all she could expect. "Well, let me pray with you before you go." She pulled out her prayer oil and placed it on Mercy's forehead and began to pray.

Mercy thought it was funny that her momma was there now when she didn't need a mother any longer. But hating her wouldn't do any good. Who knew what would happen? Maybe she and Cleezy would have kids someday, who might want to meet their old grandma.

Mercy's momma looked closely at Cleezy just as they were getting up to leave.

"You look familiar to me," she said. "I wonder where I know you from?"

Cleezy shook his head and shrugged.

"I guess you just look like someone I used to know in my past life," she said. "Mercy, I do hope you'll call me when you get back. I've missed you."

"Sure, Momma," Mercy said, and then they were out of there and on their way home.

The next night Mercy was in Chicago for another premiere event. Cleezy had business to attend to, so Chrissie came with her instead. As Mercy was about to take the red carpet in front of the beautiful old theater, a guy bumped into her.

"Hello, beautiful," she heard a familiar voice say. She turned to look and gave a little smile. "You look stunning," he added as he looked Mercy over. "Besides being the woman of my dreams, I know you from somewhere. I just can't place it right now." Taymar scratched his head as if trying to place her.

"*Merci, merci,* we need you. We need you to pose for photos with the president of the NAACP and Condoleezza Rice," one of her French publicists said as she tried to pull her away. Mercy turned back to Taymar.

"Look, I've got something for you. Please give me one minute and wait for me," she said to Taymar, who by then had turned into a washed-up boxer who could not win a fight if his opponent was blindfolded. Although he played the stock market big, Mercy knew that his trophy, dime-piece, size-4 baby momma milked him for everything she could. The judge never cared that she had poked a hole in the condom to guarantee getting her claws on his riches. Radio personality Wendy Williams kept the public abreast on the latest lowdown on Taymar. He was the ongoing joke on her radio show and every other urban radio show.

He beamed and made goo-goo eyes at Mercy as she smiled for the flashing cameras. Once she was done, she was notified that she only had a few seconds before she was to make her grand entrance on the red carpet. She headed back over to Taymar. Standing before him, she dug into her three-thousand-dollar clutch and pulled out the small, worn Liz Claiborne wallet that her father had given her for her last birthday before he was killed.

"You are so beautiful. Have you ever experienced love at first sight?" he said to her in a sincere tone, admiring her flawless makeup and shapely figure.

"Only once," Mercy answered him.

"Well, I am experiencing it now. I really want us to build something from here," Taymar said.

"Look, that was possible at one time," she said, and handed him a piece of paper.

"What's this?"

"It was my inspiration, and I owe it all to you." She pointed to the boarding pass he now had in his hand. "I have been saving this for you for a while now. My dad always told me to be careful what you say, because if you speak it you can make it happen. I think the last thing I told you was 'See you on the red carpet.' And look at us now."

He hadn't realized that the beautiful woman before him was Mercy. After running through so many women in his day, he had forgotten about her, but now everything was coming back to him. He tried to recover by saying, "I know, and you looking real good, too."

"Well, maybe I was off a bit. You're not on the red carpet; you're just a spectator. Lost your A-list status, huh? Well, as it

stands, you ain't a good look for my image, so if you'll excuse me."
Mercy's publicist called out to her. "Do you know what *my* publicist would say?" she said to Taymar as she walked off.

Chrissie walked up after Mercy left to finish Mercy's statement. "Be careful of the toes you step on today, because they may be connected to the ass you have to kiss tomorrow."

CHAPTER 33

Ain't No Stopping Us Now

A couple of months after the opening of her new movie, things had calmed down for Mercy. Zurri had dropped off Deonie to spend the night three weeks ago and, as she had done in the past, had not returned. Mercy and Cleezy didn't mind, and neither did Deonie. She felt as if Mercy was her mother anyway. Mercy and Cleezy loved to spoil Deonie and spend time with her.

One day Deonie asked to go to the zoo, and they took her.

"The monkeys look hungry," Deonie said to Cleezy.

Mercy interrupted. "The sign says that we can't feed them."

"Aw, come on, what's going to happen?"

"I don't want to know what's going to happen, but I know we can't feed them."

As soon as Mercy turned her back, Cleezy and Deonie were discreetly feeding the monkeys. "Is this what you are going to do when I tell our baby no? Are you going to go behind my back and let the baby do what he or she wants to?"

"Probably, but we got to cross that bridge when we get there."

"Well, we are there!" she said, smiling.

"What you mean? With Deonie?" He wanted her to make herself perfectly clear.

"No," she said, rubbing her stomach. "That's what took me so long in the bathroom this morning."

"Word?" Cleezy smiled.

"Yup!"

He took her into his arms and grabbed Deonie, and then he started singing, "Ain't no stopping us now." She wished her father could have met Cleezy, and for a moment, she felt sad because her child would never know his grandfather. She quickly brushed those thoughts aside and laughed at Cleezy's antics. He was dancing around, drawing the attention of people. "We're having a baby," he sang, and continued to dance around. Deonie started repeating after him and was dancing around, too.

Mercy laughed. She had never been so happy.

From the time Mercy found out she was pregnant, she was obsessed with making the perfect life for her child, the life she'd never had. She wanted her baby to have a mother and father who not only loved their child but who loved each other. Most important, she wanted her baby to have a father who was there, and not in jail or in a cemetery.

"Baby, remember when you told me when we were in Miami that I don't need to be out there on I-95 anymore getting my hands dirty?" Mercy said one morning when they were still lying in bed.

Cleezy looked at her.

"I did what you asked me to do and didn't argue."

"That's right."

"Well, I am coming to you, my soul mate, and I am asking you to leave the streets alone so we can focus on a regular life for our baby. I want our baby to have two parents and a good life. A life I never had with my parents. I want us to continue to be major instruments in Deonie's life like we've been doing, because God only knows when her momma's going to get it together. And I want our child to have the closeness that I had with my father. Baby, please, throw in the towel."

He listened but didn't respond.

"You've stacked enough paper. Now, you're being greedy. We got money, my shit is selling, and the residual checks coming in are worth more than our house."

"I feel you, and I want the best of everything for our child, too. Understand I am a man; I am a provider. So I can't live off of your residuals."

"Baby, it's our residuals. It ain't never mine. It's us. Don't you remember we decided in Miami that it wasn't anymore *me, I,* or *my* in this relationship. It is always *our, we,* and *us.*"

She snuggled into Cleezy's arms, and he squeezed her.

"I guess you's right, baby," Cleezy said. "It can't happen overnight, but I promise you that I'll slow it down and our child won't grow up with no dope-dealing daddy."

CHAPTER 34

When the Dealing's Done

As he promised, Cleezy slowed down the trips up and down I-95. Instead he spent most of his time hanging out at the horse races and gambling. He took Mercy with him from time to time, which she didn't mind. As a matter of fact, in a strange way it made her feel a lot closer to her father. One day when she was six months pregnant, Cleezy was at the racetrack with Mercy right by his side. At the last minute he put in a bet in a superbox, which is the ticket that pays the most, and the horse won. They both were excited as he walked up and collected ninety thousand dollars.

"See, baby," Mercy said to him, "when one door closes, another door opens."

"I hear you, ma," Cleezy said.

"Let's quit while we're ahead."

"You're right. Let's go put the baby's college money in the bank," he said, rubbing Mercy's stomach.

They were so excited as they headed for the car. Of course Cleezy had had his hands on more money than that before, but this was the first time he had had his hands on that much money and it was clean money, legal, legit. As he sat down on the driver's side he began singing: *"You gotta know when to hold 'em, know when to fold 'em, know when to walk away, know when to run."*

Chills went up Mercy's spine. She hadn't heard anyone sing that song before, other than her father. "Where you get that from?" Mercy asked.

"What?"

"What you know about that song?"

"My pops used to sing that shit. He used to be a big-time gambler."

"Stop playing?" Mercy was surprised. She and Cleezy never really talked a lot about their fathers. Staying on the subject too long always made them both emotional, so it was one subject they tried to avoid.

"Yup, he used to sing it because this guy he knew sang it all of the time, so that song stayed in his head."

"For real?" Mercy was stunned.

"Yeah, how crazy is this shit? Funny thing is, he ended up killin' that nigga. After that, I don't think I ever heard him sing that song again."

"What?" Mercy looked sick.

"True piece," he nodded. "This dude was one of the best gamblers of all times. Knew everything to gamble on. He bet on everything: cars, people, bugs, everything. It didn't matter."

Tears formed in Mercy's eyes.

"This dude had owed my pops some money, and he had a tip on a game so he didn't pay my pops. Just like a nigga, he ducked my pops, saying he had a family emergency. Instead of giving my pops the tip so they could all break bread together, he kept it to himself and collected a whole bunch of money. When he showed up to pay Pops, Pops wanted his part of the big game and dude told him he ain't giving shit but what he owes."

Mercy was silent, and Cleezy could feel tension in the car but that wasn't unusual because Mercy had been having mood swings since the pregnancy, so he kept on with the story. "He turned his back on my father, and one of my father's boys shot him. Dude had so much heart that as he was taking his last breath, he told my father to suck his dick." Tears flowed down Mercy's face. Cleezy didn't notice because he was keeping his eyes on the road. He continued the heart-wrenching story. "My pops was so mad that he had to find a way to get revenge on him, so he left him lifeless, shameless, and faceless. My Pops was so wild he went to the funeral and—"

Mercy cut him off. "And stole his body, took it to the middle of the street, shot it up, and then set it on fire." She cried out loud as a combination of snot and tears came down her face.

"How'd you know?" Cleezy asked in amazement.

"Because your father did it in front of that man's little girl—he did that shit in front of his little girl," she screamed. Cleezy knew right then and there who the little girl was, but before he could say anything, Mercy yelled, "Your motherfucking pussy-ass daddy killed the only thing that ever meant anything to me! Your pops destroyed my fucking life."

Mercy started to pummel Cleezy, as if he was the one who had pulled the trigger. Cleezy took the licks like a man and pulled over into a McDonald's parking lot and tried to comfort Mercy. "Baby, I am so sorry. I never knew that shit," he said.

Mercy broke down and sobbed. Cleezy hopped out of the car and ran to the passenger side and opened the door to embrace her.

She tried to push him away. "I hate you! I hate you so much!" She didn't want his apology or hug. She didn't want anything from the son of the man who killed her daddy. He ignored her words and hugged her. "I know, baby."

Cleezy wiped every tear that fell from her eyes. "I love you, baby," he kept saying, and although he wanted to be strong he couldn't sit and watch his queen, the woman he loved so passionately, cry. As he held her tight in his arms, he couldn't hold back his own tears of hurt. Her pain was his pain, and it hurt like hell that he couldn't do anything to make the pain disappear.

Everything within her wanted to tell him to get off of her, to go to hell. But then Mercy felt one of his tears hit her arm. She looked into his eyes and saw the hurt she felt reflected in them. It started to feel as if Cleezy's tears were washing away her pain. Maybe there was a reason they found each other—and it wasn't for revenge, it was for forgiveness. She couldn't end it with him; she couldn't kick him out of her life. He was her everything, her baby's father, her king. How could she blame him for the sins of his father? As bad as she wanted to, she couldn't. Instead, she embraced him and every single tear that she had held back for so long poured out onto his shoulder.

"I love you, baby, and I promise I ain't going to ever leave you or our baby," Cleezy said. "I swear. This is from the bottom of my heart.

"We gonna be the parents that we both wanted," he vowed.

CHAPTER 35

Bulletproof Love

Now that Mercy knew that her and Cleezy's pasts had been tragically entertwined, her love for Cleezy became even stronger. Their new bond went beyond this world and their love was bulletproof. Nothing could stop their love—no jails, bars, walls, people, illness, nothing. They made sacred vows to be everything their parents weren't, no matter what. Mercy and Cleezy were convinced that with the love that they would pour into their baby, not to mention their street savvy, charisma, and the best education that money could buy, their child would be someone great, someone who promised to change the world one day.

The expectations started with Deonie. They loved her as if she were their own. In her time with Cleezy and Mercy, Deonie had blossomed. She was already older beyond her years from having to fend for herself when her mother left her in the house alone and was too busy for her. Because she was smart and independent and had already learned how to take care of herself, once she began living full time with Cleezy and Mercy, Deonie's grades began to soar. Her teacher sent home a note saying that Deonie was being placed into accelerated classes in order to keep her challenged.

Cleezy had changed as well. He put everything on hold so he could be there for Mercy. Mercy had been trying to get Cleezy to go to church with her for months. Since she had found out that she was pregnant, she'd started going to the local church with a so-called "hip-hop minister." Cleezy knew the minister was a player and wasn't going to go, but this particular Sunday, since he knew that Mercy was still dealing with the past, he willingly accompanied Mercy and Deonie to church. Mercy's mother had invited them over to a dinner she was having for Nayshawn, who had just been released from prison the day before. Although Nayshawn wasn't biologically Pearl's child, he was Nate's youngest child, a child he had while married to Pearl, and she embraced him like one of her own. In his young days before his father's death, he had spent a lot of time at her house, and since Mercy was pregnant, Pearl decided to have the dinner to bring them all closer together, and they were making it a family day. After they were halfway to Pearl's house, Mercy had to go the bathroom.

"I gotta pee," Mercy said, "and I don't think I'm going to be able to hold it."

"You can't wait till we get to your mom's house?"

"Nope, I really got to go. I got this baby right on top of my bladder."

Cleezy hopped off on an exit on I-95 and decided to take a shortcut through the hood. As he sat at the light, Deonie asked, "Auntie, are you and my uncle Cleezy going to get married?"

Cleezy turned to look at Mercy as she answered Deonie. Out of nowhere—*boom, boom, boom*—gunshots were fired. *Boom, boom, boom, boom, boom.*

Cleezy reached for his hammer, but it wasn't there. It had slid down to the back floor of the car. "Oh shit! Get down, get down," he screamed as he took off and put the accelerator of his Audi A8 to the floor. But the swervin' 'Burban that was beside him was too high up, and the shots rained down on his vehicle. *Boom, boom, boom.*

Cleezy kept reaching for his hammer until he was finally able to grab it. Once he felt the cold steel in his hands, he was about to shoot back, but as he lifted the gun, he glanced over and saw Mercy on the passenger side of the car with blood gushing out of her wounds. He froze, slamming on the brakes as he bent the corner, causing the swervin' Suburban to keep going. He headed straight for the hospital. He knew there was no time to call an ambulance. "Baby, just hold on."

"Okay, Cleezy." She nodded. "I love you!"

"I know," he said, tears rolling down his face along with the balls of perspiration. "I love you, baby!"

"Take care of the baby and remember I love you," she said in between breaths. She wanted Cleezy to know that it didn't matter what her destiny was, if she lived or if she died. It was forever for them. She would always be in his heart, and he was everything that she needed and longed for. "Until . . ."

"Baby don't talk." He interrupted her as he rubbed her hand as he tried to keep his eyes on the road. He didn't want to hear those words from Mercy, "until death do us part," because those words, the same words Paula had uttered to him before she took her last breath, seemed to be a curse to him.

Cleezy knew there wasn't much time. She had been hit by bullets meant for him. They were no .22 bullets; they were assassin's bullets.

"Hold on, baby. Please, please hold on. I'm begging you," Cleezy pleaded as tears ran down his face. "Deonie," he called out while glancing to the back of the car.

"Huh?" she said, her little voice trembling.

"Stay down. You okay?"

"Yes, but what about Auntie?"

"She's going to be okay."

"Yes, baby. I'm okay," Mercy said in a weak tone. "I love you. Auntie loves you."

Cleezy pulled up to the emergency room, screaming for the doctors. Two attendants rushed out and took Mercy away. While the doctors fought for Mercy's life, Cleezy paced the hallway. His mother had not heard from or seen Cleezy since he'd found out the truth about her. But bad news travels fast in the hood, and as soon as Lolly found out what happened, she came to his side to comfort him.

But her thoughts were only for herself, as usual. *I know he doesn't want me here, but I feel I should be here,* Lolly thought as she stood there watching Cleezy pace back and forth. *Plus it looks good. I've never seen him love anything or anyone, not even his money, like he loves this girl. So I'm going to sit here as long as it takes. If she dies, I'll stick around and be the supportive mother and can reestablish our relationship. And with her being gone, he'll feel bad and want to draw closer to me. When he does, it will put me closer to his money again. Times sure have been hard without him, I know that much. And if she makes it, I'll be at her bedside waiting on her hand and foot. He'll see that I really care, and that will get me back into his good graces.*

Pearl, Mercy's mother, also showed up. When she heard what happened, she fell to her knees and cried, begging God to have mercy because she had spent so many years of her life taking her daughter's life for granted.

"God, please forgive me," she prayed. "God, please don't take her away from me. Don't punish me. I will never be able to live with myself if I can't make the relationship right with her. God, take me instead." She began to whimper silently.

Nayshawn was down in the hospital lobby with Cleezy's cell phone, calling around town to find out who was responsible for the shooting. He wasn't supposed to be using the cell phone at the hospital, but with that look of murder written across his face and in his eyes, none of the hospital staff dared say a word to him. He hung up the phone and then decided to go outside and take a smoke. He exited out of the automatic doors, lit, and took a pull off of his Black and Mild.

Whoever the fuck did that shit is going to fucking die, Nayshawn thought as he took another pull. *They say this nigga Cleezy is supposed to be a stone-cold killer. This nigga is going to have to kill these niggas or be killed. That's how it's going to go down. Punks thought he was getting soft 'cause he was scaling back his business. They didn't know shit. Now they got to deal with both of us crazy motherfuckas.*

Zurri was nowhere to be found, but Chrissie was there in the chapel praying. *God, I know for years my dear friend ran up and down I-95 carrying them packs and breaking the law, but she has finally gotten herself together, and now things are coming together for her. Please don't let her die. God, I promise I will give you my soul and my heart. I will never sleep with another married man. God, right here and now I give you my life. I will dedicate my life to you, my God. I feel this was a wake-up call for me and the lifestyle I have been living. But please don't take her. If it meant that I never get another dollar from another man, I'll sacrifice for Mercy and her baby to live. Please, God, please.*

Although Ms. Pat wanted someone to take Deonie home, Deonie refused to go, so Ms. Pat told her that she would just have her daughter take her down to the cafeteria to get something to eat. Deonie was young, but she knew what was going on as her own thoughts filled her head.

I sure hope that God lets my auntie Mercy live, little Deonie thought. *If God takes her away, I am doomed. My auntie is all I got. My momma, all she wants to do is rip and run the streets, the streets that Auntie promised that over her dead body will I end up in. I am trying to walk slow, dragging my feet, taking my time so I can hear what the doctors are saying or see how their faces look, but Ms. Pat's daughter Teisha keeps pulling me along. My aunt said that God only hears fools' and babies' prayers, so therefore, God, I hope you are listening. Please keep my auntie in your care. She promised me that my life would not be anything like hers. I believed her, but if she dies, my life will crumble. I can feel my heart breaking now. I'm only ten years old. I've learned so much from listening and watching her that I know she has so much more for me to learn. I know that my auntie always said, "You never know what hand God is going to deal you and never question God," but God, I'm begging. I'm pleading with you to please spare my auntie's life, if not for her or her baby's sake, then for me.*

Cleezy's thoughts were of revenge. *If it take everything in me, I swear to God I am going to get the motherfuckers who did this shit to Mercy and our baby. I can't believe this shit. Motherfuckers gonna die around this town. Richtown is about to be Redtown, all the blood that's about to be shed. Motherfuckers' mommas, daddies, grannies, kids is going to die. Motherfuckers gonna pay. Even if it means my life, I don't give a fuck.*

Every time the nurse walked by, everyone looked at her trying their damnedest to read the look on her face. Cleezy looked like he was about to grab the nurse and take her hostage to get information from her. After Ms. Pat told him that he was frightening the nurse, he decided to go smoke a cigarette.

As Cleezy left the building the room continued to be filled with prayer, hopes, and wishes that everything would be all right. Two women had been sitting in the waiting room for the last hour. Everyone assumed they were waiting on loved ones to come out of surgery, but then one of them said to Pearl, "So you are Mercy's estranged mother?"

Pearl acted as if she didn't hear her, but Lolly gave the lady an ugly look. "And you are?" she asked in a nasty tone.

"I am Wanda Juve, and I work for Channel Six, *Insider*, and we are covering the story of Mercy—"

And before she could get it out, Chrissie had slapped the cowboy shit out of her. "Get out of here. You fucking people are out of control."

The woman took the pimp slap like a champ and headed to the door, but the other lady began to rattle off questions as they left. "Who could want to kill your daughter? Does she have a lot of enemies? Who will the profits of Mercy's movies go to if Mercy dies? Are there any more screenplays she has finished that no one has seen?"

CHAPTER 36

Man to Man

It had only been several hours since the doctor informed Cleezy that it would be at least twelve hours before Mercy was out of surgery. He never did promise that she would come out of it alive.

Since then Cleezy had tried getting into the operating room three times. He needed to see her. He was fully aware that this might be his last chance to see his soul mate alive. He needed and wanted to be by Mercy's side. On the third attempt a security guard told him if he didn't calm down, the hospital would be forced to call the police and have him removed. Cleezy really didn't give a fuck if they called the fuckin' National Guard, but he didn't want to distract the doctors from doing their jobs. Saving Mercy's life.

He needed some fresh air again so that he would be able to think straight. He and everybody in that waiting room knew he had to regain his composure if he was gonna be of any help to Mercy. Before leaving, Cleezy gave the guard a mean look. He knew the toy cop was just doing his job, but Cleezy also knew that if he ever ran into the rent-a-cop outside of the hospital it would take more willpower than he possessed to keep from tearing into his ass. The guard would have to pay for keeping him away from

Mercy and his unborn child. It might cost him a little, it might cost him a lot, but it was going to cost him and he was going to pay every iron dime.

Cleezy walked into the parking deck of the hospital, where he spotted Nayshawn on the phone, smoking weed.

"You probably need this." Nayshawn handed Cleezy the lit blunt. "How's Mercy?" Cleezy inhaled the high-powered smoke before answering.

"It's bad. Doctors ain't sayin' shit, but it's real bad." Neither of them spoke for a minute. Both men were thinking of fond moments they'd shared with Mercy in the past. Cleezy broke the silence first.

"Have you heard anything?" Cleezy probed. "I just can't sit round like this and do nothin'. Somebody gotta pay." That's exactly what Nayshawn needed to hear. Nayshawn didn't really know Cleezy, but he'd heard, while incarcerated, that the nigga took care of his business. It was time to find out for himself.

"I heard you had put money out on the streets but was coming up with lint. But I managed to get the names of the two chumps that pulled the trigger. They go by Lil' Ali and Baby Hova."

"I never heard of them." Cleezy had a puzzled look on his face.

"I didn't think you would've. They both are 'bout twelve or thirteen years old, lil' wil'-ass twins from the Westend. They supposed to be Bloods or some shit."

"Bloods!" Cleezy echoed.

"Word is," Nayshawn said, "it was a red-light special on you. Another OG Blood red-lighted you for death."

"Do you know who place the hit?" Cleezy had done so much wild shit it could've been anyone.

"Naw, not yet. But the two that tried to execute you are now in hiding. They were just tryin' to make a name like their pops had." Nayshawn saw a murderous glare appear in Cleezy's eyes.

"Well, they 'bout to get their names in the obituaries," Cleezy said in a death tone. "I'm goin' to kill two people in both their family every other day, until they come out of hiding. If I run out of family members, then I'll start with friends of the family." Cleezy took another toke of the blunt filled with hydro and exhaled. "They just made the biggest mistake of their lives."

"I feel ya!" Nayshawn said, never looking at Cleezy. "I know their momma name is this ho name Tressa that used to live 'round Eastgate Village, and their pops was this crazy-ass motherfucker named Lucky."

CHAPTER 37

The News

The family gathered around to hear what the doctors had to say. Judging by all Mercy's blood on their smocks the doctors looked like they had been operating on soldiers in Iraq instead of Mercy.

"We've done all we can do," one doctor said, and Pearl screamed at the top of her lungs, *"Noooo!!!!"*

The doctor put his hand up to try to get Pearl to calm down and listen.

"Nooo!!!! Lord, don't do this to me," Pearl continued with a heavy, guilty heart.

Ms. Pat put her arm around Pearl. "Let him finish," she said in a comforting way, and looked to the doctor to continue.

"As I said, we've done all we can do at this time. At this point it's all up to Mercy. The next hours to come are vital. If she can make it through the next seventy-two hours, then she and the baby should be all right. We were not comfortable giving an emergency C-section, but the baby is fine. As I said, if she can fight and pull through the next seventy-two hours, she should be able to make a full recovery. At this point it's up to her, how hard she fights and how badly she wants to live."

"There's gotta be something else you can do," Nayshawn said.

"Honestly, sir, it's out of our hands. We've done everything we could."

Cleezy spoke up. "Look, money ain't no issue. We ain't no poor black people with no insurance."

"Money won't make a difference," the doctor said.

"Can't we fly some more doctors in and do something? More experienced?"

The doctor looked at Cleezy and said with a bit of cockiness, "We are the best. In the late eighties, early nineties, Richmond was the murder capital, and we saw countless gunshot victims and pulled them through. So we are the best at what we do, but as good as we are, unfortunately it's out of our hands."

The doctor looked at the family as if he wished there were more he could say, but there wasn't.

Cleezy muttered, "It's got to be something else we can do."

The doctor looked him with a solemn face and said, "All any of us can do at this point is pray."

CHAPTER 38

A Gangsta's Prayer

Cleezy sat by Mercy's bedside. As her heart monitor line crawled across the screen and beeped slowly, he took heed to what the doctor had said and prayed like never before.

God, I know I ain't never really asked you for nothing or been big into the whole religion thing, but in the message in church today, the minister said, "I have not because I ask not." God, I am asking you, I am begging you to spare Mercy's and my baby's life. God, you know like I know that I had turned into a cold nigga with an iron heart. Never did I think it was possible for me to love again, and especially after that mess with my momma. So I know the only way I could ever end up loving like I love Mercy was your will, and I thank you for that. I know God giveth and taketh, but please don't take her from me. I know I have to be accountable for all the lives I've taken away. I ask you for forgiveness of my sins, and please don't take her. God, you know my heart.

Never in his life had Cleezy called upon God like this. After the longest hours of Cleezy's life, as he studied the green line on the life-support machine, he finally surrendered his own will and gave in to the will of God.

Tears came to his eyes as he talked to Mercy. "Baby, I always wondered what would you ever want with a nigga like me. I always felt like you deserved so much more, but you always said that I was all you needed. Well, I need you, baby. I know you know that I ain't nothing without you. Never was I ever complete until you came into my life. Not only do I need you, I need you to be strong for our baby." He poured his heart out to her. "This is the baby that we promised that we would devote our lives to. Remember in Miami you made me promise that I will never leave you. Well, please don't leave me. I love you, baby. Please don't make our life in vain. You have made an important impact on my life." He tried to wipe his tears away, but he couldn't stop them from coming. He began to sob, and when he did, he heard the beeps go quicker and the lines begin to go higher.

Was that a sign that God had heard his prayers and Mercy could hear every word he was saying and that she was going to fight like hell to make it through?

CHAPTER 39

The Final Round

As Mercy looked at the white light, she made out a smiling face. It was her father, Nate, and he was wearing all white. He looked so relaxed, well rested, young, and rejuvenated. Mercy smiled and ran over to give him a hug.

"Dadddyyyy, I love you. I am so happy to see you."

"I am so proud of you, baby girl."

"Are you?"

"Yes."

"That's all I really wanted was you to be proud. Daddy, that's all I was living for."

"I know. I was watching over you every step of the way, and I am so pleased with the woman you turned out to be. I know there were some things that I could not have prepared you for but—"

"It's okay, Daddy. We're together now," she assured her father.

The beeps on the heart monitor in the hospital room became slower and fainter.

"Are you sure you want to be with me?" Nate asked.

"Yes, Daddy. You have always been my world. I always strived to have your blessings even if you were not there. I have longed for this day. The day that I could see you smile and hear you tell me a job well done and that you love me."

"Job well done, Mercy. So you ready to go with me?"

"Yes, Daddy, I am ready," Mercy said, like a little girl. "Yes, Daddy, I am ready."

He extended his hand for her to go with him. Mercy walked closer and smiled. Her life was complete.

There was a long *Beeeppp!!!! BEEEEPPPP!!!!* on the heart monitor. Cleezy started screaming, *"Noo!"* Cleezy hit the buttons to call for help, and screamed, *"Helppp!!!! Nurse!!* Nope, this shit ain't going to go down like this! Lord have Mercy!" He started praying, begging God, "Please, God, take me and let them live." Never did Cleezy ever think that he would see the day that he would be willing to trade his life in for someone else's, and a woman at that. Cleezy whimpered and begged and pleaded to a God that just days ago he never believed existed, but these words or feelings Mercy never heard, because she was with her father now.

In the hospital room the nurses and doctors rushed in, pushing Cleezy aside. Hearing the machine go completely dead froze him. At that moment it was all real to him. It was that exact second that Cleezy realized he wasn't God. He wasn't Superman, and life wasn't for him to spare or give. The only life that he had ever truly valued was Mercy's, and no matter what he had done, it was out of his control. Cleezy had put Mercy before him and sacrificed so much of himself: his freedom, his money, his heart and trust. The only two lives that ever meant anything to him had been taken away, and there was nothing he could do. He was helpless. No money, power, drugs, or respect could give him what he needed or wanted most: his wifey and his unborn child.

Mercy was hand in hand with her father.

"There is no pulse, and no vital signs," one doctor said in the hospital room. "I'm afraid—"

As Mercy took the first step to walk alongside her father, she heard a sound—"Maa-maaa, Maaa-maaa,"—a baby's cry, her baby. Her mother's intuition kicked in. She knew it was her baby calling out for her. Without saying good-bye or thinking twice, Mercy let go of her father's hand and began running, racing to save her baby's life.

All of a sudden, the chaos and distress that filled the room turned to relief as the machine began to seem as if it had a mind of its own. Cleezy had lived an elaborate street life. He had seen, heard, and done a lot of things; but nothing could prepare him for the miracle that God gave him when he heard the doctors say, "Oh, my God, she's been stabilized. Her heart rate has stabilized, and pulse is almost normal."

Cleezy felt like he was dreaming as he watched from the corner, as the stunned doctors looked around at each other. One of the doctors finally said, "Ladies and gentlemen, you have just witnessed a miracle."

There was a brief silence, but then one doctor broke the silence with a bit of humor. "All bets are off on Roy Jones, Trinidad, Bernard Hopkins, Tarver, and The Razor. I am putting my money on Ms. Jiles. This is a real fighter we've got on our hands."

Cleezy took a deep breath, looked up, and thanked God. Then all he said was, "Lord have Mercy!"

THANK YOUS

Thank you, Father, for all blessings that flow. I now know what it's truly like to walk in the FOG (Favor of God). Thank you for the favor upon my life. I thank you for using me in such a *huge* way so that I may touch the lives of others. Thank you, God, for giving me such a great vision time and time again. I love you, and I will place no other above you. All Glory to you!

Writing these acknowledgments was such an overwhelming process. As I thought about each of you, right down to my dedicated fans, it was confirmation of just how blessed and highly favored I am. Timmond and Kennisha, you two continue to make Mommy proud! I thank you for always keeping me encouraged and inspired. My family, which has continued to support me through all my endeavors. Mom, thank you for everything you do, but most of all, thank you for birthing me. My Aunt Brenda, for loving me and being my official event planner. Aunt Robin, for being you, and Aunt Yvonne for never saying no when I need a babysitter, or whatever, while on deadlines or out of town. I truly appreciate you. Craig, what can I say? You are a constant reminder of just how deep love is. You keep me so encouraged, grounded, and sane, especially when insanity doesn't seem that far away. My cousin Lisa, you inspire me, and I love our lunches. Cousin Dre, Andy, VanShawn, Shay, Natalee, and Cha, I love you! There are so many more I could name, and I thank you all!

Over the years I've learned that just because you don't have the same blood doesn't mean that you can't be family. You all have added to my life tremendously! Brenda (BT), my official travel partner, you are quick to snatch me back in line. Courtney, my prayer warrior, sister in God and heart, you are such a special person. You resuscitate me when I am literally down to my last ounce of energy, and you remind me that it's not easy being a virtuous woman, but it's worth it. I hope I've exceeded your expectations as a friend. DeAudrey and Deena, you both love me like the daughter you never had. DeAudrey, from day one you've pushed me to reach for the stars. Deena, you are such an impeccable friend and a constant motivator. Thanks for being my protector and confidante but most of all for understanding who I am behind the pen, never judging! Joy, always finding a piece of good in the bad and ugly! Kells, my best friend; Niecy, my other best friend, neither of you ever falling short of holding your title. My dear Virgo friend, Monique Wise: Thank you for always taking on my problems as if they were your own and responding with such heartfelt advice. Jake: Thank you for being my friend.

Melody, for making sure my work is always in tip-top condition and for always going to bat for me. Marc, for getting the best deals and hearing all my ideas. Robinette, my personal assistant, thanks for taking your job so seriously. Never think that I don't appreciate you. Santa, my other assistant, I truly appreciate you. You keep me worry free. You two have such a hard job, but you do it with such ease and no nonsense. My authors in the Street Chronicles series, each one of you holds a place in my heart. You are all so special to me, and I wish you the absolute best! Stay focused and remember the sky is the limit, so propel those wings and fly!

Kermit of Gresham Photography, for such beautiful pictures every single time. Dina and the whole Alan Furs family, for keeping me in the newest exotic furs and supporting me in everything I do. Sakia, for making sure every strand of my hair is in place. Here's to all those early mornings and late nights you've accommodated me to make me beautiful.

Special thanks to everyone who made *The Glamorous Life* such a *huge* success. Thank you for coming out to meet me and chat with me. I love the e-mails and all the letters. Thank you! Thank you! Thank you! That makes it all worth it. To all the bookstores and every bookseller and street vendor who pushes my book. Last, but certainly not least, an enormous and special thanks to you, the reader! I thank you in advance for making this one a bestseller too! Without you there would be no bestsellers!

ABOUT THE AUTHOR

Nikki Turner is a gutsy, gifted, courageous new voice taking the urban literary community by storm. Having ascended from the "Princess of Hip-Hop Lit" to being the "Queen," she is the bestselling author of the novels *A Hustler's Wife, Project Chick,* and *The Glamorous Life,* and is the editor of and contributing author in *Street Chronicles: Tales from da Hood.* Visit her website at www.nikkiturner.com, or write her at nikki@nikkiturner.com, or at P.O. Box 28694, Richmond, VA 23228.

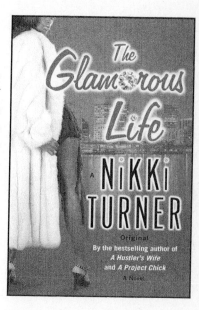

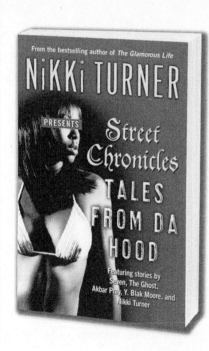
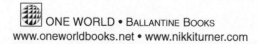